ALUMNI

David Lloyd

Pen Press Publishers Ltd

Copyright © David Lloyd 2008

All rights reserved

No part of this publication may be reproduced,
stored in a retrieval system, or transmitted
in any form or by any means, without
the prior permission in writing of the publisher,
nor be otherwise circulated in any form of binding or cover
other than that in which it is published and without a similar
condition including this condition being imposed on the
subsequent purchaser.

First published in Great Britain by
Pen Press Publishers Ltd
25 Eastern PLace
Brighton
BN2 1GJ

ISBN 978-1-906206-51-2

Printed and bound in the UK by Cpod, Trowbridge, Wiltshire

A catalogue record of this book is available from
the British Library

Cover design Jacqueline Abromeit

In this work of fiction, the characters, organisations, places and events are either the product of the author's imagination or they are used in an entirely fictitious manner. Any resemblance to actual persons, living or dead, or organisations, places and events is purely co-incidental.

Dedication

For Chemin… again your love, support and encouragement have made this book possible.

About the Author

David Lloyd first started writing in 2001 and worked in the ICT industry for more than 20 years before leaving to pursue other interests. *Alumni,* his second novel is part II of the Mike Fabien trilogy that is due for completion next year. He lives in Bristol, England with his wife Chemin and daughter Nadia.

For more information visit: ***www.davidlloydauthor.com***

With thanks also to Alexa.

From the author of *Ascension*.

Prologue

A violent shudder ripped through the cockpit of the private jet carrying William Calvert, his personal assistant Gillian Taylor and attorney David Forrester on the start of its descent towards Washington DC. In response to the pilot's startled gaze his colleague informed him that the port engine had failed but when the plane's sensors indicated a sharp increase in engine temperature his face whitened. Relatively inexperienced as he was, he knew that the engine must have caught fire and began to panic as he watched the pilot grapple with the controls in a vain attempt to steady the plane. Without thinking he released his seat belt, stood up and headed for the door that led to the cabin. The pilot's stern order for him to return to his seat immediately had not the slightest impact on him. Moments later he was forced to grab the door handle to steady himself as the plane tilted suddenly.

'The passengers!' he cried out, pulling himself erect again.

The pilot repeated his order with dire urgency but this again was ignored. The door to the cabin would have been opened had it not been for the sudden rocking of the plane. He was thrown instantly to the floor and his attempt to stand up again proved practically impossible; the plane's pitch and yaw had become increasingly unstable resulting in him having no alternative than to crawl back to his seat. When the next explosion occurred ten seconds later, the plane plummeted.

The co-pilot was hurled towards the cockpit windows, colliding with the reinforced glass with such force that his neck was instantly broken and he became sprawled and unconscious across the flight desk.

In the cabin, Gillian – unable to breathe – stared bug-eyed at the gaping hole in the side of the plane where the door had been; she had seen it disappear at high velocity just moments earlier and now she watched in terror as the wing fractured. Piece by piece the air shredded it into fragments and hurled the debris into the sky. Forrester was floating to the side of her. He clutched the jagged edge of the remains of the cabin doorframe with his blood-drenched fingers for no more than a few seconds before being sucked out, and as his briefcase flew open the documents from within it were blown around the cabin like leaves caught in a winter gale.

As she began to suffocate the sudden realisation that she was going to die paralysed her every joint and muscle. Before the second explosion she had had complete faith that the pilots would get the plane down safely. Even in the miraculous scenario that they could still do so there was no time; the agony she felt within her chest cavity and the panic that was overwhelming her made her pray in an instant that she could swap places with her boss already lying dead in the seat next to her. A large piece of shrapnel was embedded in his forehead and had probably killed him instantly.

The memory of the conversation she had had with Calvert and Forrester minutes earlier was being sucked from her mind like the air from the cabin. She had been told that the contents of Forrester's briefcase would destroy the corporation for whom she had worked for the past eight years. Moments before the first explosion, Calvert had also revealed that he had secretly arranged for them to meet with a man named Dan Riley on arrival in Washington but there had been no time for him to complete the mid-air briefing. Likewise, as she began to black out, her lungs void of oxygen, there was no time for her to fathom out what this all meant.

The pilot pushed the lifeless body of his colleague onto the cockpit floor in order to regain full control of the plane's steering mechanism. His efforts, however, caused him to let go, resulting in the plane rolling over in mid-air. With a cluster of houses on the northern edge of Baltimore approaching at speed he had only a few seconds to correct the yaw and try to steer the plane away from them. Droplets of blood appeared on his forehead as sweat from under his hairline as he agonisingly tried to force the plane just a few critical degrees – it would make the difference between the loss of five lives or 50. As the houses disappeared from view and the grass of the approaching field appeared like a giant green blanket that was about to envelope the plane he closed his eyes and changed from being atheist to believer. In an instant the plane hit the ground, a fireball rose into the sky casting a dark cloud of smoke over the surrounding neighbourhood, and David Forrester's papers burned slowly in the corner of the flame-engulfed cabin.

1

The crash site north of Baltimore had become a hive of activity following the arrival of a team of investigators at around 3AM. They had erected a canopy over the wreckage of Calvert's jet after the fire fighters had finally managed to extinguish the flames and sufficient time had passed for the wreckage to cool down for a safe inspection to take place. The paramedics had arrived early at the scene but had realised immediately that there would be no survivors as soon as they had viewed the carnage before them. The crash team had begun to unload and set up their equipment and had been joined by several colleagues during the course of the morning. The police were still present when Ross Chievney pulled up in his four-by-four and parked it alongside the multitude of vehicles that surrounded the site.

As he climbed out he looked around him and surveyed the site. The field was cordoned off and the police were still talking to the local residents, many of whom had assembled moments after the plane had made impact with the ground. He was then greeted by one of the officers who had been present for most of the night.

'Are you Ross Chievney?'

'Yes.'

'Sergeant Tomlinson, Baltimore police department.'

'How can I help?'

'Your colleagues asked me to look out for you. I'll fill you in on the details.'

'Thanks,' replied Chievney as he began walking towards the tent.

'The plane was en-route to Washington from Allentown, Pennsylvania when air traffic control lost it at 22.14 last night. There were five on board – two men, one woman and the two pilots. The paramedics have found only four bodies. The remains of the pilots have already been recovered. They're retrieving the other two bodies from the cabin as we speak.'

As the two men approached the scene the paramedics were leaving with the charred remains of a man and a woman. Chievney had seen many images of this kind before but these corpses looked like they belonged to two people who had been sacrificed in the fire to Molech. Even after all his years in the profession his stomach would still turn as crash victims were wheeled past him; this morning was no different. Occasionally he had felt physically sick; today for the first time in many months he felt an uncomfortable sensation in his throat and had to take a couple of deep breaths before continuing on his way with the sergeant.

'One of them bailed out then,' he said as they walked on.

'I'm sorry?' replied Tomlinson in surprise.

'Have the families been informed?'

'About four hours ago.'

'OK, let's take a look.'

Tomlinson followed Chievney through the curtain into the covered crash scene and stood behind him as he surveyed the wreckage.

'What in the name…' said Chievney as he saw the space where the cabin door had been on the buckled remains of the aircraft.

At that moment one of his team approached him hurriedly.

'Alec, what do we know so far?' he asked him.

'It looks from the preliminary that it just fell out of the sky. I think there was more than just engine failure here. Come, let me show you something.'

'Do you think it landed on the starboard wing? That may explain the extent of the damage to it.'

'I don't think so. The shear at the point of the wing's connection to the fuselage is not sufficient. I think the wing started to disintegrate in the air. The trajectory mapping and the state of the nose section suggests that initial impact was at the cockpit.'

'I see.'

'No sign of the engine yet,' his colleague added. 'But come and take a look at the other one.'

The three men walked around the front of the fuselage to the port side of the plane and over to the wing that was still largely intact. Chievney and Alec Jameson then began a close examination of the port engine.

'Do you notice the condition of the rotor blades and the discolouration on the internal surface of the engine casing?'

'Yes Alec, I think I know where you're leading.'

Tomlinson watched and listened with eagerness as the two men looked closer into the engine.

'The damage to the rotor blades is clearly consistent with an internal explosion, do you agree?'

'Yes I do.'

'What puzzles me is the discolouration,' said Jameson signalling to one of his colleagues to join them. 'Matt, can you bring a swathe and sample bag with you,' he added.

'You think the engine exploded in mid-air then,' commented Tomlinson.

'It certainly looks that way,' replied Alec as his colleague arrived. 'Matt, can you see if there's any trace of residue in there. Sergeant, can you hand me that large flashlight over there.'

Tomlinson returned and handed the lamp to Jameson who then shone it into the engine as his colleague inspected the walls of the internal casing.

'Can you shine the light at five o'clock? Thanks.'

'See anything?' asked Chievney.

'Not yet, try two o'clock.'

'What's he looking for?' asked Tomlinson.

'Evidence of foreign matter,' replied Alec.

'Eleven o'clock. Come forward. Wait, a few degrees clockwise.'

'What is it?' asked Chievney.

'I've got something,' said Matt as he started to scrape the internal wall of the engine casing.

A few moments later he emerged with a sample of ashes in a polythene bag.

'I'll get this to the mobile lab outside straight away.'

'When do you think you'll be done here?' asked Chievney.

'Twenty-four hours and then we'll get the wreckage cut and removed.'

'Good work Alec, I'll wait for the report.'

In the comfort of his Manhattan apartment Milton Porter lie asleep as the telephone beside his bed began to ring. He stirred and reached over to pick up the receiver.

'Hello,' he said quietly, trying not to disturb his wife. It took a few moments for him to recognise the voice speaking to him from the other end of the line.

His wife turned towards him, still snugly covered in the duvet.

'Who is it?' she asked, her eyes still closed.

The caller's words began to register, causing him to sit up suddenly and swing his legs out of the bed. In the darkness he fumbled for the switch of his bedside lamp, almost knocking it over.

'Milton, what's wrong?' his wife asked, now looking on.

'I'm so sorry, I really don't know what to say,' he continued, impervious to his wife's presence. There was a long pause.

'Yes of course I will. Goodbye Margaret, I'll call you.'

Porter put the phone down and gazed into the space surrounding his bed, his face riddled with shock.

'What's happened?'

'It's William.'

Located in the financial district of downtown Manhattan on the eastern side of Pearl Street near the intersection with Wall, the building housing Mason-Wainwright's corporate offices saw the usual stream of financiers and clients flowing in and out of its panelled foyer as another day of trading began. The corporation shared the sparsely designed building with a number of other financial organisations and occupied floors six through nine. The rotating glass doors led Milton Porter and two of his executives into the spacious lobby and they headed straight for the elevators a few strides to their left. They walked at pace towards the silver doors and waited for a descending carriage to arrive, neglecting to bid their customary good morning to the security guards as they passed the front desk.

When they reached the seventh floor the doors opened and the three men walked into the executive lounge – a stylish room from which the board members' offices were accessed. The lounge was full of employees from executive to front-line associate; Porter's PA had gathered them all for an announcement after she had received a call from him earlier that morning. He had given nobody except the two men with him an explanation as to why the meeting had been called and as the buzz of conversation began to diminish, Porter signalled for everyone to finish talking.

'Thank you all for joining me here this morning,' he began. 'I've called you together to inform you of some distressing news. Our president, William H Calvert and his personal assistant Gillian Taylor were killed in a plane crash last night. I don't have all the facts at present but I know that he was travelling to Washington on business and the plane went down over Baltimore. As soon as we know more, I'll let you know. This is clearly a grievous time for their families and so I'm sure you will keep them in your thoughts and prayers over the coming days. William was a trusted friend and a great colleague. It's a shock to us all so please take whatever time you need to let this sink in while Simone organises some coffee. I really am lost for words. This comes at a time when the corporation is prospering, thanks mainly to William's unswerving dedication. That's all I can really say for now and I thank you for taking the time out of your busy schedules. I'll let you know the date of the funeral in due course.'

Porter then signalled for the vice-presidents to assemble in the boardroom. One by one the six men and one woman filed in like officers to the bridge of a ship and stood around the oval table in the centre of the room waiting for their captain.

'Why was he going to Washington? He never informed us of this,' asked one of them after Porter had joined them and closed the door.

'I have no idea, but David Forrester was travelling with him,' replied Porter coldly.

'Forrester? What's going on, Milton?'

'I intend to find out right now. Apparently he didn't take a flight from Newark or JFK and that, coupled with Forrester's presence, troubles me deeply.'

'Simone,' he said, after pressing the call button on the table's speaker phone, 'will you get hold of Carlton Hayes for me please.'

As he waited for the call to come on the line he sensed the

air of concern emanating from his colleagues but said nothing as he nervously tapped his fingers on the table.

'Mr Hayes is on the line now,' said Simone.

'Good morning Carlton... Yes it's come as a shock to us all; we don't really know where to put ourselves. I'm sorry to hear about David, I'm sure you're feeling the loss too... I know this is not a good time to ask but I need to know exactly why he was travelling to Washington with William last night.'

Porter listened with contempt to Hayes' response, needing to provide him with a believable reason for asking the question.

'We're just trying to close a deal with a prospective client in Washington at this time,' he lied.

'I understand that but we were due to meet with them today and there are things that William hadn't communicated to us of late; it could save a lot of embarrassment... Well then call me as soon as possible! And please pass on our condolences to David's family, he was a fine attorney.'

'Well?' asked a voice from the opposite side of the table as Porter ended the call.

'Lawyers!' he exclaimed, giving no further comment.

'This is serious, isn't it, Milton?' asked another of his team.

'There's no cause for alarm yet, let's wait until Hayes gets back to me.'

'Hadn't one of us better visit Margaret and arrange for a wreath?' asked Sarah Claiborne, the sole female to have worked her way onto Calvert's board.

'Yes of course,' replied Porter. 'Can you take care of that please?'

'It's the least I can do,' she replied.

'Let's reconvene this afternoon. I should have some news from Hayes by then,' he said, concluding the meeting. 'And not a word of this to anyone, is that clear?' he added finally, gesturing for them to leave.

2

Celina McCallen walked elegantly along the central corridor of the residency occupied by her boss, Senator Robert Gouldman. She was a well-groomed woman who had held the position of personal secretary for the past six months having taken a promotion from her previous role as a senior administrator for one of his colleagues. This promotion had meant everything to her and now at the age of 32 she felt that she had finally begun to walk in the Washington corridors of power, which had been her ambition since graduating from college. Her colleagues hated her 'to die for' looks; Gouldman liked blondes as long as they were upward of 5ft 8in. In her eyes she was the senator's personal advisor and had already made her mark on him by assuming a familiarity with the man 16 years her senior the moment she had arrived.

Upon entering the spacious office she had recently acquired, Celina placed her handbag underneath the desk at the end of the room before reclining on her crimson leather sofa to look through the day's correspondence. Capitol News was broadcasting a story as she switched on the television opposite and a few minutes later a particular report came on air that diverted her attention, drawing her to the screen.

'A private jet belonging to the president of a New York based investment corporation crashed on the outskirts of Baltimore last night killing the three passengers and two pilots. Crash investigators were on the scene soon after fire fighters had quenched the flames, but a spokesman for the team was as yet unable to comment on the probable cause of the accident. Crash investigators are still at the scene, where we now join our correspondent, Steve Goodman. Steve, can you tell us anymore at this stage?'

'Very tragic,' said a voice from behind her.

Celina looked over her shoulder to see her boss leaning on the edge of the sofa, his eyes fixed on the screen.

'Good morning, Senator,' she replied, noting his keen interest in the story.

'... Yes Jennifer, unconfirmed reports say that the bodies of only two of the passengers were recovered, that is of a William Calvert of the New York firm Mason-Wainwright and a female colleague...'

'Celina, can you take a look at this and tell me what you think,' Gouldman asked, handing her a bound document.

'Did you know him?' she asked curiously as she took hold of it.

'No, and I can't say I'm familiar with the organisation either,' he replied, still attentive to the reporter's words.

Celina turned back to the TV as Steve Goodman concluded his report.

'What is it?' she asked Gouldman, referring to the document.

'We'll talk later,' he replied, sounding dismissive, something she was used to by now.

'I have an important speech to deliver to the senate tomorrow,' he added, before leaving the room.

Gouldman closed the door of his office and stood near the entrance, surveying the room for a few moments before walking to his desk to make a call to one of his colleagues. There was no answer at first but as he was about to put the receiver down a reply came at the other end of the line.

'Harvey, it's good to hear your voice at last; I thought you were avoiding me. I'm calling to make sure you're ready for tomorrow – I'm counting on your support ... Good, and are the others on board? ... Then talk them round, this is going to be a close one ... Sure, I realise that but you know this is not at all popular in certain circles and if we don't get the vote ... Yes I am well aware of the threats. I'll see you in the house tomorrow.'

He placed the handset back on the phone and then walked over to one of two ornate windows that gave him a view of the front of the residency. Looking out into the late summer morning he could see the trees that shielded the building from the busy road behind shimmer gently in the breeze. As his anxious face looked down he could see a couple of the residency staff conversing on the steps before noticing a car drive through the gates. He watched as it stopped in one of the allotted parking spaces near the main entrance. A man got out of the car, looked around and was then escorted to the entrance by one of the security guards. Gouldman's eyes followed him all the way to the front doors until he was in the entrance and out of view. The fully stocked drinks cabinet in the corner of his office met his eyes as he turned around and he became enticed to pour himself a glass of Bourbon before returning to his desk. There he lay back in his swivel chair and waited.

Celina jumped as the telephone rang loudly. She quickly fumbled for the volume control before even thinking to answer the call. The ring was much too loud; perhaps someone had been using the phone in her absence and had hit the dial volume control by accident. On the other end of the line was Sophie Griegson, one of the staff from the front office.

'There's a Mr Markham to see the senator. Can you come to the front office please, Miss McCallen. He's quite insistent.'

'I'll be right down,' she replied.

There was nobody by the name of Markham on her appointments list for this week, so this was an unscheduled visit that she would have to politely send away for security reasons. Incidents like this always worried her. In her previous job she had heard of an incident where a woman had arrived to see a resident official unannounced and had somehow weaved her way through security with an undetected gun and had almost shot her intended victim. Had it not been for a vigilant colleague, the woman, a known protagonist, would have succeeded in her goal. What had brought the incident home to Celina was the fact that she had been working in the adjacent office at the time and had been impervious to the near assassination.

She walked briskly to the door and back along the corridor to the entrance hall, the sound of her stiletto shoes echoing loudly as she did so. When she arrived she turned to her right and entered the administration office from where Sophie had called and saw the man sitting on a chair in the corner. He stood up as she walked towards him, his outward appearance initially portraying a man in his early 50s yet behind, a strangely youthful look that gave the illusion that she was meeting two different men. The striking head of light-brown hair, parted at the left, seemed to her to be too natural for a man with a face of that age, but it was his piercing eyes that unsettled her the most.

'Mr Markham, I'm Celina McCallen, Senator Gouldman's personal assistant,' she said politely, with a tremble in her voice.

'Your receptionist has informed me that I will not be able to see the senator today. Is this true?' he asked.

'Yes I'm afraid so, it's not policy to….'

'It's OK, Celina,' said Gouldman, standing in the doorway behind her.

'But I wasn't informed of this,' replied Celina.

'I'm sorry. I forgot to mention it yesterday. Please come through, John.'

Markham stared at her as he approached the doorway causing her skin to creep and turn cold. Then the senator led his guest up the large staircase to the first floor where his office was situated. He opened the door, allowing Markham to enter first and then closed it firmly behind them.

'Drink?' he asked when they were safely inside.

'No thank you, this meeting must be brief,' replied his guest. 'Did you see the report on the news this morning?'

Celina sat at her desk and opened the document that her boss had left her to read. She was surprised to see that it was the draft of a speech, perhaps the one he had told her he would be giving the next day. He had never asked her to look over anything of this nature before and with the encounter with John Markham fresh in her mind she began reading nervously. By the time she had got to the third page she could feel the tiny hairs on the back of her neck stand on end.

'He can't really mean this!'

By page four she was forced to close the document, casting it away from her as though it were something evil, something she wasn't supposed to see.

'He's given me the wrong document.'

Greatly disturbed by what she had read and unable to get the senator's visitor out of her mind, she paced at speed back to the hallway and walked briskly up the stairs towards Gouldman's office. When she reached the landing she slowed down and cautiously walked to the door, stopped, calmed herself, and placed her ear to the door to attempt to distinguish the words being spoken in the office behind.

'So everything's been covered?' asked a nervous Robert Gouldman.

'There's no trail if that's what you're eluding to.'

'Good. The money will be in the agreed location by close of business.'

'I hope so, Robert. The last payment was late.'

'Technical hitch, I apologise for the inconvenience.'

'No need.'

'John, you're looking well,' said Gouldman with a smirk.

'Let's just get this business completed as soon as possible and then we can both get back to being the people we really are.'

Gouldman laughed and patted his visitor condescendingly on the shoulder.

'Eavesdropping now are we?' said a voice from behind her, causing Celina to jump and knock her head against the wooden panels of the door.

The conversation inside the room suddenly ceased and she could hear footsteps coming towards her from within. Her heart racing, she signalled for her colleague to leave quickly before heading for the stairs and disappearing from view only moments before Gouldman and his visitor emerged from the office.

Gouldman surveyed the landing suspiciously and saw a female member of staff walking in the opposite direction to the stairs.

'Did anyone knock the door?' he called out to her.

'No Senator, maybe it was a draught. I'll close that window on the stairwell if you like.'

'That won't be necessary.'

He turned to Markham, who looked at him nervously.

'Probably nothing,' he said, trying to be reassuring.

'I'm telling you, I heard someone,' replied Markham insistently. 'So deal with it and we'll talk again. I'll see myself out.'

3

At an inopportune time the phone rang during what was becoming a cumbersome resource-planning meeting in Ross Chievney's office. He allowed his voicemail to cut in, leaving it on audio in case any messages were urgent.

'Ross, this is Alec. I've got the results from the Baltimore crash. Call me as soon as you're free.'

He immediately pressed the auto-dialler to return the call and moments later Alec Jameson was on the line.

'Alec, what have you got?'

'That sample we took from the port engine – we've found traces of an incendiary device.'

'Are you certain of that?'

'Absolutely. We've had the results verified by the FBI.'

'OK, thanks. Leave it with me. I'll need a copy of the report as soon as possible. We'll talk again,' said Chievney, ending the call and turning to his colleagues. 'I'm sorry but we'll have to adjourn this.'

After his colleagues had left, Chievney returned to his desk and picked up the phone again.

'Lawrence Henderson please... Yes I'll hold.'

Agent Rachel Kirby was opening an envelope she had been expecting, the contents of which would provide needed information regarding a drugs syndicate she was investigating.

As she pulled out a series of photographs from the envelope and sifted through them, her hopes of finding an immediate lead quickly diminished. In her opinion the photographs had been taken by an amateur, mainly because the subject of the pictures did not appear as visible as she had hoped – she had only the man's profile, not his facial features. Even the best shot was not enough to clearly identify him and she doubted they would get another chance to photograph again for a few weeks based on the timing of the shipments that she had been compiling.

When her chair tilted slightly she looked up to see the 6ft figure of Sam Durrell standing over her. He was a Virginian of Jamaican origin and had previously served as a uniformed officer in the Washington police department before joining the FBI as a special agent.

'I got a call from Henderson. He wants to see us in his office in one hour. He told us not to wander off.'

'What's it about?' she asked.

'I thought you might be able to tell me.'

Kirby noted the time and immediately returned to the photographs. Henderson had said one hour and he hated tardiness.

Durrell had great respect for the single, 29-year-old redhead. Her father, a senior official in the bureau, would in Durrell's view ensure that she would be destined for great things and in his opinion she deserved it. Due to her tenacious nature he was confident that his colleague just two years his junior would find the man in the photograph, eventually.

Sat on the edge of his desk, a perturbed Lawrence Henderson stared at the photograph on the wall taken on the day of his graduation to the bureau back in 1974, remembering his days at the academy. Within his first year he had been identified as material for fast track promotion. Now he was in charge of just 16 front-line agents. He should have been running a department by now but 90 minutes earlier what was probably the final chance of reaching that illusive goal had again been snatched from him. Before he could indulge his memories further there was a knock at the door; Ross Chievney had arrived for their meeting. When Chievney entered the room Henderson greeted his long-time colleague with a half-hearted smile.

'It's been a while, Ross,' he said as they shook hands.

'A welcome distraction from budgets, Lawrence.'

'Indeed,' replied Henderson, hearing a second knock on the door.

'This will be agents Kirby and Durrell. I'm assigning them to investigate this case.'

'Are they your best?' asked Chievney.

'They're up there. Come in,' he then called and sat down as the two agents entered the room.

'Kirby, Durrell, this is Ross Chievney, Chief Air Crash Investigator, northeastern region. Please sit down all of you – Mr Chievney will brief you on the reason I have called you both in. Ross…'

'Thanks. A private jet came down in a field just outside of Baltimore the night before last – three on board, plus the two pilots. My team found traces of a foreign substance on the port engine and we have had it analysed and verified by your labs. It was the remains of an incendiary device. We are assuming that the saboteurs planted a second in the starboard engine that was destroyed in mid-air.'

'That's why I want the pair of you to investigate this,' said Henderson. 'Durrell, you've got experience in this area. Ross will fill you in and give you anything you need. Also check with the lab. They'll point you in the right direction in finding out where that incendiary device may have come from.'

'Sir, why am I involved in this?' asked Kirby.

'You were investigating Mason-Wainwright last year,' replied Henderson.

'Yes, for financial irregularities.'

'What did you find?'

'Nothing.'

'I see.'

'That doesn't mean we weren't on to something. Mr Jackson took Dan Riley and myself off the case. A priority came up and we were reassigned.'

'Really?'

'I stated my feelings at the time, sir.'

'Yes I'm sure you did. William Calvert was on board, so I think it's time to re-open the Mason-Wainwright case and find out what's happening here, don't you?'

'Who else was on board?' asked Agent Durrell.

'His PA and a David Forrester.'

'Of Hayes-Coleman?' asked Kirby.

'Correct.'

'We spoke to them during the investigation. They weren't as helpful as we would have liked.'

'An interesting case then,' added Henderson. 'Ross, has the crash site been cleared yet?'

'No. Another 12 hours maybe.'

'Good. I need your team to comb every inch of the cabin. If Calvert's lawyer was on board I'm sure agents Kirby and Durrell will be interested if there are the remains of any documents, however fragmented.'

'Sure. If there's nothing else…'

'Thank you, Ross, I'll be in touch.'

Chievney got up, acknowledged Durrell and Kirby and then left the room.

'This investigation takes priority. There has to be a connection to this recent incident. Find it. And I want to know immediately if Jackson starts meddling. Do you understand?'

'Yes sir,' replied Durrell.

'I trust you both to keep me informed then.'

Celina McCallen was absorbed in a letter she was writing to James Stephen Eckhart, a professor of politics at Harvard. She had recently purchased a copy of his book *The Modern Machine of US Politics,* designed to enlighten the new generation of politics students on the changing face of the world's greatest democracy. The letter expressed her gratitude for this timely publication and was to include a request to meet him personally, when her boss entered the room and demanded her attention. She took off her reading glasses and saved her letter document.

'Someone was listening outside my office yesterday. Was it one of the staff?'

'I've no idea,' she replied nervously.

He stared into her eyes momentarily; if she knew something he would detect it. Celina stared back emotionless. Two could play at that game, she thought.

'Keep an eye on them, will you.'

'And how do you expect me to do that?' she replied with dissent. To say nothing, she thought, would only amplify his suspicions.

'You're right, how indeed. I'm sorry about John Markham's unannounced arrival yesterday; it was thoughtless. I know how you feel about security protocol and I could see the concern on your face.'

'Who was he?'

'Just someone I'm using for a bit of research.'

She was sure he was lying.

'Robert, about yesterday... The speech,' she said impulsively, then wishing she had kept silent and let him leave.

'The speech?' he replied, looking perplexed as she abandoned eye contact for the first time.

'Yes, the one you are giving today.'

'What of it?'

His tone had changed. She was uncertain whether this was just another of his ploys to unsettle her. He often did this to reaffirm who was really in charge.

'I think you gave me…'

'Thanks for the reminder!' he exclaimed, his tone again changing completely. 'I need to change something before you and I head off later. Well done, Celina!'

'I'm sorry, you and I?'

'Yes. I want you to accompany me to the senate today. It's time you became more familiar with the place. Put whatever else you are doing on hold, OK.'

'But…'

'Come, Celina; don't tell me you're turning down an opportunity like this.'

'No! It's OK, really, I'd be delighted.'

'Settled then,' he said, walking to door.

After he had left Celina quickly checked that the document was still in her bottom drawer. It was.

He has no idea, she thought.

At 11.00 a limousine arrived to take the senator to Capitol Hill. The chauffeur parked it in front of the steps outside the residency and stood ready for his passengers to arrive. As they got near the entrance door, Gouldman turned to Celina and held her arm.

'This is a special day. I have something for you,' he said, holding out a small velvet box.

'What is it?' she asked.

'Open it.'

Inside was a round golden broach with a single emerald in the centre.

'It's beautiful, thank you.'

'Aren't you going to put it on?' he asked.

'Yes of course,' she replied, fastening it to the lapel of her jacket.

'Shall we?'

Upon seeing them at the top of the steps the chauffeur opened the rear door of the limousine. As they got in Ed Hamell, one of Gouldman's advisers, was sat inside going over some papers, his glasses resting on his nose. He was a stocky man, balding and in his late 40s, who appeared to Celina as a seasoned political aid who knew his job.

'Ed, have you met my assistant, Celina?'

'Ed Hamell, I've never had the pleasure,' he replied, shaking her hand.

'Celina McCallen.'

'First visit to the senate?'

'Yes.'

'You must be special. He's never done this with any of his former secretaries.'

'Really,' she replied, faking her smile.

'So how do you think the vote will go?' asked Gouldman as the chauffeur closed the door and then climbed into the driver's seat.

'It'll be a close one.'

'We may have some late-comers joining us,' said Gouldman. 'I've been working on those wavering.'

'What do you think, Celina?' asked Hamell as the limousine headed towards the iron gates at the end of the driveway.

Taken aback by the question, she considered her response carefully.

'I think the senator will deliver. I've every confidence in him.'

'See Ed, my staff trust me implicitly,' said Gouldman, smiling.

'The speech of course is crucial,' added Hamell.

Celina looked quickly out of the window to avoid eye contact with either man. She did not want to be drawn into conversation about the speech, not after what she had read. She remained deeply disturbed as the fantasy she had created surrounding her role began to be replaced by the stark realities of the darker side of the workings of the US political system, something that Professor Eckhart had obviously omitted from his book. The smiles and the compliments were a mere façade; inside a voice was crying for help – she did not want to be here.

As the limousine continued on the short journey from the residency towards Capitol Hill, the three sat quietly looking out of the front of the vehicle as the dome of the White House appeared in the distance and the traffic lights immediately ahead turned red causing the driver to bring the limousine to a halt. To the left, Celina could see a group of protesters with placards gathered on the corner of the intersection. She could not see with clarity the slogans featured on the boards but whatever the message she presumed that they too were on their way to Capitol Hill to take their rightful place in contributing to the democratic process, albeit outside the gates of the edifice that supposedly represented the free world. As the limousine moved forward again and passed through the green light, she looked back at them for as long as she could before they disappeared from view.

After a few hundred yards the driver turned left and began to increase his speed down a street that she didn't recognise at first, and at that moment Gouldman looked at Hamell.

'He must be taking the scenic route,' Gouldman joked.

After passing two other junctions the driver turned left again and Hamell realised that something was wrong.

'Driver, are you new? You're going in the wrong direction,' he said.

There was no reply.

'What's going on here?' he exclaimed. 'This isn't the way! Driver?'

The chauffeur continued on his course, ignoring the voice behind him. Before they could comprehend the situation, they realised that they were suddenly descending at speed into an underground parking lot and the car was being swung violently around as the driver accelerated towards the entrance to the lower level.

'Stop! Where are you taking us?' cried Hamell.

Celina looked at Gouldman expecting a reaction from him, failing to understand the reason for the detour. Her boss remained calm; Hamell became frantic. It was then that she realised that something was very wrong and a look of helplessness covered her face, like a child who was about to experience something awful.

The car descended another level and the driver again turned sharply causing the wheels to screech loudly. Ahead they saw four men waiting in the distance beside a black Dodge carrier with its custom alloy wheels shining in the light that was filtering in from the street above.

'What's going on?' shouted Hamell as the limousine came to an abrupt stop causing the three passengers to jolt forward.

The driver leapt out and as he opened the rear door, two of the men who had been standing by the Dodge sprinted over and poked their heads inside. Celina screamed as the masked faces stared at her. They were mannequins that had come to life, reminding her of a terrifying Halloween experience she had had as a young child. As Hamell lunged forward in a pitiful attempt to defend the senator, one of the men sprayed him with a canister and its gaseous contents caused him to fall to the floor of the limousine. Before she could do anything the two men grabbed Gouldman, injected a fluid into his neck, and covered his head with a black hood. She looked on in horror as they dragged him away, watching him turn his head violently as he tried to shake it off.

She screamed again as another arrived and pulled her out

of the car causing one of her shoes to fall off, and when she felt the stab of cold metal in her back and realised that it was a gun, her legs gave way as she was dragged towards the carrier.

'No, leave her!' called a voice as they bundled Gouldman into the Dodge. Her captor removed the gun from her back and pushed her to the ground as the driver pulled up. He quickly jumped on board allowing the last man to slam the side door shut, leaving Celina and Hamell alone as it sped off out of the parking lot with Gouldman inside. Celina looked up and saw the Dodge disappear up the ramp that led to the upper level, leaving a mist of exhaust smoke hanging in the air.

She slowly picked herself up and stood trembling, trying to come to terms with the events that had just engulfed her. The engine of the limousine was still running and as she looked around in hopelessness she saw about ten other vehicles parked on the level, their owners nowhere in sight. Realising that she was alone with the situation she froze, unable to think or reason. Only the faint groaning of Ed Hamell from within the limousine brought her back and at once she called out to him.

'Mr Hamell!' she cried, running to the car, tripping almost immediately and forgetting that she was wearing only one shoe.

As she lurched forward into the rear of the car, Hamell was lying on the floor, groaning and covering his eyes.

'Can you see?' she asked.

'Yes, just give me a few moments,' he replied, taking a handkerchief from his trouser pocket to wipe his eyes. 'I can't find my cell phone!' he added anxiously.

'Use mine,' she replied, reaching for her bag.

'I should have known this would happen,' said Hamell as he glanced at her with his reddened eyes.

Celina, shocked and unable to assimilate his words, handed her phone to him.

4

Mike Fabien entered FBI headquarters, meandered through the maze of desks that stood between him and his workstation and noticed that the area was only partially occupied. Placing his copy of the Washington Herald beside his laptop he sat down, booted it up and waited for the logon screen to appear. When he had entered his user id and password he clicked on his e-mail icon and hoped he would receive something interesting. Most of the new entries he had been receiving of late were in his opinion mere e-junk consisting of, yet not restricted to, broadcasts of new operational policies and procedures, new appointments and career opportunities, none of which interested him at present. In his confused mind career prospects were, to say the least, limited at present.

Three of the e-mails, however, looked vaguely as though they were actually work related and so he opened them and browsed them briefly. 'I'll get back to you soon' was a phrase that came instantly to mind as one of the senders informed him that he was becoming a little impatient regarding information he urgently needed which Mike had promised him yesterday.

The last e-mail looked a little unusual. The sender was a user named 'Spiral Architect' and the title 'A friend in need' captured his attention. It was unusual for a misdirected e-mail intended for a civilian to get through the bureau's computer system firewall. Assuming it was internal the user's name was not compliant with internal e-mail id standards and he did not recognise it as belonging to any of his contacts outside the bureau or associate organisations. He was intrigued. As he was about to open it the phone on his desk rang. He recognised the extension number on the digital display screen immediately.

'Fabien.'

'About time; I was looking for you this morning,' said the voice at the other end of the line.

'I was working from home, reading up on something.'

'Well now you're here I'll see you in my office in five minutes.'

With that he hung up, secured his laptop screen and told himself that 'a friend in need' would have to wait. He made his way back out of the double doors through which he had entered and into the corridor towards Lawrence Henderson's office. His relationship with his boss was strained of late and he was getting used to being spoken to abruptly. Things had changed since his return from Ashbury Falls and he was finding the new regime difficult to adjust to.

On his way he decided to visit the men's restroom for a brief freshen up and turned sharply to his right, entering the dimly lit room to discover that he was the sole occupant. The mirror that stretched the entire length of the washbasins revealed his darkened eyes that did little to complement his unshaven face. A feeling of rejuvenation came over him as the ice-cold water with which he had filled the basin tantalized the pores of his face and the lids of his tired eyes. He ran a comb through his light brown hair ensuring that it was parted neatly to the left, the side to which it naturally fell, and then pulled out the plug. As he looked up to adjust the fall of his fringe he saw for a split second the figure of a man in the mirror looking at him from behind. He turned around quickly only to find that he was alone in the room just as he had been upon entry. He had not heard anyone else enter nor was anyone about to leave. Cautiously he walked over to the toilet cubicles and noticed all the doors were ajar. Darting to the entrance door he swung it open and looked in both directions along the corridor. There was no sign of anyone except for two women walking past in opposite directions.

He returned to the dimly lit restrooms and felt a drip land on the collar of his shirt. Realising that his face was still wet he walked over to the paper towel dispenser in the corner at the end of the rank of basins, but as he approached he noticed that the basin he had been using was still full of water and upon closer inspection he discovered that the plug had not been removed. He *had* emptied it – he was certain, yet he could not deny the possibility that with the amount of sleep he had been losing of late his mind may be playing tricks on him. Recurring nightmares were waking him in the early hours. He would be taken back to the jetty by the river in Ashbury Falls and encounter a hooded figure casting stones into the misty waters of the dream. Then frogmen would appear through the mist as their dinghy approached the jetty. They would pursue him up the walkway with a syringe and each time they would get closer to capturing him. It was obvious that he was recalling events that had happened to Ronnie Jebson during his investigation into the Ascension project, but the identity of the stone thrower eluded him; this causing greater distress than the frogmen.

He took out a small bottle of pills that was in his jacket pocket and swallowed one before leaving the restrooms. Aware of his sleeping malady the bureau medics had been requested to prescribe them and he had become dependent on them of late. Checking periodically to see if anyone was behind him, he marched to Henderson's office speedily and upon arrival he knocked and waited.

'Come in,' said a voice he recognised.

He opened the door and stepped inside. Three men were waiting for him.

'You're late,' said Henderson.

'Did you get lost, Agent Fabien?' asked Thomas Jackson sarcastically.

'Sir?'

'We've been waiting over 15 minutes,' replied Henderson.

He could only have been late by two or three minutes. What Henderson had just stated was impossible. What was he talking about? he thought.

'I'm sorry,' he replied. Anything more would not only have been pointless but damaging; he had to just take it on the chin.

'Good. Don't keep us waiting again,' said Jackson.

'Let's get on shall we? Fabien, this is Agent John Carlyle, I believe you've met before,' said Henderson.

The two men acknowledged each other and sat down opposite their superiors. Fabien remembered that he and Carlyle had met a year ago during a training exercise just outside the capital.

'What do you know about a Senator Robert Gouldman?' Henderson asked Fabien.

He waited briefly before answering.

'He was elected to the senate in '92. His re-election two years ago that coincided with Clinton's was, to say the least, surprising. A Democrat with questionable views on euthanasia, he has caused a storm in some circles. Some say he's dangerous; others hail him as the voice of reason. I understand that he is giving a speech today in the senate on the very subject.'

'You've done your homework.'

'Not really sir; I have an interest in him among others, seeing as I tend to agree with those who think he's dangerous. I've followed his career over the years.'

'Yes, we're well aware of *your* views on this subject,' said Jackson. 'Some might even think they're bordering on dangerous too.'

'My views would never interfere with my work.'

'Well he won't be giving that speech today,' said Henderson re-focusing.

'Sir?'

'At around midday today he was abducted in an underground parking lot about a mile from the White House.'

'That doesn't come as a surprise to me.'

'Why not?'

'I understand that he received threats a few months ago from anti-euthanasia protestors. They warned that they would have to take action if he continued to press forward with his agenda. Anyway what's this got to do with me? I suppose Mr Jackson thinks I had something to do with it.'

'Did you?' asked Jackson.

'Mr Jackson has decided not to keep you deskbound for the rest of your career so I suggest that you cut the cute talk and listen to him,' said Henderson.

'Good advice,' replied Jackson. 'So far there has been no communication from his abductors. The only witnesses were his associate Edward Hamell and his PA. Go and pay her a visit. Her name is Celina McCallen – you'll find her at this address.'

'Why the sudden change of heart?' Fabien asked Jackson.

'I don't intend to waste my resources any further on paperwork. But remember this, Fabien, you're not out of the woods yet, not by a long shot. Play by the rules on this one and you'll redeem yourself – play Maverick and you're history.'

'Agent Carlyle will be your backup,' added Henderson. 'And remember, Fabien, don't get personal with this. I want him found alive and well. Nobody cares about *your* views.'

'And if he's already dead?'

'Is that what you think?' asked Carlyle.

'There are many who would like to see his demise,' replied Fabien coldly. 'Some look upon him as a cancer in the system

ALUMNI

that should be eradicated without fail.'

'And you are no doubt one of them,' said Jackson, glaring into his eyes.

'I didn't say that, besides, as Mr Henderson said – who cares about *my* views?'

'Who indeed,' added Jackson.

Sensing the standoff, Henderson interjected.

'I want regular updates from both of you. You're dismissed,' he said and glared at Fabien as though to tell him to make a speedy exit.

Fabien stared at Jackson for a brief few seconds before turning to Carlyle.

'We have work to do.'

'Watch him carefully,' said Jackson to Henderson the moment the two agents had left the room.

'Don't worry, I don't intend to take my eye off him for one second.'

'Good. Now I have other business to attend to.'

'Wait,' said Henderson.

'What is it?'

'We both know it should have gone to me.'

'Don't delude yourself, Henderson, the position was never yours.'

'I realise that, but that doesn't change a thing. I don't know how you did it.'

'That's of no consequence now. Just watch Fabien. If he goes down he won't be the only one.'

'Well let's just remind ourselves of something, shall we. Fabien is *my* operative and as such he reports to me. I'm still running things on the ground… sir.'

'Then I expect you to keep me posted; every detail, every lead, every movement, is that understood?'

5

As another working day came to its end the streets of Boston were bathed in a warm stream of air that flowed in from the Atlantic, whilst the early evening sun cast innumerable shadows across the city. A little under 15 minutes ago Jamie Farrington had said goodbye to a friend she had joined for cocktails after work and left Quincy Market to head home to her apartment just a few blocks away. Checking her watch she realised she was going to be late in meeting Malcolm Kemp for drinks that evening and so she hurried along the last block towards the entrance lobby, hoping she would get just a few precious minutes to unwind when she arrived.

She entered the lobby trying to avoid eye contact with the security guard who, as part of his daily routine, would engage her in a brief conversation regarding the weather, stories from his past or the things of interest from the newspaper he would read from cover to cover. Today all she wanted to do was summon the elevator and get into the sanctuary of her apartment as soon as possible.

'Have a nice evening, Miss,' he called out as the elevator arrived.

She thanked him and hurried in, pressing the button for the eighth floor a number of times, once being sufficient except when she was desperate to avoid unnecessary contact with someone she was forced to humour on a daily basis. As the elevator ascended she realised how much moving to Boston had altered her temperament in such a short space of time. Had she been back at the Farrington hotel in Ashbury Falls she would never find herself having that kind of attitude towards a lonely middle-aged man who merely wanted to talk to someone in the course of his eventless day. She had met many a soul in his situation loitering in the hotel reception over the years. She hoped her politeness and tolerance had not been as a result of such individuals being paying customers.

Her apartment, number 805, was just three doors along the corridor from the elevators and opposite a window that looked down on a small, enclosed courtyard leading to the underground parking lot. It was a luxury two-bedroom apartment at the front of a complex that had been converted from a multi-storey brick-fronted warehouse used mainly as a storage repository for businesses or domestic property moves. Jamie had added a few personal yet essential touches to make it her own; otherwise it was as she had found it when she had moved in earlier that year.

As the door closed behind her she threw her bag and jacket on the floor, kicked the shoes off her aching feet and lay down on the sofa opposite the window, brushing her hand through her hair as she put her feet up and rested them cosily on the arm. She lay there for a few minutes trying to exorcise all thoughts of work from her mind before getting up to pour herself a glass of freshly made juice she had concocted that morning, and to listen to any messages on her voicemail. There was only one. It was from her boss, Paul Burgess, asking her to be in for 07.00 the next day to go through some figures prior to a meeting he was holding with one of the accountants.

After gulping down the rest of her juice she lay back down on the sofa and reached for the latest copy of *Elle* Magazine on the table beside her. She began to flick through the pages that she had already read a couple of days previous in a pointless exercise to try to switch her mind off marketing budgets and the new advertising glossies that would launch the bank's latest product line. They had gone over budget and there was insufficient time to make the needed changes to meet the accountant's targets. Running a hotel seemed like a walk in the park compared to this.

Nice hair, she thought, as the girl with the long shaggy style on page 74 caught her attention.

After flicking further through the magazine she stopped and threw it back on the table, knocking a small glass ashtray onto the floor. She left it where it had dropped as it had been emptied of her cigarette butts that morning and she felt no compulsion to get up as her eyelids became heavy.

Her head jerked suddenly, causing her eyes to open. It was 19.35 – her catnap had turned to a sleep.

'Malcolm!'

She was meeting him at 20.00 in a wine bar just off Boston Common. He would not appreciate her turning up dressed in her work clothes and looking tired as though he were the last appointment of the day. She had no choice than to be late, make up a feasible excuse, and look a million dollars. She quickly entered the bathroom and turned on the shower. Moments later she was being caressed by the hot streams of water from the three-way shower that surrounded her. After a day that had turned out to be a mini Chernobyl she wished she could have remained in there for hours.

By the time she had wrapped a warm bath towel around her wet slender body it was 19.47. She quickly opened the door of her wardrobe, took out a silk blouse, a black evening trouser suit and her shoes, and dried herself before getting dressed. She was really going to need the perfect excuse now.

The top drawer in her bedroom contained her jewellery box. A finishing touch would make the difference. If she were 'complete' in Malcolm's eyes, his agitation would be countered by her appearance – it had worked many times before. She picked up the box and carried it to the bed. In transit a small white card that had somehow loosely attached itself to the underside dropped suddenly to the floor. She placed the box to the side of her and bent down to pick up the card. When she turned it over she saw that it was the card that Mike Fabien had given her with his address and phone number before he had left Ashbury Falls the previous year. She had forgotten all about it and wondered how on earth it had turned up in there.

Remembering the number of times she had thought about picking up the phone and calling him in the immediate days after seeing him disappearing down the sloped driveway of the hotel on that breezy autumn day brought her to a realisation she had been trying to deny for months. Three weeks after she and Fabien had parted she had boarded a 12-seater plane at the airport in Burlington, Vermont, bound for Boston. She had settled, got a job, caught up with a few old friends; everything had been fine until New Year's Eve. She had been invited to a party by a couple of girls who had previously rented room 611 of the apartment block, but had declined. At around ten minutes to midnight she had been about to pick up the phone and dial his number to wish him a happy new year. It never happened. Instead she had sat with her head in her hands, tears running from her eyes, realising that her world really had been turned upside down.

The tears that were now beginning to swell in her eyes felt as bitter as the ones she had actually shed that previous lonely New Year's Eve. She put the card away immediately and put her middle fingers to each eye to stem the flow of water. She couldn't smudge her eye makeup now as she would almost certainly turn up at Philbys and find that Malcolm Kemp had already left. Even her stunning appearance would not be enough to quench the flames of Malcolm's anger if she stood him up. She had learnt that sobering fact the hard way back in their college days when they had dated the first time around.

She quickly picked up her bag and put in her purse, makeup, keys and cigarettes before closing the door and heading to the elevators.

Philbys wine bar was half full as Malcolm Kemp checked his watch for what must have been the seventh time since his arrival. Despite its up-market ambience, fine wines and in his view, a clientele of status, he was not relaxed. It was now 20.40 and he was getting frustrated, angry and worried at Jamie's tardiness. He had already finished off two large glasses of a ten-year-old Merlot and was waiting for Jamie before seeking the waiter's attention for the third time that evening. Finally he saw her enter the bar and hurry over to where he was seated. In his opinion she looked perfect.

'What happened to you?' he asked her, trying to conceal his temper.

The mother of all excuses had failed to enter her mind.

'I was working late. How difficult is it to get a cab in this town?' she replied, preparing for the worst. She could not under any circumstances reveal that she had been for cocktails earlier with her friend.

'Well at least you're here now. What can I get you?' he said, his voice softening. She looked surprised.

'Just a glass of red, anything will do, you choose.'

Jamie wasn't a wine connoisseur like Malcolm. She would have been happy with a bottle of Rolling Rock in one of the bars on the other side of the common rather than drinking in this stuffy establishment. Malcolm summoned the waiter.

'Yes sir?'

'Another of the same for me and a house Shiraz for the lady,' he replied.

'We took on another client today,' he said turning to Jamie. Having lived in the states since starting college, Malcolm's dialect was starting to reveal a tang of Bostonian, which, mixed with his native English accent, made him sound somewhat unique.

'I bumped into Jason McMeans today. You remember him, don't you?' he continued.

'Small guy, ginger hair?'

'That's the one. What a surprise that was to me. He's changed you know, for the better of course. Who'd have thought he'd end up in commercial real estate! Making a small fortune in LA by all accounts. I remember when we were at college when he and Ben had that competition to see who could drink the most Boston ale. I thought he was going to die!'

By the time the waiter arrived with their wine, Malcolm's voice had faded until it could no longer be heard. She was alone with her thoughts; wondering whether the figures would be signed off, how her friend's date was going and why she was back in Boston. Uppermost in her mind, however, was the white card she had found on the floor.

'Jamie?' she heard a voice say. 'Jamie!'

'Sorry.'

'Are you OK?'

'What are the plans for tonight?' she asked.

'I've booked us a table at Bairdes.'

'Bairdes, how lovely.'

She hated the place.

'Jamie, I have something for you.'

'What is it?'

Malcolm put his hand inside his jacket pocket and took out a small box. He held it in his hand in front of her and opened it. Inside, surrounded by red velvet was a gold ring with a cluster of sapphires sparkling in the dim lights that surrounded them. He lifted it out and gently took her by the hand.

'It's beautiful,' she said as he placed it on her finger.

'Marry me Jamie – for real this time.'

At that moment she began telling herself that she had been given an opportunity that most women would never get; a second chance initiated by what some might call a stroke of fate. What were the odds of leaving a restaurant and forgetting to take an expensive tailor made jacket with you, then returning to retrieve it at the very moment that Malcolm Kemp and friends were arriving? Moments earlier she would have missed him, moments later he would have been seated.

Malcolm watched soberly as Jamie gazed at her hand, rotating it slightly to see the full effect of the glistening sapphires. She seemed mesmerised.

'Well?' he asked her gently.

She looked at him for a moment and then gazed back at the ring, asking herself whether everything had been pointing to this moment since her return to Boston. When the answer came her eyes once again focused on Malcolm, the man who had left a hole in her life that she had thought might never be filled again.

The look of hopeful anticipation on his face slowly evaporated as she placed the fingers of her right hand around the ring and began to remove it. Gently she placed it in his palm and looked at him consolingly.

'Jamie?' he said in disbelief.

'I'm sorry Malcolm.'

'Why, what's wrong?'

'I can't do this,' she replied, tears swelling.

'Jamie, I don't understand…'

'I can't marry you Malcolm, I'm sorry.'

'Why not?'

She offered no explanation.

'But…'

Picking up her bag she got up to leave.

'Jamie!'

'I have to go.'

She paced out of Philbys hurriedly. When she had reached the bottom of the steps leading up to the entrance doors she began a brisk walk towards the common where she knew she could get a cab quickly. Malcolm rose from his seat and raced to the entrance, slapping a $20 bill into the hand of the nearest waiter. He pushed the doors violently and they flew open, one almost hitting an adjacent wall. He chased after her and began to catch up – her Dolman stilettos were no match for his Italian seam-panelled lace-ups.

Grabbing her arm he pulled her back, almost causing her to fall, and looked into her eyes with a silent pleading.

She was scared. She remembered when this very same thing had happened back in their college days. The doctors had been concerned that the blow had caused some internal damage to her right eye. Fortunately it had not, but the bruising had taken several days to heal.

'Jamie, this was meant to be, I won't lose you again.'

She sensed that he was calming down a little. Surely he would realise that he could never get away with hitting her again.

'No Malcolm, our meeting again was just chance, nothing more. This isn't right. Please, you have to let me go.'

His grip tightened.

'Please Malcolm!' she entreated him.

'OK, I understand. Maybe this is too soon,' he said, trying to compose himself. 'We'll wait.'

'No Malcolm.'

'It's OK. I know you've been under stress lately. Quit the job; you won't need to work now anyway.'

'It's not that.'

'Then what is it?' he asked in a menacing, agitated tone.

She was unable to speak.

'Tell me!' he shouted, now enraged.

'Let go Malcolm,' she replied calmly.

To her surprise he loosened his grip, allowing her to pull her arm free.

'Goodbye Malcolm,' she said, drying her eyes and then she turned and walked up the street. Boston Common was in view and she could see a vacant cab on the corner. He did not attempt to follow her. When she reached the end of the block he called to her one last time.

'You'll regret this Jamie, I promise you! Keep walking and it's…'

Moments later, Malcolm Kemp watched as the cab on the corner disappeared from view, and Jamie from his life.

6

It was late afternoon as Fabien and Carlyle made their way across a bustling Washington DC to Gouldman's residency. Fabien was quiet, saying very little to his new partner regarding the case. With memories of the disciplinary hearing in the back of his mind he felt daunted at the reality of being assigned to such a high profile case so soon. Carlyle, bored with the small talk, eventually sought to draw Fabien out. His next words came as a surprise.

'So you've been given a reprieve then.'

Fabien ignored the comment – the topic was not up for discussion, especially with someone he hardly knew who had just been assigned as his partner. Changing the subject Carlyle tried a different approach.

'I dealt with an abduction about three years ago,' he added. 'You get led down so many paths only to meet dead ends. We found her eventually, in the nick of time. Don't you think Gouldman's got a point though Fabien? I admit his views may be a little extreme but the principles merit consideration.'

Carlyle's words reminded him of something a former colleague had said during a case four years previous involving a surgeon who had been killing off his terminally ill patients. Henderson had been forced to take him off the 'Doctor Death' case because in his view Fabien was becoming unbalanced and failing to be objective in the investigation. Fabien chose his words carefully before replying.

'Do we have the right to play God?' he asked.

'That depends on whether you're religious,' replied Carlyle. 'How much further?'

'We're almost there. So how did you end up being transferred to Henderson?'

'Not transferred, just seconded. I've spent the last couple of years dealing mainly with corporate investigations, irregularities, tax evasion – the usual stuff. This is a welcome change.'

'So you were involved in the abduction case before this?'

'Yes, a few years ago.'

'So why the change to corporate?' Carlyle didn't answer. 'You must be in favour with someone,' continued Fabien.

'Maybe.'

'Jackson?'

'Yes, he asked for me.'

'He assigned you to keep an eye on me.'

'Do I need to?'

'About the case,' said Fabien. 'We'll probe a little, see what this Celina McCallen comes up with and then if necessary we'll speak with Gouldman's colleagues in the senate. We're here, that must be it behind the gates – there's a couple of police vehicles parked outside.'

Fabien drove his car towards the gates and was stopped by one of the officers. He showed his ID and was then signalled to proceed. The driveway curved to the right circumventing a quadrant-shaped lawn containing two diametrically positioned park benches for the staff to use during breaks. He parked by the side of the entrance and then opened the door. The two men got out. Carlyle surveyed the house before following Fabien up the steps and into the building. He noted that it was a white-coloured period building, probably built in the late 1800's, at the end of a terrace of similar properties and cordoned off with its own security gates and fences. Standing inside the entrance lobby was another police officer observing them closely as they entered.

'FBI?' he asked.

'Yes.'

'Miss McCallen's office is down the corridor and first on the right. She's expecting you.'

The two men made their way towards the rear of the building and saw a well lit room approaching.

'This must be it,' said Fabien as he approached an open door that led into a spacious office.

He knocked before stepping inside. As he did so he saw a slender blonde woman talking to a man holding a handkerchief to his left eye. She turned around quickly and then walked over to the door.

'Agent Fabien?' she asked, almost startled.

'And you must be Celina McCallen,' he replied, holding out his hand.

'Yes,' she replied as she shook it.

'This is Agent Carlyle.'

Disturbed, Celina glared at Fabien.

'Is everything OK, Miss McCallen?' he asked.

'We've met before, haven't we?' she replied.

'No, I don't think we have… no I'm positive we haven't.'

'Your face… I'm sorry, it's just…' She paused. 'This is Ed Hamell, Senator Gouldman's advisor.'

'Good afternoon gentlemen.'

'What happened to your eyes?' asked Carlyle.

'They sprayed me with gas, non-toxic luckily.'

'Were you hurt Miss McCallen?' asked Carlyle as Celina's eyes continued fixed on Fabien. 'Miss McCallen?'

'No… I was fine,' she recalled, realising that she was now staring. 'Mr. Hamell tried to stop them, that's why he was sprayed.'

'How many?' asked Fabien.

'I saw four, I think. There was also the driver, maybe there were others. They were wearing these awful masks.'

'And was anyone else in the parking lot?'

'No.'

'Why do you think he was abducted Mr Hamell?'

'I think you already know the answer to that, Agent Fabien.'

Celina looked on, concerned.

'You know something?' she asked.

'I'm sure you must be aware of the senator's views on certain sensitive matters, Miss McCallen?'

'Well I am now.'

'What do you mean?'

'I knew his views on euthanasia, well at least I thought I did, until he gave me this.'

'It's a draft of a speech. The one he was due to give today?'

'Yes, but I don't think he meant to give it to me.'

'Why not?'

'Read it, there on the third page.'

Celina pointed to the fourth paragraph. She looked at his face again as he read through it.

'Take a look,' said Fabien, handing the document to his partner.

'What do you make of it?' asked Hamell.

'Some areas of politics interest me Mr Hamell, particularly controversial subjects such as this. I've been following Senator Gouldman's career for some time now, wondering how far he would take matters. Clearly he's crossed the line here.'

'Do you think that's the reason for the abduction?' asked Celina.

'Possibly, but I have a bigger question regarding the contents of this manuscript.'

'Which is?'

'How he could have possibly got away with saying this in the senate! It would probably have ended his career.'

'Let me see that again,' said Hamell anxiously.

'Are you the only person who has seen this?' asked Fabien.

'I don't know,' replied Celina.

'When did he give you this?' asked Hamell, stunned.

'Yesterday morning.'

'Well, I looked over the speech a few days ago, and this certainly wasn't included.'

'Would he have changed it without your approval?' Carlyle asked Hamell.

'I don't know, I don't understand what's going on here.'

'Someone must have seen this and decided action was necessary,' concluded Fabien.

'I was very disturbed when I read it. It's unnerved me,' added Celina.

'So who got hold of the speech? That's our first port of call,' said Fabien confidently.

'Where do we start?' asked Celina.

'Faxes, e-mails, any correspondence.'

'OK, but I don't have access to his computer.'

'True, but I do,' said Fabien smiling.

'How?'

'Can you get the staff to check any recent faxes, telephone calls, visitors etc. In the meantime I need to get back to the office. Can I take the speech?'

'Sure.'

'Will you be here this evening?'

'Well I do need to catch up on a few things.'

'I'll be back about seven and then we can check his computer.'

'I am rather busy. All this has put me behind somewhat.'

'I'm afraid this can't wait.'

'OK,' she said reluctantly.

'Is anything wrong, Miss McCallen,' asked Carlyle.

'No, everything's fine.'

'Fabien, can I talk to you for a moment?' said an annoyed Carlyle.

The two men moved towards the door.

'What's the story here, Fabien? We're both assigned to this case.'

'I need you to check something out for me while I deal with this. Can you dig out as much information as you can on any known organisations whose causes included anti-euthanasia, any major protests or any known threats to leading politicians. I'll see you in the office tomorrow morning, we'll touch base then and go from there.'

'I'm not used to working this way. Jackson warned me about this. I'll agree to this just this once, Fabien, but no more.'

'I'll be back at seven,' said Fabien, turning to Celina.

The police were still guarding the senator's residence as Fabien entered for the second time that day. Approaching him was a younger officer, again asking for his ID, and after parking his vehicle he climbed the steps to the entrance and was met by a second officer stood in the hallway.

'How long will you have to stay here?' asked Fabien.

'Orders are for tonight and tomorrow,' replied the officer.

'Have a good evening,' said Fabien as he turned and headed down the corridor towards Celina McCallen's office.

As he arrived he noticed that it was dimly lit. The door was open and Celina was busy working on her laptop under her desk light.

'Miss McCallen?' said Fabien as he placed his jacket and briefcase on the sofa.

Celina was not only startled but also appeared scared as she looked across the room at him.

'Who let you in here?' she asked, reaching immediately for the phone.

'Celina?' said Fabien as he moved closer to the light.

'Agent Fabien! Oh, it's you!' she replied, utterly relieved.

'Do I have that effect on you?' he asked guardedly.

'Yes.'

'Did you check out the phone calls and faxes?'

'There was nothing irregular. He called a couple of his colleagues in the senate. The only visitor he had was a guy called John Markham. Do you know him?'

'Should I?'

'I didn't see him leave.'

'Then we'll need to check the senator's computer.'

Celina opened the top drawer of her desk and pulled out a gold-coloured key.

'The senator's office is upstairs, follow me.'

'Does he always leave you a key?'

'No, he always locks up before retiring to his private flat. It's just that yesterday for some reason he didn't, maybe he was planning to return. I found the key in his drawer and decided to lock up myself.'

'I didn't notice his wife and family here today.'

'His estranged wife lives in San Francisco. It's been two years now. His son died in a sailing accident four years ago and his daughter doesn't want to see him again.'

'Maybe she'll get her wish.'

'Shall we?' she asked as she unlocked the door and opened it.

The room looked untouched and strangely vacant. Everything was in its place as though it had been put away prematurely.

'Have you tidied up in here?' asked Fabien.

'No, why?'

'It all looks so prepared.'

'I'll boot up his computer. You said that you can get in.'

'Yes.'

Fabien took a CD out of his briefcase. It was the one he had used to break the security code on the mainframe at Sterling Medical Research the previous year. He inserted it into the 'D' drive and about 30 seconds later, the logon screen appeared.

'OK, all yours,' said Celina.

Fabien entered the activate command for his software and within seconds the logon id 'RGOULDMAN' was written in the logon box.

'Now for the password,' said Fabien.

'Does the FBI let all its agents have toys like this?' asked Celina.

'No. This is illegal. Here comes the first letter.'

Celina looked on as the first character of the password appeared. It was the letter 'C'. Gradually the full password was revealed.

'CELINA98, how interesting. Not exactly hard to crack,' remarked Fabien.

'Are you going to check all his e-mails?'

'Yes,' replied Fabien, browsing the list of sent messages.

'Anything obvious?' asked Celina.

'Not yet.'

'Could someone have hacked into the system?'

'Possibly but not likely. This computer isn't on a network is it?'

'I don't think so.'

'Difficult then, unless you knew how to get in or it was logged on.'

'I can't see anything either,' said Celina. 'Let me check all the ones with attachments.'

Fabien watched over her shoulder as she sat in Gouldman's seat and went through the e-mails. He could smell the fragrance of her perfume as it wafted up and danced on his senses. Then he pulled up another chair so that he could sit beside her.

'Nothing,' she said despondently.

'Let me try something,' said Fabien.

'Go ahead.'

Fabien pulled another CD out of his briefcase.

'Something a computer geek friend of mine wrote a while ago,' he said as he took out the previous disk and inserted the next one.

'What does it do?'

'It looks for deleted e-mails,' said Fabien as he entered a command in yet another box that appeared on the screen.

'That's impossible. How can it do that?'

'Can't say. Trade secret.'

'An old boyfriend who used to work for an IT company told me once that data is never really deleted. It just can't be found anymore.'

'He was right. We'll just have to wait a few minutes.'

'Do you want a drink?' she asked.

'No thanks.'

'Do you mind if I indulge? It's been a long crazy day.'

'Not at all.'

Celina poured herself a scotch from her boss' crystal glass decanter and sat back down next to Fabien before taking a sip. Her eyes were turned towards him. She watched him as he stared at the screen. His eyes – it was his eyes.

'OK, here we go,' said Fabien as a list of e-mail titles appeared on the screen in the command box that had been created by Fabien's software. As he turned to her, her eyes shifted away to her glass by reflex.

As he returned to the screen and scanned the list, one message stood out. It was addressed to 'william.calvert@masonwainwright.com', and entitled 'The truth hurts'. He opened it and read the single line of text:

Silence is golden as long as you won't tell.

'What's that all about?' asked Celina curiously.

'Secrets I guess. Let's take another look.'

Fabien browsed the list again for a few minutes and then gave up.

'Nothing else. Looks like "silence is golden" is our only lead.'

'What do we do now?' asked Celina.

'Someone must have known about the speech. It has to be some pro-life group that have been forced to go to the extreme.'

'But why kidnapping? Why not an assassination?' asked Celina.

'A lot more can be achieved if you catch your prey alive, Celina. Killing him would achieve nothing. Someone else will pick up the torch eventually. Let me know as soon as you get a communication from the abductors will you.'

'Of course,' she replied. His words chilled her.

'One more question. Can you describe this John Markham?'

She looked at him and then backed towards the door.

'Are you alright Celina?' he asked.

'I think you'd better go now.'

'Really?' said Fabien, puzzled.

'Yes, I need to be somewhere, soon.'

'Well thanks for your help – it was worth the trip.'

Celina smiled nervously, looking at the floor.

'If there's something you want to tell me…' said Fabien.

'It's been a long day Mr Fabien, I'm confused and upset, you understand…'

'I'll be in touch.'

'Before you go, there was something that I noticed the other morning. Maybe it's nothing but the senator seemed more than casually interested in the Baltimore plane crash that came on the news, do you know the one?'

'Yes, making that e-mail to William Calvert all the more intriguing. I'll check it out. Did Gouldman have much in the way of dealings with them?'

'I wouldn't know. But when I asked him if he knew Calvert he denied it and told me that he knew nothing about Mason Wainwright either. Why would he lie about this?'

'Good question.'

'I'll escort you to the entrance,' she added.

'There's no need. Goodnight Celina.'

She followed him to the door. He turned to her as he opened it.

'I think it would be a good idea if you closed the senator's computer down. We can't be too careful.'

'Yes, of course,' she replied.

'I'll see myself out,' said Fabien as he closed the door behind him.

7

New York's bustling financial district could be seen with clarity from the windows of Mason-Wainwright's boardroom, where a nervous Milton Porter waited for his colleagues to join him for an emergency meeting in the wake of William Calvert's death. Carlton Hayes, the head of the law firm that had represented the corporation since its founding in the early 60s, had given information that had now caused Porter to recollect the events of the past couple of weeks.

Calvert had been unusually secretive during the days leading up to the fateful trip to Washington and had been particularly cagey about disclosing his whereabouts. The daily briefings had become unusually short and two days before the flight, Porter, suspecting that something was wrong, confronted his boss who had quite calmly denied that anything was untoward. Calvert would never lock his office; later that day Porter had not been able to gain access to it.

Rising from the table he walked over to the window and as he stared out he could see the busy street below him. He caught sight of a couple of men who looked like dealers on their way to the New York stock exchange and it reminded him of his days on the floor as a trader and how far he had come since then. Moments later the door to the boardroom opened and three of his colleagues entered and took their places at the table. He continued facing the window until the other four arrived and then turned to face them all.

'Good, we're all here,' he said, breaking the silence.

'Your note said this was urgent. What's the news, Milton?' asked Sarah Claiborne.

Porter stood for a few moments trying to find the right words to say, his colleagues becoming uneasy at his silence.

'I have news regarding William, but there's a matter that needs our urgent attention first. The last few days have been a shock to us all. William was a close friend as well as a colleague and his presence will be sorely missed in this boardroom. But I'm sure that he would endorse the inescapable fact that there's a company to run and we have to move on. We wouldn't want the stock price falling; our friends on Wall Street would have a field day.'

'I think they already are,' remarked a colleague, sceptically.

Porter continued.

'I've been the senior vice-president for five years and now I have to step into the breach by default as it were. I am asking for your support and vote to take over as president of this corporation. We'll need a steady hand at the helm so will you support my proposal?'

Having not seen eye-to-eye with some of them on many occasions, the delay in their response proved almost intolerable. They had been loyal to Calvert over many years but slowly five of the board put their hands up. Morgan Wendt was one of the two whose hand had remained down.

'Morgan, do I take that as a no then, or are you abstaining, sitting on the fence as usual?'

There was no answer.

Wendt was near retirement and was notorious for sitting things out and waiting to see the response of his colleagues before making a decision on anything. Porter had wanted him out long ago and had tried to persuade Calvert that a good severance package and early pension arrangement would do the trick. Calvert had had other ideas and deemed Wendt as 'still useful'.

'I need the support of you all. So what's it to be, Morgan?'

'OK I'm in,' he replied reluctantly.

'Thank you.'

He then turned his attention to Peter Vincent, the corporate finance vice-president. His hand was down, which came as no surprise. Vincent had always seen himself as a future company president.

'You know I can't support this, Milton,' he said.

'The lone voice of dissent – why not, Peter?'

'Personal reasons.'

'I'd like to hear what they are. This is an open forum. If there is a genuine reason why I should not lead this corporation I think the board has the right to know before this is made official.'

Vincent's disconcerting look brought delight to Porter's heart as his colleague's position became more precarious by the second. He knew exactly what to say next.

'Peter, I know you were close to William but...'

'Save it, Milton!' he replied, getting up.

It had worked.

'You've always been after William's job since the day he made you his senior vice-president. He's still warm in his grave and you want his job. You're not worthy or capable of filling his shoes. No, this is not in the best interest of the corporation and if the rest of you can't see that then this corporation is in more jeopardy than I thought.'

'I'm disappointed Peter,' replied Porter, 'but I appreciate your honesty. Six to one it is then,' he added coldly. 'I'll draw up a resolution for you all to sign. We'll inform the shareholders.'

Vincent stepped away from the table and began to walk towards the door.

'And Peter...' added Porter.

'Yes Milton?' he replied, stopping in his tracks.

'I'll have your resignation letter on my desk by close of business today. There will be full severance of course; we owe you at least that much.'

'Wait a second – is this really necessary?' asked Sarah.

'It's OK; I have something lined up anyway. It'll be on your desk within the hour, Milton.'

'Peter!' she called as he closed the door behind him.

'Let him go Sarah – it's for the best,' said Porter, trying to be reassuring.

Sarah and Vincent had had an affair lasting nine months. They had remained close friends and Porter knew she was clearly unhappy at his departure. The others sat looking attentively at the man who had just become their new president and as Sarah turned around her eyes met Porter's. He had been staring at her with prejudiced eyes as she had watched Peter leave the room.

'We go back a long way, Milton, I'm sure you appreciate that much,' she said courageously, hoping that he would view her words as an emotional reaction rather than a questioning of his judgement.

Morgan Wendt was not so diplomatic.

'Firing someone already? Not a good start. Remember Milton, you need our support – your words not mine.'

Porter paused for a moment. He didn't want to lose face, not today.

'Of course,' he replied in a mellow tone, and then sat down. You'll be next, he thought, smiling at Morgan.

'So now that's sorted out, what's the news on William?' Wendt continued.

Porter considered his words carefully.

'This is to go no further. The crash was sabotage. Hayes also informed me that Forrester was carrying documents regarding the Haedenberg account. He'd been under scrutiny the week prior to the trip.'

'How can this have happened, Milton? Especially with the FBI investigating us a year ago. Their files are still warm!'

'I can't be certain. But let's not panic yet shall we. Whoever he was going to meet he didn't get there, did he.'

'But we could be implicated in this. The Feds will be all over us now!'

'Relax Liam, there's no evidence that we had anything to do with this.'

'That may be so but if we end up under investigation again, Milton… Remember, we lost two major accounts.'

'Until then and if anything does happen, its business as usual. Let's just get on with the job, shall we?'

Max Beresford was the last to leave. Porter had requested him to remain behind. As the last one left the room, Porter closed the door and walked over to the window.

'Come see the city, Max,' he said, now relaxed.

Beresford joined his boss at the window and the two men gazed out over the Manhattan skyline.

'I need someone I can trust implicitly. You've always supported me, particularly during the investigation last year. I think William started to lose it from then on and I owe some of why I'm still here to you. I'd like you to become my senior vice-president. Will you accept?'

'Of course.'

'Good, then we need to make plans.'

'They'll bury us if they find out,' said Beresford.

'Nobody will find out. Hayes will destroy the files.'

'We'll have to keep this from the others.'

'Agreed,' said Porter.

'So who sabotaged the plane?' asked Max.

'That I do not know, and it's probably better that we leave it that way. There's only one thing that matters now and that's our own survival.'

'What do we do now?'

'Nothing. I expect the FBI to be paying us a visit in the near future. As long as we co-operate fully there won't be any problems.'

'What if they decide to re-open the investigation into the Haedenberg account?'

'They have no grounds to do so, besides I have made sure that all the holes have been patched up. They wouldn't find anything this time. Let's hope this whole incident and tragedy is yet another near miss.'

'Do you think William was trying to bring the whole corporation down? Did he have an attack of conscience? Why else would he be flying to Washington with one of our lawyers? He was going to blow the whistle, wasn't he?'

'William was the victim of his own stupidity,' replied Porter. 'Now he has paid the ultimate price.'

8

'We may have a lead on the Gouldman abduction,' said Henderson, addressing Fabien from across the table in conference room C4F, around which Carlyle, Durrell and Kirby were also sat. Thomas Jackson had insisted on attending all meetings regarding the case and his presence grated at Henderson continually. His disdain for Jackson was beginning to fester like mould in a bowl of dough.

'Have you ever heard of an organisation called the Haedenberg Foundation?' he asked.

'No Sir, I haven't.'

'Agent Kirby was investigating Mason-Wainwright last year. This corporation manages the Haedenberg funds. Agent Kirby...'

'I was investigating irregularities in Mason-Wainwright's accounting process for this client with Dan Riley.'

'Dan Riley, that name rings a bell. Whatever happened to him?' asked Fabien with keen interest.

'Please continue Agent Kirby,' said Jackson.

'We suspected that the Haedenberg account was really a façade and that whoever or whatever was behind it was using Mason-Wainwright to facilitate illegal monetary transactions.'

'What do we already know about the Haedenberg Foundation?' asked Fabien.

'It's a conglomerate of trustees who look after the interests of the terminally ill... the rich terminally ill,' said Jackson, interceding. 'Contrary to Agent Kirby's beliefs, there's nothing sinister about this organisation. They merely make provisions to ensure that the companies of their clients continue to run smoothly and make money during such periods and, of course, to ensure that whoever is destined to take over is not going to make the company bankrupt after 18 months of incompetence. There are many who aspire to hold the reins but few destined to achieve greatness.'

'Very honourable – a way to let the president pass away peacefully, counting the dollars as he slips away,' said Fabien.

'That's one way of looking at it,' said Jackson.

'Is that why you took Kirby and Riley off the case?' asked Henderson.

'There was no evidence in my opinion to merit any further use of the Federal government's resources in this matter,' replied Jackson.

'Anyway,' continued Kirby, 'the crash investigation team found the charred remains of some papers in the wreckage of William Calvert's plane. We had the lab analyse them and try to identify anything from the fragments that may have given us an indication of the contents of the documents. They found a few references to the Haedenberg Foundation and so it's very likely that Calvert was on his way to meet someone here in Washington. To discuss what, we can't be certain.'

'What's this got to do with Gouldman?' asked Fabien.

'Intelligence sources have revealed that Gouldman had links with Haedenberg, but we don't know much more than that,' replied Durrell.

'Some co-incidence that he is abducted after Calvert's plane crash,' added Fabien.

'So what have you got so far, Fabien?' asked Henderson.

'A copy of the speech that Gouldman was due to give in the senate the day he was abducted and a suspicious e-mail that Gouldman sent to William Calvert prior to the crash.'

'Then there has to be a link somewhere. Someone wanted them both out of the way,' added Durrell.

'But why kidnap Gouldman, why not just assassinate him?' asked Kirby.

'You're not the first to ask that question,' replied Fabien.

'Durrell, Kirby, as of now you are both off the case,' said Jackson. 'I want Fabien and Carlyle to take this over. Keep me posted.'

'I suggest that you get yourselves up to New York and pay Mason-Wainwright a visit,' said Henderson.

'Milton Porter should be your point of contact. He's the senior vice-president,' added Kirby.

'I want to speak to Dan Riley first,' said Fabien.

There was a momentary silence. Fabien watched as a perturbed Rachel Kirby looked nervously at their boss.

'Agent Riley was killed in action a month ago,' replied Henderson.

'To New York then,' said Fabien sombrely to his partner.

'I'll pack an overnight bag and meet you back here in two hours,' replied Carlyle as he went to leave. Jackson, Durrell and Kirby followed.

'I'd like a word Agent Fabien,' said Henderson, calling him back from the door.

'Sir?'

'You've been deskbound for the best part of a year now,' said Henderson after the others had left. 'How does it feel?'

'If you really want to know I feel like a busted cop reassigned to traffic duty,' replied Fabien, remembering the disciplinary hearing nine months previous.

'Your career would be over if I hadn't stepped in.'

'Perhaps.'

'Make no mistake, Fabien; Jackson will have a long memory now he's been promoted. You need a result here… and so do I.'

Fabien left the conference room and headed back down the corridor to his desk. After a few moments he could hear footsteps running behind him. As he turned he saw Rachel Kirby catching up with him.

'We need to talk,' she said.

'OK, let's go outside,' replied Fabien.

There was a door just along the corridor that led to a passageway at the end of which was another set of double doors that were card-key controlled. The two agents went out and stood on a patch of lawn to the side of the building that was just shaded from the sunlight.

'Strictly off the record, Fabien,' said Kirby hesitantly. 'We were getting very close to something on the Haedenberg Foundation. It's not what it seems to be and Porter knows something, I'm sure of it. He's the key.'

'In light of what you've just said, I would suspect that William Calvert's death was very timely, wouldn't you?' said Fabien.

'Definitely. Be careful, Fabien. I don't think it was a coincidence that Dan Riley and I were taken off the case.'

'I need you to dig deeper into the Haedenberg Foundation for me.'

'I can't, you heard what Jackson said.'

'He needn't find out.'

'I'm not sure, Fabien.'

'Please, I have a missing senator to find.'

'I can't promise anything.'

'What happened to Riley?'

'I don't know. It was all very hush-hush – on a need to know basis. Look, I've got to go; I shouldn't be seen with you, OK.'

'Kirby, wait!'

'I have to leave,' she replied, and then hurriedly went back inside.

From the window of his office Thomas Jackson could see the two agents part company. He watched for a few seconds as Fabien skirted around the edge of the building towards the main parking lot and then he returned to his desk.

It was around three in the afternoon when Fabien and Carlyle entered the lobby of the Stanley hotel on 31st Street and 5th Avenue, having left their car in a parking lot a few blocks away. They checked in and proceeded to their respective rooms to dump their bags. As Fabien entered his dark and sparse room he turned on the light, opened his bag and took out his map of Manhattan to check the location of the Mason-Wainwright building in the financial district. He had arranged to meet his colleague in the lobby in ten minutes, but it had taken him at least four minutes to finally call the elevator and get to his floor. It must have stopped on most of the floors en route to his room. He had been put in accommodation that was located at the rear of the building and all he could see from his window was the back of the surrounding buildings and a series of fire escapes that seemed to the eye to cross each other as they descended to the dark, untidy ground below. There had been cutbacks in his department of late and budget accommodation was the only option.

He poured himself a glass of water and rummaged through the contents of his bag to find his medication. When he discovered that it wasn't where he expected it to be, he reached his hand into each corner of the bag only to find that it was missing.

I must have left it in the apartment, he thought to himself, and then began to feel uncomfortable.

He rummaged again and then checked the external pockets to see if he had put it in one of them. He hadn't and so in desperation he pulled the bag right open and tipped everything out on the bed. He had to find them – he was dependent on them now. As his clothes fell onto the bed he scattered them like a crazed man looking for gold, and then to his relief a plastic bottle of pills rolled out onto the sheet of the bed from his underwear. Gulping down one of its small torpedo shaped contents he picked up the map and car keys to leave.

The elevator was only a short walk from his room. He stood waiting for it to arrive, pushing the call button several times. It appeared to stick on the first attempt and did not illuminate. He watched painfully as each floor lit up, tracing the path of the elevator on its tired journey to the 12th floor. He checked his watch. It was 15.29 and he realised that if Carlyle was a studious timekeeper he would have been waiting for him for around ten minutes by now.

Eventually the bell rang and the doors opened. The elevator was empty – there could be nothing worse than a slow descent with an elevator full of people in his opinion. Being on the 12th floor meant that inevitably he would soon be pinned to the back of the elevator by numerous bodies by the time he reached the lobby. He got in and hit the button for the ground floor. The doors slowly closed, clanking as they did so, and he began his descent. Two floors down the elevator stopped. 'Here we go,' he said to himself, but as the doors opened, to his surprise, nobody was there – they must have grown tired of waiting, he thought.

Then for no apparent reason, he fell against the side of the elevator and felt the controls dig into this back. Unable to move, he started to feel drowsy.

When the opened elevator doors came back into focus he stood erect, causing the doors to close again. I must have been leaning on the buttons, he thought, as the elevator continued its descent to the ground floor. When he arrived there were around eight people waiting to get in. They appeared not only to be annoyed but also looked as though they had been waiting for an eternity. As he passed through the crowd their pointed expressions told him that he was solely responsible for their delay.

Carlyle was sat on a chair at the other end of the lobby and as he saw Fabien approaching he got up, looking agitated.

'Are you habitually this late, Fabien?' he asked.

'I'm sorry?'

'Do you realise the time?'

'It's 15.54,' replied Fabien, staring at his watch. 'That's impossible!' he thought as the fact dawned on him.

'I've been waiting over half an hour. Are you coming?' said Carlyle dismissively as he strode towards the hotel entrance.

'Have you taken care of the Haedenberg files, Carlton?' asked Milton Porter, lurched over his desk and exasperated at Hayes' delay in returning his calls. 'Good! That's all I wanted to hear.'

'Mr Porter, Max Beresford is on the other line,' said his secretary only seconds after he had ended the call.

'Put him on.'

'Milton, we've got trouble.'

'What's wrong?'

'FBI, in the lobby, they want to speak to you.'

'Have them escorted in discreetly and meet me in my office immediately. Let's just play it cool and see what they want.'

He put the phone down, closed the files that he had been reviewing on his computer and sat motionless in his chair waiting for his unwelcome visitors to arrive. A few minutes later Beresford escorted Fabien and Carlyle into his office and the two men stood at a short distance from Porter's desk as he stood up to greet them.

'How can I help you gentlemen?'

'I'm Agent Fabien and this is Agent Carlyle. We'd like to talk to you about the Haedenberg Foundation and your late colleague.'

'What do you want to know?'

'Mr Calvert was travelling to Washington with a representative from your lawyers with documents pertaining to the Haedenberg account. We'd like to know why?'

'So would I, Agent Fabien.'

'Come, Mr Porter, you're the vice-president of this corporation. Are you telling me that you didn't know what your own president was up to?'

'William was very secretive towards the end.'

'So you believe he was involved in something irregular?'

'I didn't say that,' replied Porter, feeling at a disadvantage already.

'Then what did you mean?'

'William did not involve me much in his dealings of late; for what reason, I do not know.'

'Did you speak to him about this lack of communication?'

'What relevance does this have? He was my boss; that was his prerogative.'

'Didn't it bother you?'

'Only if it affected my ability to act in my capacity as senior vice-president.'

'Have you spoken to your lawyers?'

'Yes, and they are as much in the dark as I am.'

'So William Calvert and David Forrester were in league somehow?'

'I have no idea.'

'It appears that they were on their way to meet someone in Washington. No doubt to discuss Haedenberg. I can't help thinking that there's something that you're not telling us, Mr Porter.'

'I cannot help you, Agent Fabien.'

'Haedenberg must be extremely sensitive if someone was prepared to sabotage his plane, do you not agree?'

'We are all shocked by what happened and I am trying to make sense of it all, but again I do not know why William undertook that trip.'

'What dealings have your corporation had with a Senator Robert Gouldman?'

'Nothing to my knowledge. I know that he and William were acquainted in some way but that's all. Why do you ask?'

'We believe that they were more than just acquainted, Mr Porter.'

'Really. Well I'm sorry but I can't help you any further. I am a busy man with a company to run now, so will you please excuse me.'

'We will be reopening our investigation into the Haedenberg account. I will have a team of agents up here within days and we will get to the bottom of this. Your lawyers will also be investigated.'

'On what grounds?' asked Beresford.

'Three people were murdered on that flight to Washington, Mr Beresford, and Mason-Wainwright is implicated.'

'What's the next move, Milton?' asked a sombre Max Beresford, standing next to his boss at the window after Fabien and Carlyle had left.

'I need to think about this,' he replied abruptly.

'There isn't time, Milton.'

'Then I'll find time! I'm president of this corporation now and nobody is going to take that away from me; the FBI, William Calvert or Robert Gouldman!'

'This is not a one-man show, Milton. We have to inform the board.'

Without warning, Beresford was grabbed by the lapels of his jacket and forced against the window.

'We will do nothing of the kind, Max!' said Porter, wide-eyed and crazed.

'Let go of me, Milton,' said his subordinate calmly.

Porter released him and stepped back. Max, lost for words, began to doubt the merits of his decision to approve Porter's presidency.

'I need to make some phone calls,' said Porter, turning away to face the window again.

'Think very carefully about your position, Milton,' said Max. 'If you go down, the others will distance themselves, believe me.'

'And what about you Max, what will you do?' he asked coldly.

Beresford decided to leave; silence was the wisest course. As he left the room, Porter's eyes followed him all the way to the door.

Returning to the window, Porter stared out of it as before. As he did so a seagull landed on a ledge near to it and perched there for a short while. He watched it as it made small jerking movements with its head and became enchanted by it.

'Where the eagles are gathered, the doves cannot enter therein,' he said quietly to himself before it took to the air again and flew headlong towards the street below. Recalling those words made him shudder.

9

'Is everything OK, ma'am?' asked a concerned uniformed officer standing guard in the hallway of Senator Gouldman's residence as Celina stepped off the central stairwell and onto the floor of the hallway. She clearly wasn't.

She walked as gracefully as the last whiskey she had taken from Gouldman's decanter would allow, her stiletto shoes disturbing the icy silence that now permeated the building as she returned to her office.

When the door closed at the end of the hall the officer turned towards the front of the building to resume his vigil. In view were two of his colleagues, one guarding the entrance, the other patrolling the grounds. It was time that he performed his own periodic checks of the building and so he climbed the stairs towards the first floor and disappeared down the passageway past the senator's office. A fourth officer, a detective from the Washington police department had arrived minutes earlier. He was sat on the sofa in Celina's office reading a newspaper as she returned.

'Miss McCallen?' he asked.

'Hi,' she said quietly, glancing at him as she walked to her desk.

Her hair was covering her face slightly and he observed traces of tears around her eyes.

'I'm Detective Slater from Washington PD.'

'Did Mr Henderson send you?' she asked, seeing as he was casually dressed.

'Yes ma'am, I'm your date for this evening.'

'Date?'

'We're going for a drink after we leave here. Mr Henderson will join us there.'

'Where are we going?'

'I guess you weren't expecting an undercover cop, were you? We don't know who will be following us, do we?'

'Of course, I understand.'

'We'll also provide you with 24 hour protection.'

'That won't be necessary, really. I'll be back in a few minutes.'

Celina had arrived at her office at 08.30 that morning and had had to face an onslaught of pressure and threats that seemed to have assaulted her relentlessly throughout that day. On her arrival a barrage of reporters from the Washington and national press had descended unmercifully upon Gouldman's residence. An hour later Ed Hamell had arrived with two of Gouldman's closest allies from the senate, during which Gouldman's estranged wife had called for news after having finally heard about the abduction. Celina knew that this was merely a token gesture of concern on her part but had felt obligated to provide some information. It was only when she had received the first of two threatening phone calls from an unknown source that she realised that the nightmare of Gouldman's abduction had just begun for her personally.

Celina had arrived at the iron gates of the residency in her open top BMW. As she approached she realised that a crowd of journalists had assembled there and immediately started to feel a sense of unease. She had never faced the press before and as she swung the car into the driveway they suddenly turned their attention to her and swarmed to her as she headed into the parking lot. She opened the door, but before she could step out she was inundated with questions from journalists and a barrage of photographers taking shots of her, battling vigorously to get her attention.

'Miss McCallen, is it true that Senator Gouldman has been abducted by anti-euthanasia extremists?' called one of them, almost hitting her in the face with his microphone.

Celina froze. Confused and overwhelmed, she tried to force her way through the crowd that surrounded her.

'Tell us about your ordeal, Celina. What was it like to be confronted by the kidnappers?' asked another.

'Who's behind this? Can you give us any information?' asked a young female reporter.

Celina stopped and looked at her for a moment almost with sympathy, remembering the breaks she had been given. Then, coming to her senses, she realised that the less said at this time the better.

'I really cannot comment, I don't know what has happened to Senator Gouldman. I'm sorry, please let me through.'

At that moment two of the police officers ushered her into the building and closed the front door behind them. Celina was shaken and hurried down the corridor to her office where she slumped down on the sofa and brushed her hair from her eyes, calmed herself and then tried to think clearly. After a short while Sophie turned up with her morning tea and placed it on the table in front of her.

'Why are all those reporters out the front?' she asked.

The administration staff had not been informed of the details of recent events but knew that something was wrong due to the police presence. They knew that the senator had been absent but that was all.

'I guess I should tell you,' replied Celina. 'Senator Gouldman has been abducted. I can't tell you any more than that at this time.'

'Who would do such a thing?' asked a startled Sophie.

'I don't know,' she replied. 'Haven't you got work to do?'

'Yes, of course I'll…' she replied, before a knock at the door interrupted them.

Ed Hamell entered the room with two colleagues; one she recognised, the other she had not met before.

'Good morning, Celina. You remember Senator Harvey Allen.'

'Yes,' she replied, shaking his hand.

'This is Senator Eugene Sylvian.'

'Miss McCallen.'

'Sophie…' she said, telling her young subordinate to leave immediately.

She waited for Sophie to close the door before asking Hamell how his eyes were.

'Still a little sore, but no permanent damage,' he replied. 'Anything yet?'

'I'm afraid not. The FBI is looking into connections that Robert had with Mason-Wainwright. That's all I know at present.'

'Mason-Wainwright,' commented Sylvian, raising his eyebrows.

'Celina, we want you to go home. There's no need for you or your staff to be here right now. We'll call when things get back to normal,' said Allen.

'I don't understand.'

'We'll take care of things from here. We'll liase with the FBI and we'll call you when we get news.'

Celina looked at Hamell suspiciously.

'No. I'm part of this. I was there when he was taken. I'm not just going to sit at home and do nothing.'

'It's out of your hands now, Miss McCallen,' added Sylvian.

'What will I do?' she asked.

'Take some vacation. We'll make sure that your pay

cheques keep coming in,' said Hamell, trying to reassure her.

'This is irregular, what's going on?' she said, feeling extremely uncomfortable.

'Like we said, Celina,' replied Hamell insistently.

'I'm not happy about this,' she added.

'I wouldn't be either,' replied Allen. 'But under the circumstances you must do as we request.'

Celina considered her words carefully.

'OK, but I have some things to sort out today. I'll finish up tonight and then I'll leave.'

'Very well,' acknowledged Allen.

'I'll notify the staff,' said Celina, getting up to leave the room. Her exit was halted by a telephone call. It was Sophie.

'Mrs Gouldman is on the line. She wishes to speak with you.'

'Put her on,' replied Celina, reluctant to take the call. 'Hello Louisa, this is Celina McCallen.'

'So the rumours are true then? He's finally upset someone big. I heard what happened and I'm just calling to see if there's been any news.'

'Do you really care?' asked Celina coldly.

'He's still my husband unless you've conveniently forgotten.'

'I can't tell you anything,' replied Celina.

'Well I would appreciate it if someone could call me and put my mind at rest when you do know something.'

'Sure, we have your number.'

'How has he been lately?'

'OK, a little secretive.'

'Holding secrets from *you*? That does surprise me, Celina.'

'What do you mean?'

'I know all about you and Robert – I wasn't blind you know. I couldn't satisfy his needs but at least he could have been honest with me. But then he is a politician, isn't he.'

'Robert's a good man,' replied Celina.

'You poor naïve girl! You don't know him at all. A word of advice: don't get sucked in by his charm, you're not the only young blonde he's taken along for the ride, believe me.'

'It takes an embittered woman to say that,' replied Celina indignantly. 'Who are you to bring my integrity into question?'

'His wife!'

'I have to go. Goodbye Louisa.'

Celina slammed the phone down and turned to her three visitors.

'Robert's wife,' she said, looking embarrassed.

There was no reply, only a cheap smile from Ed Hamell.

'We have a few things to collect,' said Sylvian.

'Please excuse us, Celina,' said Hamell, his eyes watering slightly.

'We'll be in touch,' added Allen, and then the three men turned to leave the office.

'Make sure you've wrapped everything up by this evening, won't you,' added Hamell as he left.

11.00: Sophie came marching into Celina's office. She didn't even knock, something she would always do in token respect.

'You're not telling me everything, are you?' she said abruptly.

Celina was startled. None of the staff had ever spoken to her in that way. That was not the issue here – she would have to lie.

'The matter is being dealt with, Sophie. We'll be on extended vacation until things are cleared up, me included. That's all I know.'

'Why does everything you say have to be so orchestrated?' said Sophie angrily. This had been building up for a while now.

'Not now, Sophie,' replied Celina dismissively. 'You'll still get your pay cheque.'

'Don't worry about it, Miss McCallen, I'm quitting anyway.'
'Sophie?'
'I've had something else lined up for a week or so. I got the offer yesterday.'
'Oh, I see, well… just put it in writing and leave it in the front office. I'll pick it up on my way out. I'm sorry you're leaving.'
'I'm not,' replied Sophie.

11.23: Celina's cell phone rang.
'Celina McCallen, it's good to talk to you finally,' said a distant spectre-like voice down the phone.
There was a long pause before the voice spoke again.
'You are alone, aren't you?'
'Who is this?' she asked frantically.
'Do not leave the senator's residence under any circumstances,' said the voice.
'Please tell me who you are.'
'The senator is quite safe for the time being, but all that depends on you.'
The voice sounded strangely familiar. Paralysed with fear she paused to think what to say next.
'What do you want?' she said, beginning to shake.
'You will receive another call tonight. Do not miss it. And remember we're watching your every move. The police officers guarding the building – do not talk to them, Celina, under any circumstances.'
'Please don't hurt Robert.'
The voice on the phone laughed, the sound of which rippled through her very nerve endings.
'Tonight, Celina, and *do not* miss the call.'
The line went dead.
Celina picked up her handbag and ran out of her office to

the hallway. As she approached the officer on duty, she slowed down and tried to look calm.

'Everything OK, Miss?' he asked as she tried to slip by quietly.

'Yes, I just need some fresh air.'

As she climbed down the steps another of the officers looked around and nodded at her. She waved awkwardly, leant against the wall and opened a packet of cigarettes. Her hands were shaking as she lit it and took the first deep drag.

17.47: Celina entered the office where her three administration staff were beginning to clear their desks. None of them knew what to say.

'I'll call you when we're able to return,' she said, looking exhausted.

Nobody responded and only one of the girls smiled briefly. None of them particularly liked Celina. They regarded her as aloof and out of touch.

Celina made a prompt exit and then headed upstairs into Gouldman's deserted office. She poured herself a drink, stared at Gouldman's empty chair and swallowed the potent smelling liquid in one mouthful. The photograph of him and Louisa on the corner of the desk spoke out to her. Confused, she knew everything had changed. Hearing the front door close downstairs she realised that Sophie must have left and so she placed the empty glass on the drinks cabinet and walked to the open door. Everything was silent now; she had never experienced the feeling of isolation that now overwhelmed her. She had to get downstairs.

In the front office Sophie's letter of resignation lay on the desk before her. It was addressed simply to 'Miss McCallen'. She decided not to open it but placed it back where she had found it, turned off the light and closed the door.

22.02: The streets surrounding Gouldman's residency had become almost deserted as darkness enveloped the capital, but traffic from the main roads a block or two away could still be heard by the new shift of police officers now on duty. There was very little activity on the street outside and they had seen very few people walking past the iron gates that fortified the premises they had been assigned to patrol. Only a tramp had showed any interest in the place. He had stood there for a moment clutching the railings with one hand to steady himself as he grasped tightly onto a brown paper bag that contained a depleted supply of liquor. One of the officers had moved him on and he had subsequently staggered off into the night, singing something about the moon as he went on his way.

Moments after the tramp had disappeared from view a car drove slowly by the gates and stopped just past the entrance. One of the officers decided to open the gates and take a look out onto the street. A Mercedes Benz was parked by the side of the road with its lights on but the engine cut. As he approached he could see a man sitting alone in the driver's seat. The officer tapped on the window and the occupant of the car wound it down.

'May I see your driver's licence sir?'

'Here,' he said, handing it over.

'Where are you headed?'

'I'm lost, I'm trying to find the freeway.'

The officer handed back the driver's licence and began to give him directions. On the other side of the car was a streetlight with a garbage bin attached. As the two men were speaking a third approached along the sidewalk and stopped for a moment. He knelt down momentarily and then rose, continuing on his way. The officer, aware of his presence seemed disinterested as the man passed the iron gates and gradually disappeared into the darkness.

'Thank you officer,' said the driver as he started the engine.

'Drive carefully,' replied the officer, looking back towards the gates in the distance. The driver pulled away in the opposite direction.

Inside the residency Celina was becoming tired and anxious. The phone hadn't rung; it was getting late so she had decided to go outside for another cigarette, hoping to be left alone. As she stood on the steps she fondled the emerald broach that Gouldman had given her. She had put it on again that morning; it was all she had of him now.

'You're working late tonight Miss, haven't you got somewhere to go?'

'Not really,' she replied, trying to give nothing away.

'It's a warm night,' said the officer, trying to make conversation.

'Yes it is.'

'Not much happening around here,' he added. 'That's a nice emerald you've got there. Present from your boyfriend? He must think a lot of you.'

Celina was in no mood for empty conversation and ignored him. When she had finished her cigarette she stubbed it out with the long, slender heel of her shoe.

'Got to go,' she said, reaching into her jacket pocket to pull out her cell phone.

Her blood ran cold when she realised that she had left it on her desk. She ran back into the building and down the corridor towards her office, almost tripping and twisting her ankle in the process. As she got near she could hear it ringing on her desk. She darted over, only to hear it ring off just as she picked it up. Her LCD told her that she had missed two calls. She checked the origin but the number had been withheld.

'Oh God no!' she said with her heart pounding. Then it rang a third time.

'Celina McCallen!' she blurted immediately.

'You missed the call,' said the voice.

'I'm sorry!' she said instantly, her voice raising a pitch.

'This was the last time I was going to ring. Never mind. Go to the front gate, turn left and you will find a streetlight with a garbage bin attached. In the hedge behind you will find a package. Open it and follow the instructions.'

'I will! I promise!' she said, trembling.

'Speak to no one except Agent Fabien. Is that clear?'

'Yes!'

'Remember we're watching you. Not even your home is a sanctuary,' said the voice as the line went abruptly dead as before.

Celina gazed across the room, petrified.

The package! she thought.

She walked hurriedly out of her office to the hallway but slowed her pace as she reached the steps that led to the parking lot. The officers could suspect nothing, she thought, as she headed for the gates. There she was stopped by one of the officers. Her heart was still thumping the inside of her chest and she knew it would be difficult for her to get any words out without seeming extremely nervous.

'Is everything alright, ma'am?'

They know something's up, she thought to herself. 'Yes, I just need to go for a walk. It's been a long day. My back and neck are stiff,' she replied, trying to think of something.

'Our orders are not to let you out of our sight.'

'Please, I just need some air, that's all. Five minutes.'

The officer reluctantly signalled for his colleague to open the gate.

'Five minutes, OK, then we send out the search party.'

She walked briskly to the gates trying not to look suspicious.

'Be careful, ma'am, stay within the block,' said his colleague as she stepped out onto the sidewalk.

'I won't be long,' she replied.

The streetlight loomed before her like a beacon guiding a ship to the shore. She looked behind her to make sure that she was not being watched. The gates had been closed, the officer had gone and she was confident that she was out of view. Still trembling, she knelt down and groped around the bottom of the hedge behind the pole of the streetlight and touched what felt like a package. She grabbed it and pulled it out. It was brown and padded. She opened it to find a white envelope inside. Ditching the outer package in the garbage bin, she quickly put the envelope in her handbag, realising that the officers would be suspicious if she returned too soon. She lit another cigarette and remained there for a while under the streetlight, allowing herself to calm down and look normal when she returned. In the distance she could see the headlights of a car coming along the road towards her. It slowed down as it passed her and she could see that it was a Mercedes Benz with two men inside. They looked at her and smiled, making her feel uncomfortable. As the car passed and then regained speed, she knew it was time to head back before she ended up being mistaken for a hooker or something. She paced back to the gates and then stopped to wait for an officer to open them.

'That's better,' she said as the gates were opened.

'Too much sitting at a computer? My wife suffers from that all the time,' replied the officer.

She smiled at him nervously and headed straight back to her office. Closing the door behind her, she hurriedly pulled the letter out of her bag and opened it.

Lawrence Henderson tidied his desk under the light of his lamp and was ready to call it a night when the phone rang. He noticed that it was his secure line, one that would be almost impossible to tamper with. He picked it up and recognised the voice at the end of the line. It was Celina calling from her cell phone.

'Mr Henderson?'

'Yes.'

'I need to talk to you right away, I've had a communication.'

'I'll have someone from the Washington police department come to pick you up shortly.'

'Thank you,' she replied and then hung up.

Celina put the phone to her chest and then pondered over the instructions in the note that lay open on her desk.

Celina returned from the bathroom.

'It's time we left, Miss McCallen. Mr Henderson will be waiting for us,' said Detective Slater.

'I'll be finished here soon,' she said, looking at the clock. It was 23.34.

'I'll escort you home after the meeting and then my colleague will take over. He'll keep watch outside your apartment until the morning.'

'Is that really necessary?' she asked.

Slater looked sympathetically at the woman stood before him. She looked tired, traumatised and worse for the liquor she had evidently been consuming that evening.

'Your life may be in danger,' he replied. 'Anyway, by the smell of that whiskey on your breath I'd say you were in no state to drive anywhere. My colleague will drive you back here tomorrow to pick your car up.'

'OK,' she replied, conceding to his wishes, having finally come to the shocking realisation that a dark side really existed outside her world of cocktails, Christian Dior, fast cars and expensive clothes. Conspiracy theories and her near kidnapping by armed extremists with masks had been inconceivable. Right now she badly needed some male company – a rock, if only for tonight.

Through the view of a pair of binoculars, the observer could see the gates of Gouldman's residence open and out sped a dark coloured Ford Taurus with a man and a woman inside. They were followed all the way to the end of the block before stopping at a set of traffic lights that just remained in view. A few moments later the lights changed and the car disappeared from range.

'She's left,' said a voice into a phone.

Detective Slater parked his car outside 'The Lobby', an aptly named bar just outside the Capitol Hill area, and escorted Celina inside. The place was busy as Slater led her to the back of the bar where the lighting was dimmer and more private seating was available. In the corner sat Lawrence Henderson sipping a large brandy. He looked up as Celina approached and asked her to sit down in the chair on the opposite side of the small table he was occupying.

'I'll be at the bar, Sir,' said Slater and left the two of them alone.

'Thanks for meeting with me, Miss McCallen, and well done,' said Henderson sympathetically. 'This must have been an ordeal for you. So what have we got?'

Celina produced the note from her handbag and handed it to Henderson. He began to read it.

'Can I get you something, Miss?' asked a waiter who suddenly appeared from nowhere.

'Scotch, large please, with ice,' she replied.

Henderson waited until the man had gone before responding.

'I'll hold onto this. My next move is to brief Agent Fabien in the morning. We'll take care of everything from now on. I suggest you join Detective Slater at the bar and get him to take you home as soon as possible.'

'OK,' she replied, looking over at him.

'I'm sure the detective has informed you that there will be police protection around the clock. I suggest you stay at home and do exactly as the officers instruct you. Please do not return to work under any circumstances.'

'Sure,' she replied, turning again to look at Slater. As she caught his eye, she smiled at him for the first time.

'If you'll excuse me, Miss McCallen, I have to leave now. We'll call you.'

'Mr Henderson, there's something else,' said Celina as he was about to get up. 'It's been on my mind since all of this started and then today when I got the first phone call…'

'I'm listening.'

'It's about Agent Fabien. I think he has something to do with all this.'

10

At the entrance to FBI headquarters in Washington the security barrier opened to allow John Carlyle to pull into the large parking lot outside the complex. He pulled into one of only a few spaces left within short walking distance of the nearest access point. His passenger, a weary Mike Fabien, sat quietly as the car was brought to a standstill.

'We'd better touch base with Jackson and Henderson,' said Carlyle as they got out of the car.

'I need to go to my desk first and check something out,' replied Fabien.

'Thirty minutes then,' replied his colleague before the two men parted.

As Fabien arrived at his desk a stern-faced Lawrence Henderson was waiting for him at the entrance to his cubicle.

'My office immediately,' he said.

'Something wrong, sir?' asked Fabien.

'We'll talk when we get there.'

Thomas Jackson was waiting in Henderson's office. He had summoned Carlyle the moment he had arrived.

'You have some news?' he asked.

Henderson opened his briefcase and took out the note that had been given him by Celina McCallen the previous night.

'The terms of Gouldman's release have finally arrived.'

'What do they want?' asked Jackson.

'Mark Bradovich released from jail,' said Henderson, beginning his briefing.

'The anti-euthanasia campaigner?' asked Fabien.

'Yes,' replied Jackson.

'Wasn't he sent down for the murder of the two doctors from Maryland a couple of years ago?'

'He blew up their clinic one evening when they were working late. They were suspected pro-euthanasia supporters who we think were illegally administering death drugs on the wishes of their terminally ill patients,' said Henderson.

'What's next?' asked Fabien.

'We have to deliver Bradovich to this location at 23.00,' said Henderson, handing the instructions to Fabien. 'As soon as he is safely retrieved the word will be given to find Gouldman at the second detailed location and bring him back.'

'We'll take a backup team,' said Fabien.

'No, just you and Carlyle, no one else, the note is specific. Any deviation and Gouldman dies,' replied Henderson assertively.

'Aren't we even going to try and bring these guys in?' asked Fabien.

'No, it's too risky. I don't want to endanger Senator Gouldman's life. We'll use intelligence, follow and monitor them and then we'll move in soon after,' said Jackson.

'We'll co-ordinate things at this end,' said Henderson. 'Go home, Agent Fabien, and get some rest. That's not a request – nothing must go wrong tonight.'

'I need to report to medical.'

'It will have to wait. Tonight's operation is paramount,' replied Henderson.

'You are up to this, Agent Fabien?' asked Jackson.

'Of course, Sir.'

'Good. Your chance to make amends then.'

'Here are your communications devices,' said Henderson, handing them both a small black package. 'Do not move in until I order you to do so. We'll establish communication at 22.30. Now get some rest. That includes you, Carlyle.'

As Celina McCallen was driven to the entrance of Gouldman's residency one of the police officers guarding the building signalled for the vehicle she was in to stop. She wound down the passenger side window and the officer walked around to the side of the car.

'No one is allowed in here, ma'am.'

'But I work here; I'm Senator Gouldman's personal assistant.'

'I'm sorry, ma'am; no one is to enter the premises.'

From the car she could see a large white van with the back doors wide open parked near the entrance steps and there were men loading computers and filing cabinets.

'What's going on?'

'I have to ask you to leave now, ma'am.'

'Detective Slade,' said her driver, showing his badge to the officer. 'Why is all this equipment being taken?'

'By order of Senator Allen.'

'We're almost done here,' called one of the men loading the van.

'OK,' replied the officer. 'You have to leave now, ma'am, Detective, we need to secure the premises.'

'That's my car over there,' said Celina, pointing to the metallic blue BMW parked near the entrance.

'Keys ma'am?'

Celina handed them to the officer who then turned to his colleague.

'Pete, can you check out the BMW,' he asked, holding up the keys.

His colleague came over, collected them and walked over to the car.

'Please wait here,' said the officer, and then he walked briskly over to the van and began conversing with the driver.

His colleagues slammed the rear doors closed and then got in with the driver. He started the engine and then drove the van through the gates and out onto the street as Celina began walking towards her car. The first officer approached her briskly.

'I wasn't informed that this was going to happen!'

'I'm sorry, ma'am – orders,' he replied. 'OK Pete?'

His colleague emerged from looking inside the trunk and began to walk over.

'Why are you inspecting my car?' asked Celina, getting annoyed.

'Just making sure nothing leaves here unless it's in the white van,' said the officer who had been checking the car over.

'Can I go now?' she asked.

'It's clean,' said the officer to his colleague as he handed back the keys.

'Thank you!'

'You're lucky you got here when you did,' said the first officer as Celina walked to her car.

She ignored him and got in quickly.

'OK let's finish up here.'

Celina drove out of the parking lot and down the driveway to the gates. She stopped and spoke briefly to Detective Slade through the window before heading off at speed down the street. Slade started his car and then followed her.

As the sun began to set, Fabien and Carlyle arrived in Tilghman, a small town on Chesapeake Bay located to the east of

Washington DC. They had left the main highway at Easton and turned onto a road that led them to Tilghman, meandering around the edge of three coves until they reached their destination. There was a small diner located down a short driveway that looked out onto the bay and so the two men decided to grab some food before heading to the designated location a few miles back along the road. There were only two other people eating as they entered and sat down by the window.

'What sort of a place is this to hide a US senator?' said Carlyle.

'Isolated, which gives me an uneasy feeling,' replied Fabien. 'Let's just hope this is over quickly and we can get back to Washington in one piece.'

'You seemed on edge during the journey.'

'I haven't done this kind of thing for a while,' replied Fabien.

'What was all that about visiting medical earlier?'

'Nothing. I'm getting hungry, how about you?' replied Fabien. He did not want to discuss the subject.

'So we clean up here and then get back on the Mason-Wainwright case,' said Carlyle.

'All this to get Bradovich released from jail? It's all too convenient,' said Fabien.

'He's a major player for the anti-euthanasia movement.'

'That e-mail from Gouldman to Calvert is troubling me,' said Fabien.

'Do you think that Mason-Wainwright is involved in the abduction?'

'Maybe, but it doesn't make sense. The link has to be between them, Gouldman and this Haedenberg Foundation. I can't see where this abduction fits into the equation.'

'Here we are gentlemen,' said the waitress as she arrived with the food. 'You visiting or passing through?' she asked.

'Up for a spot of fishing,' replied Fabien.

'Don't mention fishing to my husband! He spends too much time out on the water. I could use a hand in here tonight instead. Enjoy your meal.'

Fabien smiled at her and then she walked back towards the kitchen. He turned to Carlyle as soon as she was out of earshot.

'Gouldman will have a lot of questions to answer when we get him back to DC,' said Fabien unequivocally.

'This is personal, isn't it, Fabien?'

'Get out of my skin, Carlyle.'

Fabien stared out the window and cast his eyes across the cove, watching the waves as they gently rocked the boats moored along the shore. He was in no mood for further conversation. His thoughts were on the job in hand and it made him nervous. He was finding it hard to adjust to being back in action after such a long break and he began to question how sharp he would be if things didn't go according to plan later that evening.

'I'm going outside for five minutes,' he said.

'Are you OK, Fabien?' asked Carlyle.

'I'm fine.'

As night fell upon Chesapeake Bay Carlyle turned off the main road and headed down a track that disappeared into the trees as Fabien navigated the way to the location where they would pick up Gouldman. They finally came to a clearing and in the distance they could see an old house at the edge of the cove that jutted over the shore and was supported on thick wooden stilts above the water. There was a speedboat moored to a long jetty that protruded out from the front deck of the house. It was clear that the house had not been lived in for a number of years and there was no sign of anyone or any vehicles in the vicinity.

'We'd better get wired up,' said Fabien as he took out the packages that Henderson had given them.

Fabien clipped a small microphone to his denim jacket and a pager-sized receiver and speaker pack to the belt of his jeans. It was now 22.30 and so he activated the kit and called in.

'Fabien here, we're in place.'

'Acknowledged,' replied Henderson.

'Awaiting your instructions.'

The two agents sat in the car and waited. As the minutes ticked on there was still no sign of anyone.

'They must be waiting inside,' said Carlyle, tapping the steering wheel.

'They've got a vehicle somewhere,' said Fabien. 'Let's find it.'

'No! Our orders were to pick up Gouldman, nothing else,' replied Carlyle hastily.

'Where's your sense of adventure?' said Fabien.

'I don't have one right now,' replied his colleague.

Henderson and Jackson stood on the warm tarmac outside a deserted warehouse complex with a score of police cars and a FBI security vehicle containing three agents guarding Mark Bradovich. It was approaching 22.50 when a black '77 Mustang with tinted windows pulled up directly facing them at a distance of about 70 metres. A man got out, stood there and waited.

'Release Bradovich,' ordered Henderson, speaking into his comms gear.

Moments later the doors of the security vehicle opened and out walked a man in his late 20s with ruffled long hair and a short goat beard, escorted by two agents. Bradovich remained silent as he walked past Henderson and glanced briefly at him. The three walked about a distance of five meters in front of the police entourage and stopped. The man from the Mustang then signalled for Bradovich to walk towards the car and after a nod from Henderson the two agents released him. He walked slowly towards the Mustang and when he arrived he was bundled into the back. The man got in, closed the door and the car reversed a short distance before being swung around and driven at pace out of the complex.

'Fabien, this is Henderson. Bradovich has been delivered – go to work,' he said into his communicator.

Fabien and Carlyle got out of their car and cautiously approached the side of the house. They found a rear entrance door and Fabien opened it slowly. It creaked loudly as Fabien stepped inside.

'As we said, you wait outside and cover me.'

'Be careful,' replied Carlyle.

Fabien walked slowly along the dark corridor and felt the occasional cobweb brush into his face. He gripped his gun firmly as he passed what must have been a sitting room at the rear of the house. In the distance he could see a dim light shining from a room at the other end of the corridor. As he walked through a doorway in the middle he saw something move above him and quickly got out of the way as a wooden support lintel almost fell on top of him, spraying dust and fragmented plaster into the air. As he approached the room with the light he spread himself across the wall leading up to the door, his gun ready to fire. He quickly peered around the corner and immediately pulled himself back, his nerves on edge. At the moment he least needed, an overwhelming sense of fear gripped him and he could feel perspiration on his brow. Calming himself, he swung around the door again, his arms outstretched at full lock, his gun pointing at a chair in the distance. The windows in this room had been boarded up and there were no doors apart from the one through which he was about to walk.

As he entered the room he could just make out what looked like a body strapped to the chair facing away from him. He could see the back of the head above the chair rest and the hands clasping the padded arms of the seat. There was no movement from the figure. The floorboards creaked with every step he took as he approached the body. Gouldman was either dead or unconscious. As he reached slowly for the back of the chair his hands began to shake. He gripped it firmly to stop the shaking and then took a deep breath. He swung the chair around and there sat in front of him was a mannequin dressed in a suit.

'Carlyle!' he shouted into his communicator.

At that moment he heard a floorboard creak behind him and realised that he hadn't made any movement himself. Instinctively he dived to the floor as a blinding light was directed at him and flooded the room. As he hit the deck the space above his head was showered with gunfire. He curled up tightly behind the chair as one bullet after another hit the mannequin and pummelled its body, blistering the dark suit in which it was dressed.

Fabien turned over and instantly fired back at the figure standing above him. It fell towards him, opening fire as it staggered forward, the bullets splitting the wooden floor just inches from the side of his head. Fabien rolled over to his left, just preventing himself from taking the full force of the weight of the would-be assassin as he crashed to the floor.

He got to his feet quickly and raced out into the corridor from where he had come, only to meet another round of fire from a second source. Again the bullets missed him by a fraction as he crouched down against the wall. Fortunately there was a bend in the corridor just ahead of him and so he sprinted around the corner just as another bullet took a small chunk of plaster from the corner of the wall. Ahead of him was a door that led out onto a large balcony that overhung the water to the front of the house. He opened it and ran around the outside of the house until he found what he thought was a place of safety. He tried to contact Carlyle on his comms device for a second time but there was no reply.

'Come on Carlyle, where are you?' he said in desperation.

An eerie silence hung in the night air as he slowly walked back to the front of the house, checking over his shoulder continually to make sure that nobody would take him from behind. As he approached the front balcony he checked to see if anyone was on the jetty below him and then he turned his attention to a pair of large damaged louvre doors. He walked towards them, his finger on the trigger of his gun, when, without warning, they were violently kicked open. Just as Fabien was about to open fire a masked man came out holding a gun to Carlyle's head.

'Be cool, Fabien!' said Carlyle. 'Don't try anything, just do as he says!'

'Throw the gun in the water!' ordered Carlyle's captor.

'Do you really think I'd be so stupid as to do that?' replied Fabien defiantly.

'Are you crazy, Fabien?' cried Carlyle.

'Which one of us has the faster finger, my friend?' asked Fabien.

'Fabien, no!' shouted Carlyle.

'If you shoot him, how long will it take you to re-aim your gun at me?' asked Fabien as he advanced towards the two men.

The gunman dragged Carlyle back into the room as Fabien waited momentarily on the balcony.

'Stop playing games, Fabien!' called Carlyle from inside.

Fabien cast all caution to the wind as he rushed into the room opening fire at random and shooting to alternate sides of his shocked opponent. Carlyle was thrown to the floor. Fabien saw his chance, but as he stepped forward the floor beneath him splintered into large fragments and gave way under his weight. Instantly he disappeared through the hole that remained, and plunged into the water below him. As his body submerged, more debris fell into the water and then floated on the surface over the spot where he had entered. Immediately the gunman fired several rounds through the hole and into the water below where Fabien had fallen. He turned around and pointed the gun back at Carlyle, signalling him to get up and move towards a door in the corner. Carlyle opened it, revealing a large cupboard. He felt a hand push him from behind, turned and saw the door shut and then heard it being bolted from the outside.

The gunman raced back down the corridor to the room where the mannequin sat sprawled over the chair with numerous bullet holes in it. He looked down and saw his dead colleague on the floor and then headed back up the corridor to the balcony. He ran down the stairs to the jetty and jumped into the speedboat that was moored to one of the posts. As he began to untie it from the post he was stunned by the sound of a splash in the water behind him and felt the boat rock, causing him to lose his balance and tumble backwards into it. Fabien pulled himself up over the side of the boat and landed on top of him. He quickly jumped on the gunman's stomach with his knee, winding him, and then hit him with full force in the face. He caught sight of the gun he had been using to hold Carlyle, and as he pulled it from its holster the gunman returned a blow to Fabien's right cheek, knocking him backwards and sending the gun to the rear of the boat just under the engine. A struggle ensued and Fabien found himself pinned to the floor of the boat by a man at least 20 percent heavier than himself as he stretched in desperation for the gun that was just out of reach. The gunman delivered another blow to Fabien's head causing him to lose his focus momentarily. When he began to realise what was going on, a gun was pointing at his face. Fabien thrust his hands up and managed to force the gun to rotate just enough to change the trajectory of the bullet as it left the barrel and was embedded in the engine casing. Fabien kicked his attacker hard in the chest and he fell back, gun in hand, towards the front of the boat. He lunged forward, grabbing the gunman's wrist and jabbed it repeatedly against the edge of one of the seats to the side of him. As his hand released the gun, Fabien grabbed it, held it into his opponent's chest and fired three times. The gunman's arm became limp and Fabien felt him become lifeless. He pulled himself up and climbed out of the boat onto the jetty. As he stood up he felt his legs buckle and he slumped down hard onto the large wooden planks by the side of the boat, with the gun still in his hand. He felt dizzy, disoriented and his blurred vision could just make out a few lights in the distance. He heard the sound of what felt like thuds on the water in the distance that became louder each time they occurred.

The stone thrower! he thought, feeling a panicky sensation overcome him.

As the thuds got louder he began to see a hazy figure approach and then stop a few feet in front of him. The stone thrower pointed his arm out at Fabien and in return Fabien drew the gun. They had found him. Very soon the frogmen would appear out of the mist and take him.

'Fabien!' said the figure. 'Fabien, it's me – Carlyle. Put the gun down.'

Fabien maintained his aim until the figure came into focus.

'It's you,' he muttered, relieved.

'What the hell were you doing back there?'

'A calculated risk,' he replied as he got up.

'Sure. Well here's one for the road Fabien,' said Carlyle as he kicked his colleague hard in the stomach causing his legs to give way. 'Now get up! Let's get out of here.'

'This was a set-up, Carlyle,' said a winded Fabien staggering to his feet.

11

Exhausted, bruised and aching, Mike climbed the stairs to the balcony that led to his apartment as John Carlyle drove out of the complex and onto the deserted road around the front of the building. Each step he took became more painful than the last as he clutched the railings and struggled to reach the top. It had been a long time since his body had taken the blows that it had received that night and he considered himself lucky even to be alive. Every survival manoeuvre he had made seemed to him to be both clumsy and misjudged. On reflection he felt as though he had performed like a rookie on his first major assignment – inexperienced, unsteady and afraid. The time he had spent away from the front line on the orders of Thomas Jackson had taken its toll.

It was approaching 03.00. He opened the zipped inside pocket of his jacket and pulled out his door keys. The door to his apartment began to sway a little in his vision and so he leaned up against it to steady himself and winced as he felt another sharp pain in his ribs on his left side. He had been nursing the injury on the journey home, one that had seen little conversation with his partner. He wondered whether he had broken a rib during the struggle in the boat but having cracked one before during a training exercise a few years ago he realised that the pain had been far worse on that occasion. When he finally opened the door he groped for the light switch on the wall to the right and hit it hard with his middle fingers. The apartment lit up in sequences – first the lounge area then the kitchen and finally the bathroom. He squinted as his eyes adjusted to the light and he felt relieved to be home and safe again as he closed the door firmly behind him.

The dry parched feeling that flared up inside his mouth and throat was a fire needing to be dowsed. He went to the kitchen and reached for the jug of ice-cold water that he kept constantly in his refrigerator. He would try to drink at least five glasses a day. Not bothering to fetch a glass, he gulped it down like a man in a desert who had stumbled upon the last oasis. The soothing liquid quenched the inferno instantly whilst some trickled down the edge of his mouth and onto his chin before dampening the collar of his shirt.

He wiped his mouth with his sleeve as he switched off the lights, walked into the bedroom and painfully removed his clothes from his body leaving them on the floor for the morning. Clambering into bed, he pulled the duvet over him and lay there in the dark whilst his tired eyes began to adjust to see the outlines of various objects in his bedroom. Replaying the events of that evening over in his mind eventually caused him to fall asleep and within an hour he was reliving it all as he tossed and turned restlessly in his bed, imagining he had returned to the old house and was standing alone on the balcony that overlooked the water. The dim sound of stones being thrown into the water outside rippled through his mind as there, on the jetty below in the distance and in the moonlight, was the stone thrower, casting what looked like large pebbles into the water. It stopped and looked at him, but as in all their previous nightly encounters since his return from Ashbury Falls, he was again unable to distinguish its facial features. There were no frogmen waiting in the boat for him this time. Then, as before, the hooded figure lifted its arm, stretched out its hand and pointed directly at him.

He awoke instantly and felt a sharp pain in his arm. He had been stabbed with a syringe. He quickly reached for the bedside lamp but knocked it off the table and onto the floor as he did so. Getting out of bed, he crouched down on the floor and managed to find the switch of his lamp. As he pressed it the room became illuminated with red light and numerous shadows danced across the ceiling until he placed the lamp back on the table from where it had fallen. He looked at his arm and could see a mark surrounded by a small red circle of swollen flesh. He began to panic and ran into the lounge. It was the frogmen; they *had* returned. As he groped for the light he felt a sudden haziness inside his head that caused him to feel dizzy and disoriented. He could not find the light switch and began to stagger around like a drunken man. As the room started to sway he saw a figure standing in the distance by the entrance door that he could just make out from the light that shone from his bedroom.

'Who's there?' he cried hopelessly as he held the edge of the sofa to stop himself from falling.

The figure just stood there, lifeless almost, tormenting him as his whole body began to be sapped of strength.

'What have you done to me?' he added, becoming breathless.

The figure moved towards him. Mike staggered clumsily back into his bedroom in a vain effort to find his gun and protect himself. Suddenly he felt two hands grab him from behind and throw him to the floor. His body rotated as he hit the carpet with a force that sent painful shockwaves through his head. Lying on his back and staring up at the figure above him, he realised that the end had come. In what coherent moments still remained he realised that he had been drugged to make him defenceless against his assailant and that at any moment the gun would be aimed and the lights would go out forever.

Whoever had failed to get him at Chesapeake Bay was about to eliminate him now.

He felt himself being lifted up and pressed against the wall by his attacker. As the hazy figure clutched him by the underside of his jaw, the face before him came closer into focus and Mike's eyes widened in disbelief as he saw the man's facial features. He was looking at himself, except the face appeared older than his. The man stared at him, expressionless for around 30 seconds, pressing in on his throat, blocking any air from entering his lungs. Then the face disappeared from view as blackness enveloped him.

Groaning as he began to stir, his head throbbing and his body stiff, Mike pushed himself up from the floor with one outstretched arm. As he regained full consciousness he was startled when he noticed that he was fully dressed in the clothes he had been wearing the previous night. The digital clock on the shelf informed him that it was still the early hours of the morning and he immediately tried to get up. He was unsteady on his feet at first and caught hold of the arm of the other sofa to support himself. His side was bruised and his cheek still tender.

He walked around the apartment, dazed, like a man who had lost all sense of reality. As he entered the bedroom he could see that his bed had not been slept in. 'Impossible,' he said to himself, looking around the room as he recalled vividly being pinned to the wall by the intruder who had somehow broken into his apartment. The last thing he could remember was being unable to breathe due to the tight grip of the intruder's hand around his neck. He quickly ran back into the lounge and over to the entrance door of the apartment. As he examined it both inside and out there appeared to be no sign of any break-in.

He moved over to the window and lifted the blinds to look down onto the parking lot. The dimmed street lamps shone on the tarmac revealing nothing more than the stationary cars below and a light on in an apartment on the ground level that belonged to a neighbour who was a renowned early bird. He waited for a moment to see if there was any movement and then came to the realisation that he was merely chasing ghosts. He had been spared. Why?

As his head continued to throb he remembered the painkillers in the bathroom cabinet. When he returned he opened the refrigerator to get some water and as he did so he stopped and stared at the jug. It was full, just as it had been when he had arrived home in the early hours of the morning. It was then that he realised that someone must have got into the apartment with a set of skeleton keys and had waited for him, somehow observing everything he had done: the drinking of the water, the undressing to go to bed. All this, he thought, to make it appear as though it had never happened. His complexion changed as he remembered the face in the mirror of the restrooms at FBI headquarters and the incident in the elevator in New York.

He jumped as the phone rang. He had fallen asleep and it was now approaching 09.00. At first he dared not even think about picking it up, but it would not stop ringing. He picked it up and then cut the call. He stared at it for a few moments and then it rang again, seemingly louder than the first time. He waited. The phone continued to ring until his voicemail cut in.

'Fabien, pick up the phone and call me,' said a voice that he recognised. It was Henderson's.

Immediately Fabien dialled the number and waited a short while before his boss came to the phone.

'Fabien here,' he said as he heard the connection.

'I want to know exactly what happened last night! We have just released a dangerous anarchist and Robert Gouldman is still missing. You were almost killed and I've got an angry associate agent making bitter complaints about the way you handled things! And if things weren't bad enough, Jackson is after my scalp!'

'It was a set up!' replied Fabien angrily.

'Don't be ridiculous - it was just a scam to get Mark Bradovich freed.'

'With respect, Sir, I don't think you realise what's going on here.'

'Get a grip, Fabien! Firstly, Jackson wants you to report to sickbay this afternoon and when they are done with you I want you in my office. Is that understood?'

Fabien immediately dialled Rachel Kirby's number and waited for a reply. It was a long time coming.

'Kirby! Glad I caught you!' said Fabien, relieved at the sound of her voice.

'Are you OK? I heard what happened.'

'For the moment, yes. Have you found out anything else regarding Mason-Wainwright?'

'Not yet, but I'm working on it.'

'Look, I need you to do something for me today. It's really important. I need a portfolio on a John Markham, suspected anti-euthanasia activist and possibly in league with Mark Bradovich. Anything you can get on him, *anything*, and I need a photograph. Meet me in the labs at 16:30 this afternoon.'

'OK Fabien, but you owe me one.'

'I know. Thanks.'

'No permanent damage, Agent Fabien,' said Dr Mitch Coleman, one of the bureau's senior medics, as he finished shining a small torch into Mike's right eye. 'Everything looks fine, just a bruised rib and some slight concussion.'

'What about the drug that was pumped into me last night?'
'Drug, what drug?'
'My attacker injected me with something to sedate me.'
'Then we had better take a blood sample and see what we can find. Show me where the needle went in.'

Fabien removed his shirt and pointed to his left upper arm. Coleman looked closely.

'That's strange!' he muttered.
'What is?' asked Fabien.
'Are you sure it was the left arm?'
'Positive.'
'Well, there doesn't seem to be any evidence of a needle here.'
'It was around here,' replied Fabien, pointing to the approximate place that he had seen the swelling.
'Nothing there. Not to worry, we'll still take a sample, give me your finger.'

After Coleman had taken the sample, Fabien put his shirt and tie back on and got up to leave.

'I'd like to do some further tests, if you don't mind. I'll let you know when.'
'Tests?'
'Neurological.'
'Why?'
'Have you experienced any blackouts lately?'
'No, why do you ask?'
'Your superiors are concerned about recent incidents and they have asked me to investigate.'
'I am not having blackouts.'
'Well that's really for me to determine, isn't it?'

Fabien got up and headed towards the exit door.

'Don't go wandering off, I'd like to do them tomorrow, say 14.30,' said Coleman as Fabien opened the door.

'You're the doc,' replied Fabien unenthusiastically before closing the door.

A few moments later he returned.

'Yes, Agent Fabien?'

'I'm in the middle of a major assignment right now.'

'Don't worry; I have no intention of speaking to your superiors about this until I've completed the tests and verified the results.'

'Thanks,' replied Fabien, and then he left.

To admit he was experiencing blackouts would be suicidal. Was he cracking up? he asked himself on his way to meet Rachel Kirby. Passing a drinking water fountain he stopped to pull out a plastic cup. He was feeling thirst more often than usual and as he filled the cup with the running water his hand began to shake violently, spilling some of the contents. He gulped the remainder down and continued on his way to the labs. Kirby will be waiting, he thought.

When he arrived at the laboratory complex he waited at the entrance and signalled to a colleague to let him in. He did not currently have security access to this section of the building so nobody would think to look for him there. The door opened.

'Fabien, what are you doing here?' asked his colleague.

'I'm meeting Kirby here for a few minutes, that's all.'

'Alright, come in quickly and go straight into my office. I'll tell Kirby you're waiting for her there. Five minutes, that's all.'

Fabien waited in a small room that could only have been around 8ft square in area and that contained hardly any natural light. There was a filing cabinet, a small desk and a rather unusual looking houseplant tucked in the corner that towered almost to the ceiling. He did not have to wait long before his colleague opened the door and showed Rachel Kirby into the room. He waited for the door to close before speaking to his colleague.

'What did you find?' he asked her.

'It's all here. But it wasn't easy to get hold of. If they ask, it wasn't me, OK?'

Fabien nodded.

'Why do you think it's taking so long to get to the bottom of this Mason-Wainwright investigation?' she added.

'What are you telling me, Kirby?'

'I'll call you,' she replied, and then closed the door behind, leaving Fabien alone, holding the document and looking bewildered.

He sat down at his colleague's desk, opened the document folder that Kirby had given him and pulled out three pieces of paper. As the cold eyes of John Markham stared at him from the photograph he knew immediately that the face on the page was the very same one that he had seen before him when he had been pinned to the wall in his apartment in the early hours of that morning. As he read through the dossier his eyes widened as it revealed that the intruder that had been in his apartment had connections with a number of extremist anti-euthanasia action groups that had begun to emerge throughout the country in recent years. As he read on, the dossier revealed that he had been associated with Mark Bradovich and his activities.

'Time to go, Fabien!' said a voice from behind him. 'My supervisor just called and is on his way back!'

'OK, I'm out of here.'

'It *was* Markham!' said Fabien, throwing the dossier onto Henderson's desk.

'Where did you get this?' he asked, looking shocked.

'That doesn't matter. What matters is the contents of this. Read it. If that won't convince you then the fact that he was in my apartment last night makes him the chief suspect for Gouldman's abduction in my eyes.'

'And you think that this mysterious John Markham set you up?'

'Yes!'

'Then why didn't he finish the job off last night?'

'I don't know.'

'Exactly! You don't know,' replied Henderson heatedly.

'We need to bring this guy in. Celina McCallen said that he visited Gouldman before the abduction.'

'That could have been for any number of reasons.'

'It's him, Sir.'

'Have you been to see Coleman?' asked Henderson.

'You don't believe me do you? You think this is all in my mind, a fabrication!'

'I'm unable to reconcile the fact that you believe that Markham set you up, tried to have you killed and then when he had the opportunity he just left you there asleep and quietly closed the front door. Time is running out, Fabien. We have nothing else to go on and the press are lapping this one up.'

'I'll talk to Celina McCallen again.'

'No! You are not to speak to her or go near her. That's an order.'

12

Rockfields was a bar about five miles outside of the District of Columbia that attracted a clientele whose tastes in music were not for the faint hearted nor for those who didn't like the dirtier sound of the electric guitar. Within its smoky isles sat numerous bikers, truckers and urban cowboys ending the day to the beat of loud drums, heavy metal riffs and copious amounts of beer, as an entourage of rock chicks shook their heads frivolously on the dimly lit dance floor. The walls were decorated with numerous black and white photographs of Hendrix, Clapton and other guitarist legends along with posters from various tours that had etched their way into the annals of rock history.

At the bar sat the lonely figure of Michael Fabien, with a large scotch in his hand, looking directly at a colour poster of Eddie Van Halen in mid flight. He was dressed in denims and was wearing a T-shirt from the Eagles' 'Hell Freezes Over' tour that he had managed to get last minute tickets for three years previously. His face was beginning to smart a set of designer stubble that blended well with the hair that was beginning to sweep over his ears and almost touch his collar at the back of his head. All he needed was an earring to make the final transition from FBI agent to rock band roadie. He had been at the bar for about 30 minutes, drinking and playing with a small pack of complimentary matches and being content with his own company. He had not been to Rockfields for a while and apart from the apparent change in management he had noticed that very little else had changed during his absence. It was an old haunt of his; somewhere he had stumbled upon one evening not long after he had moved to Falls Church and bought his apartment. Tonight the familiar sounds of classic tracks that were belting out of the jukebox were passing over and around him. During the time spent at the bar he had attracted the attention of two women on the dance floor who watched him as they danced and spoke into each other's ears to communicate their opinions of him over the drone of the music. After a while he looked over and noticed one of them looking at him periodically. He turned his head away and took another sip of his drink, as though disinterested and to discourage either of them from coming over.

As the golden glimmer of the bottle of Southern Comfort that rested on the edge of the bar in front of him danced around his eyes he saw the figure of the lifeless dummy that was supposed to have been Gouldman. In his mind he could see the face staring at him over and over again and then hearing the floorboards creak behind him. Three seconds later and *he* would have been perforated with bullet holes. The sound of firing echoed through his mind as he saw himself diving in slow motion to the floor, almost feeling one of the bullets as it brushed through his hair. He felt his face hit the cold wooden floor but was then suddenly awoken from his trancelike state by a voice beside him. It was the girl from the dance floor. She had come over to tell him that her friend wanted to dance with him. On any other day he would have been glad to oblige.

'Tell your friend that I may be dead in the morning,' he answered with a slur. 'So I probably won't be very good company for either of you, if that's what you had in mind. Too dangerous…'

Sincere as his drunken words were, the girl was clearly not on his wavelength.

'I don't think we're in any danger by the look of the state you're in. Take it easy, OK.'

'The reaper cometh!' he added, laughing.

'I doubt it,' she replied and then returned to her friend.

'Sorry ladies, another time maybe!' he called out as he carefully stepped off the barstool.

With that he made his way from the bar through a small crowd that had begun to congregate. They noticed that he was drunk and gave him the space he needed to get to the entrance.

'Go steady, man!' said a large bearded biker as he reached the door.

As he walked out into the evening air, a soft breeze blew the fringe of his hair from his eyes. As he looked down the street the lights shone softly against the backdrop of a beautiful summer sunset and the sky was aglow with a mixture of blue and red. He stood there alone, amidst the people walking and the cars driving slowly by, and he wondered how long it would be until his world would finally collapse around him, dragging him down into a black abyss from which there could be no return. It would not be too long, he hoped, before he would sober up enough to get himself home safely – he had been getting used to taking his drink in recent months.

The cab that Mike had flagged down dropped him in the parking lot of his apartment complex. He gave the driver a $20 bill and climbed out. The cab drove off, leaving him at the bottom of the stairs that were now illuminated by lights that were activated by an auto-sensor when darkness began to fall. He started to climb the steps to his apartment but was a little off balance due to the scotch. When he had reached half way he had the sudden feeling that he was not alone. Lights were on in the other apartments, people were in, but someone was following him, he was sure of it. He moved quickly to reach the door to his apartment and stood there while he searched his pockets for his keys. He knew they were there somewhere but it took a few moments for him to remember that they were tucked inside one of his breast pockets. As he pulled them out he began to hear footsteps along the balcony coming towards him. At first he wondered if he really had seen someone, perhaps it was Markham, but then he realised that the footsteps sounded like the heels of a woman's boots. As he looked to his left he saw a woman walking towards him with long shaggy brown hair, carrying a suitcase. When her face came into view he was stunned with disbelief. It was Jamie Farrington. Lost for words, he wondered if this was a hallucination. Maybe he was cracking up. Perhaps he was seeing what he wanted to see. It must have been the drug that the intruder had given him.

'Hello Mike,' she said softly.

He was unable to speak, as though reality had turned itself on its head. He looked away for a moment but then felt himself being drawn back to look into her eyes. As he did so she started to feel uncomfortable at the way he was looking at her.

'Mike?'

He put the key in the door and as the lock clicked open he pushed it ajar. This was real – time to sober up.

'You'd better come in,' he said to her.

Jamie hesitated for a moment. She could see he had clearly been drinking but decided nevertheless to follow him into the apartment. Mike was stood in the kitchen gulping down a large glass of water. When he had finished he breathed deeply and turned to her.

'Can I get you something to drink?'

'Sure, coffee would be great,' she replied nervously as she closed the door.

The next 30 seconds of silence felt like a lifetime to Jamie and the atmosphere within the apartment could be cut with a knife. Even the sound of the coffee machine steaming on the breakfast bar couldn't remove the air of awkwardness that she could so readily sense around her. She put her case down and sat on one of the sofas, looking around the room trying to avoid speaking to him.

'Nice apartment,' she finally commented.

'Thanks,' he replied in a subdued tone.

She smiled to hide the fact that inside she was beginning to feel embarrassed at turning up out of the blue, finding him worse for drink and remembering that she had not called him for all that time.

'How long have you been waiting?' he asked.

'A few hours.'

Mike walked over, handed her a drink and sat down on the other sofa. 'Are you staying anywhere?' he asked, covering his face with his hands.

'Actually no, I've not checked in anywhere. I was about to leave before I saw the cab pull up.'

'Why are you here Jamie?' he asked, blinking his eyes in an attempt to shake off the effects of the whiskey.

She couldn't find the right words to say as again he gave her that same strange look that she had experienced on the balcony. She could see that something was wrong. He looked exhausted and lost and she was surprised at how rugged he looked. His hair had grown since they had last been together and she drew the conclusion that maybe he had either resigned or had been fired from the FBI.

'You look awful, Mike.'

'Thanks. I'm on a difficult case at the moment. Anyway you didn't answer my question.'

'So you made it through the disciplinary hearing then?'

'Only just. Jamie, why are you here?'

'I don't know, Mike.'

'Have you come from Boston?'

'Yes, I've been living there for the past nine months.'

'Are you going back?'

She didn't answer.

'When did you last eat?'

'I stopped at a service diner on the '95 earlier.'

'Can I fix you anything?'

'No, no really, it's OK, thanks.'

'Your hair looks pretty.'

'Thanks,' she replied, smiling as she ran her fingers through the ringlets that rested on her neck. 'It was a spur of the moment thing.'

'It suits you.'

She smiled coyly.

'How have you been, Mike?'

'I've been.'

The cut-dead remark acted as a signal for her to stay off that line of conversation. Like most women she was a discerning creature and she could sense that Mike's reply was more than just a rebuff. In the short time that she had spent with him she had realised that this Mike Fabien was not the one whom she had turned her back on to make a life for herself in Boston. He was damaged somehow, affected, but by what she was unsure. She would have to find out, if indeed the opportunity to do so would materialise.

'I left the hotel to Stella to look after,' she said in an attempt to keep things moving.

'How is she?' he asked.

'She's fine, she's been a rock.'

'And what about Hank and Carla?'

'Carla and Jack went to North Carolina like they said they would, but I didn't see Hank after you left. I went to see my cousin in Burlington before leaving for Boston. I got a job in one of the banks as assistant to the marketing director.'

'That's good, I'm pleased for you.'

'What have you been up to?'

'I've been desk bound for the most part since my hearing, but I'm back in the field now. I have to be up early tomorrow morning. You're welcome to stay the night and sleep in the spare room. There's a duvet in the cupboard and some sheets. I'm sorry it's not made up.'

'Thank you.'

'In here.'

Jamie followed Mike into the spare room. It was a good size and looked tidy and comfortable. Mike opened the wardrobe and lifted some bedding from the top shelf. He placed it on the bed and then closed the doors. Jamie put her case down on the bed and then looked at Mike as he walked back out into the lounge. She followed shortly afterwards and stood at the door to her room as he headed for the kitchen. He drank some more water, again gulping it down as if he hadn't had a drink for ages. He stood there and rubbed his head with his hands and flexed his neck a little. He looked like he was in some sort of pain.

'Are you OK, Mike?' Jamie asked.

He turned around, startled a little.

'I'm fine, just some slight concussion. Help yourself to whatever you want,' he said. 'There's a refrigerator full of food; there's juice, beer, and you can watch TV as long as you keep the volume down a bit.'

Jamie walked slowly over to the kitchen and then joined him behind the breakfast bar. She stood close to him as he again rubbed his forehead.

'Can you get me my painkillers; they're in a brown bottle in the bathroom cabinet. That door over there.'

'Sure.'

His eyes followed her until she disappeared into the bathroom. She returned shortly thereafter with his medication.

'Thanks. Excuse me for a second.'

Mike swallowed three pills using the remainder of the water in his glass and then put it by the sink. Jamie watched, disturbed, and yet concerned. They did not appear to be the regular painkillers that you would get from the local drugstore, nor anything she had ever seen prescribed for her parents during their final years. She approached him cautiously and then, unable to hold back, put her arms around his neck and rested her head on his shoulder.

'Mike, hold me, please hold me,' she whispered, shedding a single tear from her pale blue eyes.

Mike reached out his hands and held her around her waist. Moments later she started to tenderly kiss his face, starting by his ear, then his cheek and slowly moving around to his mouth. He tried to stop her from going any further when she finally made contact with his lips, but she wouldn't stop. He gently put his hand on her chest to move her away and with that she stood back suddenly and glared at him, hurt.

'I'm sorry,' she said, brushing her hair from her eyes.

'I need to sleep. We'll talk in the morning,' he said to calm the situation.

'OK,' she said, drying her eyes with a small handkerchief that she pulled out of her jacket pocket.

'I hope you'll be comfortable.'

'Thanks, I will.'

Mike headed into his bedroom and switched on the light. He turned back to Jamie who was stood at the edge of the kitchen with her back to him.

'Is there someone else?' she asked impulsively, remembering that she had told herself not to ask that question so soon on arrival.

'No,' he replied.

'Goodnight then,' she said softly as she closed the door to her room.

13

Jamie had slept deeply after her long journey from Boston but at just before 10.00 she pulled the duvet away from her and rolled her legs to the side of the bed to get up. In the wardrobe was her blue silk dressing gown. She put it on and entered the lounge looking for Mike; the master bedroom door was ajar but there was no sign of him. She called out but it was evident he had already left. Tucked under the edge of a glass fruit bowl on the breakfast bar was a note:

Jamie,
Hope you had a comfortable sleep. Back tonight.
Please don't leave. We'll talk later.
Mike

She smiled, put the note down and finished drinking a glass of juice. She liked the apartment. It was clutter-free, with just the occasional ornament and picture spaced around the room. The pictures on the walls were mostly either of natural scenery or city architecture. One in particular caught her eye; it was a photograph of a '77 Mustang, something she recalled Mike had mentioned he had always wanted to own when they had first met. In one corner were shelves full of vinyl record albums that surrounded a Sony music centre that must have been in excess of 15 years old. Amongst the vast collection were volumes of progressive rock, American AOR and what looked like everything that Bruce Springsteen had recorded, all of them with the sleeves in immaculate condition. When she decided to look for evidence of a relationship – photos, gifts, feminine articles that had been left lying around by mistake, there were none. Maybe he *had* told her the truth last night.

NBC news was broadcasting an interesting story as she flicked through the channels on the TV remote controls. She settled into one of the sofas and began to watch.

Lawrence Henderson was becoming increasingly frustrated. No further leads had appeared in the Gouldman abduction. He had been deceived into letting a dangerous activist go free and his new boss, Thomas Jackson, was gunning for his demise. He had switched on NBC news to catch the hourly update and had sat there waiting to see how bad the media would present things. He had suspected that news of recent events had been leaked and now he and countless millions of other viewers were about to find out.

'In other news, the FBI are no closer to finding the abductors of Robert Gouldman, the controversial Rhode Island senator at the centre of yet another debate on euthanasia, support for which is currently gaining momentum across the nation. Let's go to Alan Deacon...'

'The FBI have no firm leads on the whereabouts of Senator Gouldman the pro-euthanasia campaigner who, sources reveal, was due to give what they describe as a truly controversial speech on this very issue on the day of his abduction. This has heightened the temperature in the pro-euthanasia camp who claim that his abduction is an act by what they are calling the 'anti-league' whose aim is to silence the ever growing voice of those who want to see the decision to end life become a fundamental right for every American. Some here in Washington are praying that he will be found alive. They believe him to be the voice of reason. Leaders representing many

Christian denominations have condemned his philosophy, branding him a God player. Fuelled by a statement from one of Gouldman's staff, the FBI were forced to confirm that activist Mark Bradovich had been released, but denied that this was a failed attempt to use him in an exchange to free Gouldman. Bradovich was convicted in 1995 for the murder of two scientists alleged to be involved in euthanasia research.'

The coverage switched to a group of reporters surrounding a man as he was leaving the Washington police department. Henderson recognised that it was Jackson.

'Can you confirm what one of your spokesmen told us regarding the Bradovich release, Mr Jackson? Was it a trade for the senator?'

'I have no further comments,' he replied.

'Is it true that a bumbled rescue attempt took place in Chesapeake Bay two nights ago?'

'No comment.'

'Will you be dealing with those responsible for this incompetence, Mr Jackson?' asked another as he tried to avoid the crowd.

'Mr Jackson, do you still believe Senator Gouldman to be alive at this time?'

Henderson pushed the red button on his remote controls and the screen went black. He rubbed his chin nervously and then called Fabien's cell phone. His voicemail cut in, but Henderson declined to leave a message.

When Fabien had arrived at his desk earlier that morning there had only been three other colleagues in. They were too busy with their own assignments to notice him. Fabien had hoped for this; a chance to get to his e-mails before Henderson, or anyone else for that matter, would arrive or disturb him. The enigmatic 'A friend in need' sent by 'Spiral Architect' was now the focus of his thoughts. The text simply stated:

Friend in need,
Find me quickly. Zachary can help. Regards…

Fabien was perplexed. Who was he to find and where? He had few options. He downloaded his e-mail file to floppy disk, tucked it inside his suite jacket pocket and shut down his computer. He left again unnoticed.

Fabien rang the bell of a green-coloured single storey house on the outskirts of the capital. Visibly in need of maintenance, it stood out from the surrounding cluster of look-alike homes in the tree-lined street in which it was situated. The road came to a dead end after the house in question. There the tarmac ended and a narrow path continued on into the trees.

He waited about 30 seconds before ringing the bell again. When there was still no reply he began peering through the windows. From what he could see through the thin gauze that covered them, the inside of the house appeared dark and uninviting. Then suddenly he heard a voice from behind him.

'What's going on? Have the FBI got me under surveillance after all this time?'

Fabien swung around startled. There before him was a tall man with long brown hair and a beard.

'Zachary, is that *you* underneath all that hair?' asked Fabien humorously.

'Well if it isn't Michael Patrice Fabien! You are still in the FBI aren't you?'

'For my sins, yes,' he replied.

'They haven't kicked you out yet? Grab hold of this,' said Zachary, handing him one of three brown grocery bags.

He followed Zachary through the front door into the darkened house and was shown to a large room at the back full of computers and empty coke cans.

'I know a guy who can fix this place up,' said Fabien.

'I've no time for all that. As long as it's comfortable.'

'How's the world of computer hacking these days?' asked Fabien.

'Wouldn't know. I'm out of that now. I fix desktops and laptops, rebuild them and install software, all from here. Need anything repaired?'

'Not exactly.'

'Sit here while I put these away.'

The seat was an ochre-coloured swivel chair that was a good 20 years old. Zachary's desk was full of CDs, computer components, and laptops. He was not short of work. Short of time more like, as the house revealed.

'Want a beer?' called his friend from the kitchen.

'No thanks, I can't stay long.'

'OK, Mr Fabien, what can I do for you?' asked Zachary, returning with a can of Budweiser in his hand.

'I need you to trace this, and quickly,' said Fabien, pulling the diskette from his jacket pocket.

'What is it?'

'There's an e-mail from a sender called 'Spiral Architect'. I need to know the origin and a location.'

'Cryptic?' asked Zachary.

'Yes.'

'OK, let's take a look.'

Zachary loaded the file onto his desktop and merged Fabien's e-mail file with one of his own. He then opened 'Spiral Architect' and looked at the properties file.

'Unusual,' said Zachary, stroking his beard.

'Do you think you can trace it?'

'Give me a day or two.'

'I need it sooner than that.'

'Why didn't you get one of your boys on the case? Surely they could trace it.'

'I don't think so, and besides, it's safer with you.'

'You up to something, Fabien?'

'What's this going to cost me?'

'Well, let me see… 200 bucks to you if you want me to drop everything.'

'Done.'

'I'll call you.'

'No, I'll be back tomorrow.'

'You in some kind of trouble, Fabien?'

'Tomorrow then,' he replied, handing Zachary the cash.

As Mike opened the door to his apartment the aroma of fresh pasta wafted across the room. Jamie was stood in the kitchen serving up dinner. On the dining table was a plate of hot panini bread, salad, black pitted olives, and an opened bottle of red wine waiting to be poured into two long-stemmed wine glasses. She had lit a vanilla-scented candle and the flame's reflection glistened in the glasses.

'Perfect timing,' she said as she brought the pasta through.

'Something smells good,' said Mike as he threw his suit jacket onto one of the sofas.

'I rummaged through your larder and came up with this. Shall we eat?' she asked, directing him to the table.

Mike looked better today. She noticed he was clean-shaven and had had his hair trimmed. An encouraging sign, she thought, despite his demeanour being less than inviting.

'For a guy you keep a neat home,' she said as he approached the table.

'Thank my cleaning lady.'

'So what happened today?'

'I took a cryptic e-mail to an old friend,' he replied as he sat opposite her.

'Can he help you?'

'He has before. This is good pasta. It tastes familiar, I…'

'Thanks for letting me stay last night.'

'Sure,' he replied, avoiding eye contact.

'Look, if it's about last night, I'm sorry for being so forward,' said Jamie, deciding she had had enough of the small talk already. 'We haven't seen each other for the best part of a year and then I turn up uninvited. I shouldn't have made assumptions.'

'It doesn't matter, Jamie, it's no big deal.'

'It is to me.'

'To say I was surprised to see you is an understatement.'

'I guess it must have been a bit of a shock.'

'Like I said, it's no big deal,' he repeated pouring her some wine.

'It might be to me.'

'Whatever. Shall we just enjoy the food.'

'And then what?' she replied confrontationally.

Mike looked at her and declined to reply.

'You're right, let's enjoy the food.'

'Why didn't you call?'

She looked up, surprised.

'Protecting myself I guess.'

'From whom?'

'You of course.'

'Why?'

'I wanted to get you out of my system. Forget you. Going to Boston was supposed to be the way, or so I thought.'

'But you're here... why?' asked Mike, interjecting.

'I was having lunch with some friends not long after I arrived. We finished up and I left the restaurant without my jacket. It was kind of expensive, made to fit. I had to go back for it. When I returned, Malcolm Kemp, my former fiancé, was there, the one I told you about before. Well we started dating again. My friend Samantha thought it was fate. I think she was more excited than I was at first. She's into all that kind of stuff.'

'Do you believe in fate, Jamie?'

'Of course not.'

'If you began seeing Malcolm again why are you here?'

'I thought that we could make it work. I had a good job, he had his own business and it really looked like he meant it this time.'

'And did he?'

'He proposed to me in this stuffy wine bar. It was when he put the ring on my finger that I realised that everything was wrong.'

'So have you broken up with him?'

'I left him on the edge of Boston common begging me not to leave.'

'I always knew you were a femme fatale.'

'That's not funny, Mike. It's over, I haven't seen him since that night.'

'So what's the deal, Jamie?'

'Why are you so cold, Mike?'

'Figure it out!'

'Look, I had to leave. I had to get out of Boston, OK. I went there trying to relive some fantasy that I belonged there and that my life would somehow come full circle, back to where I had left it after college.'

'Fate then.'

'I told you I don't believe in that.'

'Me neither,' he said abruptly. 'What about your job?'

'I quit three days after. Mike, do you realise that when he put that ring on my finger I could have had everything, that's what he promised me. What girl in her right mind would turn that down?'

'Your track record isn't good, is it Jamie, and I know first hand.'

'That's not fair! We both had things to deal with.'

'But you didn't call, not even to tell me it was over.'

'I know, I feel bad about that, I'm sorry…'

'Well I guess it doesn't matter now.'

'Why?'

'Come on, Jamie, look at the situation. Things didn't work out with Malcolm and next thing you know you're here knocking at my door.'

'It's not like that.'

'It's going to take a lot more than that to convince me.'

'It's you Mike. You're to blame. I knew that from the minute I boarded that plane to Boston. But I guess I had to prove it to myself.'

Mike remained silent.

'Your turn,' she said.

'What do you want me say? You didn't call. I had no way of tracing you. I'd assumed you'd started a new life in Boston, so I moved on, or at least I tried to! You're too much of a risk.'

'Don't say that.'

'You have to leave, Jamie.'

'Are you telling me it's over?'

'It hasn't even started, besides if you stay here your life will be in danger.'

Jamie looked at Mike with disdain.

'Is that really the best you can do?' she asked angrily. 'Do you think you can ditch me by doing your FBI thing on me?'

'Someone's trying to eliminate me as a result of this case I'm dealing with. It's not safe. You have to go.'

'Let me in, Mike, will you. It was just the same in Ashbury Falls, wasn't it? You never let me in.'

'You're not listening! Someone tried to kill me the other night. It was a set-up, it's only a matter of time.'

'No, you can't do this to me! I want in, please Mike!'

'You got in before, remember? And it nearly got *you* killed.

I can't risk that again. Go home.'

'I shouldn't have come here, I knew it.'

'This is not a good time, Jamie.'

'What's going on with you, Mike?'

'Things are just very irregular at the moment.'

'Are you doing drugs?'

'I'm on medication by order of my superiors. I'm going through what they call psychological profiling.'

'What does that mean?'

'They think I'm unbalanced. Maybe they're right. I'm having nightmares about Ashbury Falls; Frogmen injecting me with serum like I'm one of the subjects of the Ascension Project or something. Then there's the stone thrower.'

'Mike, what are you talking about?'

'You wouldn't understand. Listen, you have to go!'

'OK, I'll check into a motel!'

'That might be best, but leave Washington before you do.'

She got up to leave.

'Sit down Jamie. Let's finish dinner first - you went to a lot of trouble.'

Jamie returned from the spare room with her jacket on and her case in hand.

'Well, it's been interesting, Mike,' she said with a faint hint of sarcasm.

'I'll call you when this mess is sorted out. If you're heading back to Ashbury Falls make sure Stella gives you my messages *this time,* will you.'

'What's the point? This was all a big mistake. I can see that now. Goodbye Mike.'

She opened the front door and walked out into the night. From the doorway he could hear the sound of Jamie's boots slowly dissipate as she descended to the parking lot below. Daylight was fading and as he leant on the doorpost he could just see her get into her car from the balcony. She looked up at him for a second and then drove off. He needed some air. The balcony ran the perimeter of his apartment block and he decided to walk around the front where he could overlook the street and watch the cars drive past, their lights on like beetles in the dark. The sky was a mixture of gold and deep blue and the streetlights on the side roads in front of him looked like candles amongst the trees presenting his eyes with a strangely picturesque vision of suburban Virginia. Then blackness – the lights went out around him and in his head. He collapsed and hit the floor without any warning.

There was no longer the sound of cars or any noise from the street, just an eerie silence and the sound of one of his neighbours shuffling along the balcony towards him. He looked up from the floor and felt a trickle of blood across his eyes. His forehead was cut – he must have collided with the balustrade during his fall. The sky had darkened in an instant.

'Good evening, Michael,' said one of his neighbours, staggering with a scantily dressed woman in his arms. She was nearly as drunk as he was. 'Don't mind us, we're hitting the sack, aren't we baby?'

She giggled incoherently and then started to slobber over him, misjudging the position of his mouth in a vain attempt to kiss him.

'Woe! It looks like you've been hitting the bottle too!' he said as Mike reached out his hand, hoping he would help him to his feet. 'Hey, get that cut seen to! Got to go!'

As the door opened and the two of them fell into the apartment, Mike turned his wrist slowly and was just able to make out the position of the hands of his watch. It was 02:40. He must have been lying there for several hours.

14

Half way through what had become a boring and tiresome movie, Celina McCallen switched off her VCR. The plot of the B-rate movie she was now returning to its case had featured a young renegade on the run from the law, travelling across the state of Louisiana with his less than co-operative girlfriend, pulling off heist after heist until being cornered in a shack with little ammunition left to stage a prolonged resistance to their pursuers. It had been leant to her by a friend some six months ago but she had never got around to watching it. Her friend had not pestered her for its return and tonight she had realised why.

She had become almost a prisoner in her own home with around-the-clock surveillance by detectives from the Washington police department. When she was given a reprieve to leave the premises she was under constant escort. The trips would be short, for necessities only. She had heard nothing regarding Gouldman's whereabouts since receiving the ransom note she had given to Lawrence Henderson, and she had become increasingly uneasy after seeing the report on NBC earlier that day regarding the FBI's failed attempt to retrieve him.

Her world was collapsing around her. Everything had been on an upward curve until the day she had seen Gouldman's draft speech that called on every decent politician in America to help alleviate the burden to society from those who could no longer contribute to it; a Logan's run of the 1990s.

They had been lovers for the past three months; whether it was physical attraction or the thought of being with a man with powerful connections, she was not certain. Either way, the night that she had slept with Detective Slater had not caused her to forget the way she now viewed her abducted boss nor made her feel any the more confident regarding her career prospects. As she re-read the pages of the speech in her mind she asked herself the question: could she really love a man like that? It couldn't be true, not Robert, there must have been some mistake. But it had been there in black and white and she hadn't been meant to see it.

The streets had become quiet since the night shift detective had taken over, and as he sat in the surveillance vehicle that was parked just across the street from Celina's house he was reading a newspaper, taking little notice of a dark coloured '77 Mustang as it drove slowly past him, taking a right at the next set of lights. He was reading an article that was full of speculation regarding Gouldman's whereabouts and was accusing the extremists in the growing anti-euthanasia league of touching the very eyeball of the US government in abducting a senator of Gouldman's standing. As each paragraph he read saw the debate heating up he was not enticed to get involved. He didn't much care what happened. Leave it to the politicians, he thought. As he flicked through he became more concerned with an article regarding a shooting near Capitol Hill in which one of his colleagues had been injured. He knew the officer in question and started to read through it in earnest, slowly becoming oblivious to the street outside. When he finally came to the end of the article he put the paper down on the passenger seat and laid back in his own. He hated surveillance duties; most of the time nothing ever happened and tonight seemed to be no different.

All that could be heard was the distant drone of traffic from the freeway as he looked up at the starry night sky. His neck started to ache and so he looked around briefly to flex the muscles and opened the window to get some air. From out of the calm of the night came what was at first an indistinguishable sound in the distance. Slowly, it transformed into the sound of footsteps on the sidewalk. As each second passed they were getting closer. He looked in his rear view mirror to see who was approaching. From out of the dark came a man dressed in a suit. He started to cross the road and when he reached the car he stopped by the door and caught his attention.

'What can I do for you?' he asked.

'I'm lost,' replied the man. 'I need to get to Lynch Street. Can you direct me? I know it's around here someplace.'

'Lynch?' replied the detective as he reached over to the passenger side of the vehicle. 'I'll just check the map – I've got one in the glove box, wait a second.'

'Sorry, no time,' replied the man, pulling a gun and silencer from his jacket. One easy shot and Celina McCallen's protector was sprawled lifeless across the automatic gear change of his car with his arms dangling to the floor.

Celina wandered into her bedroom with a vodka in her hand as her body tingled with excitement. She opened her wardrobe, took out a black cocktail dress and laid it on the bed. Her decision to sneak out of the house somehow and cut through her neighbour's yard to get to Auburn street made her feel like a grounded teenager escaping from her room ready to fall into the arms of the boy she was secretly dating. There was a call box some 200 yards from the end of the street and she could call a cab from there to take her downtown to a bar where she knew she would find some suitable male company. She put on the dress and found a pair of patent stilettos in her shoe rack.

She touched up her makeup and then returned to the wardrobe to get a jacket.

Her excitement turned cold when she heard a noise from the front of the house. Someone had entered the front door. Startled, she walked cautiously over to the bedroom door.

'Hello?'

With no reply forthcoming, she crept to the edge of the lounge.

'Hello, is that you, Detective?'

Peering into it she could see no one. She quickly went over to the front window and pulled the blinds apart. She could just see the surveillance car across the street but couldn't see clearly if anyone was inside. She looked again, focusing as hard as she could. It appeared empty.

'Detective, is that you?' she called again.

She immediately turned around and paced over to the table where her telephone sat and grabbing it, she started to dial a hotline number that Lawrence Henderson had given her in the event of an emergency. Her hands shook as she dialled the number. It felt like an eternity as she waited for the dial tone to end and a voice to cut in at the other end. When Henderson finally answered she felt instant relief, albeit short lived.

'Mr Henderson, I think…'

The line went dead. Celina froze as she felt a hand grab her and press the receiver button. She looked around and standing there was a man she recognised dressed in a light grey suit.

'Hello again, Celina,' he said in a soft yet menacing voice.

It was John Markham. Paralysis spread through her body like a virus as she recalled the day he had turned up at the residency to see Gouldman.

'What do you want?' she asked in a fear-stricken tone as she backed herself against the wall, knocking the phone off the table.

Markham touched her face – Celina's eyes widened in terror as he smiled at her.

'You've let us down, Celina. We thought we could trust you.'

'But I did as they…'

Markham touched her lips with his index finger before she could finish.

'Please, I don't know anything, I swear!' she said in desperation.

'Such a pity. Were you the one listening at the door when I first arrived to see Gouldman, Celina?'

'No, I swear!'

Her heart was racing.

'Yes, you were there, Celina.'

She was unable to respond. She trembled as he gently caressed her face with the ends of his fingers.

'Such a pity,' he repeated. 'I think it's time you knew the truth about me,' he continued, and then started to pull some of the skin from his face.

Celina looked both repulsed and petrified as he removed his eyebrows and then a large handful of skin from his throat. As each piece of disguise was removed his face grew slowly younger. When he finally pulled away the wrinkles from his eyes she gasped in horror at the realisation of that which she had suspected all along, but had refused to believe. No longer was the evil face of John Markham staring at her. It was the face of a man she had been asked to put her trust in from the start, yet had never been comfortable in doing so.

'No!' she exclaimed, barely able to get the words out as she looked upon the face of Michael Fabien glaring back at her.

'I'm sorry it has to end this way, Celina,' he said as the calm expression on his face was replaced by a merciless stare.

Lieutenant Jeff Cairns sat in his cluttered office at the headquarters of the Washington police department looking over some files from a case that was causing him a major headache. At more than regular intervals now he was also checking his watch with unease. Something was clearly wrong, as the scheduled call in from the detective assigned to the surveillance of Celina McCallen's home was late. It was now overdue by 25 minutes and so he got up from his desk and called out to one of his sergeants to check it out. A couple of minutes later Paul Benedict entered Cairns' office.

'I can't get him on the radio, Lieutenant.'

'What's he doing?'

Before Benedict could respond the phone on Cairns' desk rang.

'About time,' said Benedict, looking at his boss.

Cairns picked up the phone and began to listen intently to the voice at the other end.

'No!' he said moments later and looked up at Benedict, his expression sullen. 'We have to go, now!'

By 00:30 Cairns and Benedict arrived outside Celina's house. They parked their car behind the surveillance vehicle but could see no one inside. Another police vehicle arrived moments later with two uniformed officers as Cairns got out of his car. He walked over to the vacant Ford and looked in through the open window.

'Benedict! Get over to the house, now!'

His colleague leapt out, rushed towards the house and signalled to the two uniformed officers to follow. He darted through the gates and upon reaching the door he banged hard on it. The other officers joined him and looked through the front window. The lights were on.

'Kick it in!' ordered Cairns as he approached in haste behind them.

By now the neighbours had started to peer through their windows and one or two had come to their front doors in their nightgowns.

As the door flung open Cairns led the men in and called out to Celina as he searched along the hallway.

'Check the lounge,' he ordered, before entering the bedroom. The wardrobe was open and clothes strewn across the bed.

'Lieutenant!' called one of the officers.

A few moments later Cairns raced into the lounge. There behind the sofa he found Benedict and the two officers standing over the corpse of Celina McCallen.

15

'Fabien, it's Carlyle. You need to call in. Henderson wants a meeting urgently.'

The voice message woke Mike suddenly. He had fallen asleep in the lounge and had been out for at least six hours. His hand shook as he pressed the replay button on the phone next to the sofa on which he was led. He listened again to the message and this time it registered. Sitting up, he ran his hand through his ruffled hair and then lay back on the sofa for a few moments considering his response. He felt the cut to his forehead and winced as his fingers pressed the tender bruised area just under his hairline. The blood had dried and had matted his hair. Slowly he got up and walked to the bathroom to take a shower. He had no intention of calling in – he had other plans.

The morning light dazzled Zachary as he opened the front door of his house. He was just able to make out the silhouetted figure of Mike as his eyes acclimatised to the rays that surrounded it.

'What time do you call this, Fabien?'

'Time is something I don't have. What did you come up with?'

'You'd better come in then.'

The house was as dark as it had been the previous day. All the blinds were drawn and only scattered beams of light filtered through into the darkened rooms. A person unacquainted with Zachary would not be blamed for thinking they had entered the lair of a psychopath. Disturbing memorabilia cascaded the walls on the way to the room at the back of the house from where this computer geek operated, including a poster of Bela Lugosi as the 1930s Dracula. Zachary had been sent down for two years for computer hacking in 1992. He had, however, become a reformed character in Fabien's mind since his parole if you discounted the occasional job he would do unofficially for some of his former clients in the security services.

'Do you always live in darkness, Zachary?' asked Fabien, looking around him, tying not to bump into anything.

'Come into the office. I've traced your friend.'

'Who is he?'

'This was a tricky one, Fabien, don't ask me to do anything like this again in a hurry.'

'I hope I don't have to.'

'It came from somewhere in up-state New York. I managed to trace it to the Catskill Mountains area. Then it got really tricky. But with a few calls I pinned it down to Tannersville, possibly northern outskirts, but I can't be certain. My guess is that if your friend only wants *you* to find him, he's hiding out there somewhere. Maybe a house in the woods that has a communications line with minimum bandwidth capability to send e-mail.'

'No address then?'

'If they were hiding out in a city or large town maybe I could trace a zip code area, but it's not so easy once they're out in the sticks. It's the best I can do.'

'Thanks.'

'You're welcome, here's your diskette.'

'Stay out of trouble, Zachary.'

'If I can be of service again…'

As Mike walked to his car his cell phone bleeped. The message read urgent – it was from Henderson. 'There have been developments. Call in immediately,' it said.

He made the call. An apprehensive Lawrence Henderson ordered Mike to meet him in conference room 11. He was to go straight there. Placing his phone on the seat besides him he drove off at speed and headed towards town.

As Fabien entered CR 11, Jackson and Henderson were sat at the end of a large table. Carlyle was to the side of them. On Fabien's side was a solitary chair. This was no meeting.

'Sit down, Fabien,' said Jackson.

The atmosphere was icy – he could sense that something was wrong but nothing could have prepared him for what was to follow. The three men sat waiting for Fabien to open the discussion but he had no intention of doing so. He would not succumb to those sorts of tactics; after all, he had used them many times in the past himself. They were clearly not there to discuss further developments. They stared at him as though he was an accused man. Carlyle was clearly party to whatever his two superiors were withholding from him.

'Do you have any more leads on the Gouldman case?' asked Jackson eventually.

'No sir, I do not.'

'Mr Henderson informs me that you were attacked the other night by a John Markham, this John Markham.'

Jackson slid a file to Fabien, the one he had given Henderson previously.

'He's been stalking me for some time. I also think he's our only link to Gouldman.'

'The man doesn't exist,' said Henderson.

'But we have a file on him. I've seen him,' said Fabien defiantly yet with a touch of nervousness in his voice.

'No we don't,' replied Jackson. 'The file that Agent Kirby found for you isn't authentic.'

'Kirby?'

'Yes, your helping hand. I know she's been off doing little fliers for you but don't worry, I'll deal with her later.'

'Leave Kirby to me,' said Henderson.

'Whatever,' replied Jackson.

'Look, the guy broke into my apartment and drugged me,' added Fabien.

'Your blood test says otherwise – there was no drug,' said Henderson.

'What?'

'Perhaps this is all just a reflection of your current state of mind,' added Jackson. 'The results of your neurological examination reveal some disturbing facts.'

'I don't understand.'

'You've been having blackouts,' said Henderson.

'I don't know what you're talking about,' he replied, lying.

'Carlyle told us about the elevator incident in New York,' said Jackson.

'Celina McCallen is dead,' said Henderson. 'She called me last night moments before she was murdered. Where were you between 22.00 and 01.00 last night?'

'I was at home. Why are you asking me that?'

'Someone that fits your description was seen in the vicinity of her home last night.'

'That's crazy!'

'What do you make of this, Fabien?' asked Jackson, sliding another file to him.

'What is it?'

'Evidence of your involvement with the anti-euthanasia league.'

Fabien opened it to find several pages of text and a number of black and white photographs clearly showing him at rallies of the league along with contact with its leaders. He looked down at the photographs in shock and dismay.

'Where did you get these?'

'It doesn't matter.'

'Like hell it doesn't. What's going on here?'

'You tell me, Fabien,' said Jackson coldly.

'So I've done some poking around into the organisation, out of interest mainly, but I've never met these people, I wasn't there.'

'You're a sympathiser of the cause, aren't you Fabien?'

'If I am that's my business. Who are you to accuse me of...?'

'That's enough, Fabien!' said Henderson sternly.

'The papers say it's them. Did they enlist some help, Fabien?' asked Jackson.

'I'm not going to continue with this, you are out of your minds, all of you.'

'Go home, Fabien, you're off the case,' ordered Jackson.

'He can't do this, sir,' said Fabien, turning to Henderson.

'I'm afraid he can,' replied Henderson, perturbed by the inconceivable facts before him.

When Mike returned home he quickly threw some essentials into a shoulder bag in preparation for the now needed trip to up-state New York, and checked for any messages on his voicemail. Something was very wrong about the whole Gouldman case and he knew that he had to get out of town and fast. Tannersville would have to be his sanctuary until he had traced the source of the e-mail that Zachary had analysed and he could only hope that 'Spiral Architect' held the key to the reasons behind the bizarre events that were unfolding. He checked quickly to make certain he had included everything and picked his car keys up from off the coffee table. Luckily he had filled up with gas on his way to see Henderson and

Jackson. Time was of the essence and one last glance around the apartment was enough to tell him he was ready to leave.

The sudden knock at the door made him quite literally jump. At first he decided not to answer but when the second more pronounced knock sounded, he picked up his gun and stood by the wall adjacent to the door. With the third knock came the cry of 'Mike' from a female voice. With that he cautiously peered through the spy hole and could see that it was Jamie.

'You pick your moments, Jamie!' he said in an undertone.

'Mike, open the door please!' she called again.

Against his better judgment he gave in to her pleading. When the door opened Jamie stood looking hopelessly lost and vulnerable. Flashbacks to Ashbury Falls filled his mind's eye. Her expression was familiar, her thoughts no doubt also, but now was not the time for a repeat performance of his final encounter with her the previous fall.

'Your timing couldn't be any worse!' he said in greeting her.

'Mike, I have to talk to you.'

'Not now, I have to leave.'

She placed her hands in the pockets of her faded blue jeans that clung tightly to her hips and legs, and looked at him coyly.

'Mike, I'm sorry for what I said last night. I want to give this another chance.'

'Jamie!' he said grabbing her arms.

'Please Mike…'

'Shush!!' he said putting his index finger to her lips. He could hear the sound of cars arriving in the parking lot below.

He grabbed his bag and put it over his shoulder.

'Mike, the gun what…?'

'You're my hostage!'

'What do you mean?' asked Jamie as she looked over her shoulder and saw two police vehicles and a blue Ford Taurus pull up.

Before she had time to prepare herself, he grabbed her and pulled her towards him. Rotating her swiftly, he held her tightly around the chest and dragged her out to the balcony with his gun to her neck.

'Do exactly as I say!' he shouted.

The men below aimed their guns.

'Give me safe passage to the car or she's a dead woman,' called Fabien as the two of them began their descent of the stairs.

'You're finished, Fabien,' called Henderson.

'I'm serious!' Mike replied.

'Do as he says! He's crazy!' cried Jamie.

'No more dramatics!' whispered Mike to her as they reached the foot of the stairs.

He stood there for a few seconds assessing the situation. Four armed police officers accompanied Henderson, Carlyle and Agent Willis, another unwelcome face, and all of them a trigger pull away from blasting him to oblivion. Carlyle's penetrating glare projected a smugness that indicated an almost gleeful contempt for Fabien's disposition and Willis, who had tracked him down to Ashbury Falls during the Ascension case, was probably having similar thoughts. The maverick Fabien had crossed the line big time and they were there to see him go down.

'Let me through!' shouted Fabien, looking crazed and ready to do anything.

'Do as he says,' ordered Henderson. The men backed off one by one.

Fabien walked briskly to the car, forcing the gun deeper into Jamie's neck. He had warned her to leave the previous night. She wished she had been discerning and read the situation but now it was too late; she had ignored the obvious – he must have known this was going to happen.

When they reached the car, Fabien opened the driver's door and threw her inside before climbing in next to her. As her pleading scream penetrated the still air around them, the four officers moved towards Fabien's car.

He fired a shot that hit the windscreen of one of the cars and shattered it in one corner.

'Back!' he shouted, and they retreated.

Willis, who had been watching Jamie from the moment they had headed for the car, recognised her.

'It's a scam! The girl – she was with him in Ashbury Falls, stop him!'

Upon hearing those fateful words, Fabien fired up the engine, engaged drive and pulled away at speed. Bullets shattered the rear passenger door window as Fabien sped off towards the road. Jamie lay helpless in the passenger seat, crouched to avoid being hit, her dreams in tatters.

'Get after him,' ordered Henderson. 'Follow him and report your positions. I'll make sure he's intercepted. I want him and the girl alive. Aim your shots at the wheels.'

The three of them got into the Ford Taurus and followed the patrol vehicles.

As they sped out onto the main road, the officers could see Fabien's car ahead of them in the distance and began to close in on it, but as the lights ahead turned red the officers were astounded as Fabien drove straight through the narrowest of gaps between two approaching cars on opposite sides of the road that were crossing the junction before them. The sound of horns bellowed out as the respective drivers pulled abruptly to a halt and sat there in shock, blocking the needed access to the junction for the two patrol cars.

Meanwhile, Fabien's car skidded around at 90 degrees and just made the turn, correcting itself as it headed away from the junction whilst the patrol officers had to brake to avoid hitting the stationary vehicles. One of them shouted 'Move!'

at the top of his voice and within about ten seconds the junction was clear. As the police turned left to follow Fabien, they noticed him taking a right in the far distance and radioed for assistance in pursuit. When they reached the turning, the tyres of their vehicle screeched loudly as they drove at speed into the quiet neighbourhood road down which he had tried to evade them. There at the end was Fabien's car with the driver's door open. As the police pulled up behind it, they exited their vehicle and grabbed their guns from their holsters. One approached the car cautiously as the other scanned the surrounding vicinity to provide cover. As the first officer reached the open door and pointed his gun into the car, he discovered as expected that the car was empty.

16

The car in which Mike and Jamie were travelling was fast approaching Newark, New Jersey on the '95 freeway en route to Tannersville, New York. Soon Mike would have to navigate his way through the busiest maze of road network on the eastern coast to head onto the road to Albany, the place he had spent his college days before graduating to the FBI. The route would take him up the Hudson Valley past Kingston and then off the freeway into the Catskills where he would then have to find his way to Tannersville.

Jamie sat silently looking out of the window to her right and watching the New Jersey skyline flash past her. She peered at Mike through her hair in the hope that he would be watching the road instead of her, and that eye contact would be avoided. She was puzzled at his seemingly calm demeanour but then remembered that he was probably trained to act this way, which made her fear him all the more.

She had turned up at his apartment hoping that they could go out for the day and talk things over. She had almost rehearsed the things she would say to try to persuade him to give the relationship another chance and to find out what was going on inside his troubled mind. Now she was on a freeway in New Jersey, having no idea where she was being taken and why, fearing that the man she loved had joined the flip side and wondering what he might be capable of doing in his present state of mind. She was frightened, alone and wondering how her life had reached this point and if she was as messed up as he was. As the veil of love-blind stupidity began to wither away she realised just how much she did not know about him and that she might have to pay dearly for the way she had misjudged everything. What could he have possibly done, she thought, to bring his colleagues and the police armed to his apartment to arrest him, and for him to take her as hostage at gunpoint?

They had not spoken since transferring vehicles back in Washington. Jamie had been hysterical whilst the police had pursued them for the first mile or so before Mike had abandoned the car. She had shouted out to all and sundry to help her and had continually asked him where he was taking her, as if she thought he would really tell her. It was only when he had had to warn her very sternly to shut up by pointing his gun at her that she had realised that silence would be the best policy.

Jamie was forced out of the car, pulled across the road and into a wooded area behind the house to escape the police. She struggled to free herself, but Mike's grip proved too tight for her and his loaded gun was doing all the talking. When they reached the far side of the trees they walked out onto the edge of a main road and promptly crossed it to enter into the adjoining neighbourhood. As they began to walk calmly along a quiet tree-lined road leading to a shopping mall complex, Mike put his arm around her and forced his hand and gun under her jacket above her waist and told her to act normally and stop shaking. When they reached the edge of the mall's parking lot Mike found a wall to sit on, and with his arm still around her he contacted Zachary on his cell phone.

The couple sat for over 40 minutes trying to look normal as shoppers walked past at intervals, paying little attention to them as Jamie silently pleaded to them to help her. About ten minutes before Zachary arrived, a police vehicle drove through the parking lot close to where they were sat and Mike's only option was to force Jamie over the wall and onto the grass to avoid being seen. It was unclear to him whether other vehicles in the vicinity were looking for him or whether this was a routine patrol. When Zachary finally arrived in his car Mike forced Jamie into the passenger seat and thanked Zachary for his much-valued assistance in helping to apprehend one of three suspects involved in a recent heist.

It was Mike who finally broke the ice as he turned off the New Jersey freeway network onto the road that led to Albany.

'I'm being set up.'

She did not reply.

'I'm sorry that you've been caught up in all this but I warned you to leave, didn't I?'

She turned and looked at him with contempt.

'You could have locked me in the bathroom or something!' she replied.

'I had no choice; actually you're my saving grace,' he added.

'You're sick!' she replied.

'I guess that makes two of us then. You shouldn't have come to Falls Church.'

'You sad...'

'Just calm down will you!' said Mike, interrupting.

'Where are you taking me? Can't you at least have the decency to tell me that?'

'I'm not taking you anywhere.'

'What do you mean?'

'I was about to leave to find someone whom I hope will help me out of this mess. Then you and my very loyal boss and his entourage turned up. You're along for the ride now – it may get dangerous, so shut up and just do as I say and then maybe when this is all over, and if we get out of this alive we'll see where the road takes us, OK?'

'I don't believe this!'

'Believe it, lady! Welcome to the world of Michael Fabien, defender of noble causes.'

'I need a cigarette,' she said, reaching for her bag.

The conversation temporarily came to a stop to Mike's relief. Hopefully she would calm down and he could reason with her from then on.

'You didn't answer my question,' said Jamie, flaring up again. 'Doesn't the hostage have the right to know where she's going?'

'You're not my hostage; at least you won't be when I know that I can trust you.'

'Trust!'

'What's your problem, Jamie?'

'Are you trying to tell me that all the time you had that gun aimed at me it was a scam? I came to you to tell you that I wanted us to be together and I get a gun to my head! I get dragged into a car with a guy who's lost it big time, and he tells me he's being set up! I don't know what kind of a fool you think I am! There is no lead is there, Mike? You've crossed the line somehow and now you're on the run.'

'It's not like that.'

'Are you going to kill me if I call out or try to escape?'

Mike ignored the question.

'Are you?' she cried loudly.

Mike slowed the car down, pulled over to the hard shoulder of the freeway and cut the engine.

'What are you doing?' she asked, her voice trembling.

'You're free to go.'

'What?'

'You're free to go, Jamie. You're not my hostage.'

'What, here?'

'Yes. There's a service area a few miles ahead. You could probably walk it in, say, an hour. That would give me enough time to be far away from here by the time you call the cops.

Of course you might get a ride from a friendly driver, and then I would be taking a risk, wouldn't I?'

'But…'

'All I wanted was for you to call me from Boston, Jamie. You didn't. I got over it. A second chance? Maybe. Trust Jamie, that's what it's all about.'

'You are really letting me go?'

'Yes. I trust you, Jamie.'

She sat in her seat staring out of the window, a tear in her eye with a lost expression on her face.

'Well?' said Mike.

'I…'

'Look, no gun Jamie.'

As she turned to him he could see that she had no idea what to do, but a glimmer of trust was all he wanted.

'Start the car,' she replied.

'This is your chance to walk away, Jamie, take it.'

She paused before speaking again.

'Just start the car, Mike.'

It was early evening by the time Mike turned off the freeway at the Catskill junction and headed towards Cairo, a small town in the mountains on the way to Tannersville. Jamie had rested for most of that leg of the journey and neither of them felt like conversing as the day wore on. The drive to Cairo seemed endless but eventually Mike spotted a small motel as they reached the edge of town and so he turned into the parking lot and drove the car around the side of the building. Jamie stirred as the tyres of the car negotiated the uneven ground that surrounded the motel and she awoke as Mike parked the car. Her mouth was parched from the sleep.

'Got anything to drink?' she asked.

Mike handed her a bottle of water.

'Are we here?' she asked, after taking a long gulp.

'Not quite, but I'm tired and I don't want to go any further today.'

As they got out of the car, Mike released the trunk and then pulled out the bag he had packed for the trip.

'This place will have to do for tonight.'

The motel was old and looked a little run down, but it was better than sleeping in the car in Mike's opinion. All Jamie wanted was to lie down. Mike opened the door that led to reception and was greeted by an elderly woman behind the desk. Mike asked for a twin room for one night. The woman was baffled and asked Mike if that was really what they wanted. When he replied she told him that there were two singles available if they wanted to take a look. Mike told the woman that Jamie was his sister, Grace, and that they were travelling home to see their parents in Lake George. The woman, still unsure of Mike's request, was about to quiz him further when he smiled at her and took her hand.

'My sister has a medical condition and she needs constant monitoring, particularly when she's asleep. If she were to wake up in the middle of the night finding it hard to breathe and I wasn't there to give her the medication, well, my father would never forgive me. You understand, don't you?'

'Why yes, of course. I have just the one twin room left. Please come with me.'

'Thank you,' said Mike, cringing.

'No bags my dear?'

'Not today,' Jamie replied nervously. She wasn't used to scams.

They were led to a room at the back of the motel. When the owner opened the door they could see just how basic it was. The beds stood on a bare wooden floor divided by a small set of drawers with a dated bedside lamp on top. The windows were open but the large fir trees that were only a few yards from the room blocked out most of the light.

'That will be $50 cash,' said the owner.

Mike handed over the money and she nodded to him with a smile as she closed the door. Extortionate, he thought as Jamie surveyed the room, slowly pacing around it looking unimpressed.

'I hope you'll be comfortable,' said Mike clumsily.

'I'll be OK,' Jamie replied.

Mike threw his bag on his bed and then headed to the doorway that led to the bathroom, placing his gun on a nearby chair. The bathroom was basic too and in need of a good clean. It didn't matter; he needed a shower.

'This may not be the sort of accommodation you're used to, Jamie,' he said, coming back into the bedroom, 'but....' He stopped in his tracks.

'I see,' he said, drawing a breath as Jamie stood between the two beds pointing his gun at him.

'Just sit down on that chair over there and don't move,' she ordered.

'OK,' he said, doing as he was asked.

'I'm calling the police and you're going to sit there until they arrive,' she said as she sat down on the bed and reached for the telephone.

'I'm disappointed, Jamie. I let my guard down.'

'Likewise,' she replied, calmly and coldly.

'If you hand me over to the police, what then?'

'I don't know, but I'll be out of here I guess.'

'Back to Ashbury Falls, and what then?'

She didn't answer.

'I'm being set up for the murder of a senator's aid. I know who did it but I can't prove it yet. You have no idea what's been going on before you arrived. Someone in high places wants me out of the picture. I'm lucky even to be sitting here talking to you.'

Jamie pressed '9' for an outside line and in doing so Mike realised that she wasn't bluffing.

'This may be my only chance to find out what's going on, Jamie. Turn me in and I'm finished. We're finished. You'll go back to Ashbury Falls and will still be searching for what you want after you let it slip through your fingers like sand.'

Jamie's fingers moved slowly back onto the dial pad of the telephone. Mike became increasingly nervous and stood up without thinking.

'Don't move Mike or I'll fire.'

'Have you ever used one of those before?' he asked. Jamie suddenly looked uncomfortable. 'I thought not. You really do need to hold it firmly when you squeeze the trigger, else you could make an awful mess.'

Jamie's hand began to shake.

'You have to trust me, Jamie,' he said as he slowly approached her.

Jamie looked down at the gun and then back at Mike. She was out of her depth.

'Give me the gun, Jamie,' he said softly as he reached the edge of the bed. 'Come on, Jamie, give it to me.'

With that her grip loosened and the gun slipped from her hand and into Mike's outstretched palm.

'Good. Now put the phone down.'

She complied and then reached for her bag, pulling her cigarettes out. She lit one as quickly as she could then put her feet up on the bed and crossed them as she exhaled.

'You should have got out of the car when you had the chance.'

Jamie refused to be drawn by Mike's comments and continued smoking her cigarette.

'Please don't pull another stunt like that, it makes me nervous,' he added. 'I'll take that shower then.'

When Mike returned Jamie was asleep. He walked over to her bed and looked at her. She was peaceful enough, considering what he had put her through. He sat down on the edge of the bed, his hair still damp and his body wrapped in the towel that had been graciously provided, and watched her sleeping, still fully dressed in her jeans, cowboy boots and her denim jacket. He touched her face for a few moments and then quickly withdrew his hand as her cheek twitched slightly. Her presence would complicate things, but there was nothing he could do about the situation now. Had she got out of the car on the freeway she would remember him only as a renegade FBI agent on the run. Now at least he might be able to vindicate himself in her eyes as well as his superiors'. Tomorrow they would drive to Tannersville and start the quest for the source of the e-mail that might offer him a thread of a lifeline out of the waters of treachery that were slowly drowning him.

When Mike had finally dried he got up from the bed and went back into the bathroom to clean his teeth, avoiding eye contact with the mirror. They were not his favourite objects at present. As he scrubbed his teeth heavily and almost bruised his gum his mind became focused on John Markham, the ghost figure he had to find. Maybe his friend in Tannersville could help. As he climbed into bed and switched off the lights he suddenly became all too aware of the near silence and darkness that surrounded him. Even though Jamie was on the next bed, he felt an intense feeling of isolation overcome him, as though he had become detached from normality and for the first time in his life he felt almost completely alone.

17

Jamie awoke to the sight of patterned brown wallpaper that had been hung eons ago on the walls that surrounded her and remembered in an instant that she was in a run-down motel somewhere in the Catskill Mountains in up-state New York. Her back felt stiff and her skin tacky as she realised that she had slept all night in her clothes. Rolling her legs over the edge of the bed she decided to get up and go to the bathroom.

'You've got to be kidding!' she mumbled quietly to herself when she saw the state of the room before her. How Mike had dared take a shower in that was beyond her.

Mike was still asleep. It looked as though he had been wrestling someone or something in the night by the state of the bedclothes that were haphazardly wrapped around him. She had no clothes to change into neither did she have any makeup, toiletries or even a toothbrush. Mike's bag was on the chair in the corner and so she opened it and quietly rummaged through it to see if there was anything she could use. To her surprise there was a spare toothbrush, new, still in its cellophane packaging.

When she had freshened up she finished what was left of a bottle of water that Mike had left on top of the drawers and decided to make some coffee for them both.

As the quiet whining sound of the kettle boiling became louder Mike began to stir. His eyes did not open at first; just a groaning came from his mouth as his head moved slightly over the pillow. Jamie did not attempt to disturb him. She went to the window by her bed and looked out. The sun was shining through the fir trees and the morning looked inviting. The rotting wooden window proved difficult to open at first but with a push it budged enough for her to get some fresh air into the room and for her to poke her head outside and breathe in the pine-scented air. She leaned on the window ledge for a minute or two, waking herself up until the kettle clicked, signalling that it had boiled.

'I'll get the coffee,' said Mike as he got up from his bed, his hair ruffled, wearing a pair of boxers and a long grey T-shirt.

'Good morning,' she said, in a more congenial tone as Mike made two mugs of coffee.

'It's powdered,' he told her, referring to the milk.

'No worries,' she replied as she walked over to the bed.

'I suggest that we drink up and get out of here,' said Mike.

'You sure know how to show a girl a good time! I'll choose the next stay, OK?'

Mike nodded.

'In case you hadn't noticed, I have no toiletries or change of clothes.'

'Don't worry. We'll get breakfast on the way and hopefully there'll be a store where we can get you fixed up.'

Mike and Jamie finally arrived in Tannersville and parked the car on the main street running through town. There was a diner across the street and so they walked over to it and went in. They were directed to a table by the window overlooking the street, and shortly after the waitress brought them some coffee and two menus.

'I'm hungry so this is going to cost you,' she informed him.

'Be my guest. Are you OK now?'

'I can live with this for a while,' she replied from behind the menu.

'Were you really going to call the cops?' he asked Jamie quietly.

'Maybe,' she replied, her face still hidden from view.

'Why didn't you?'

Jamie kept silent and continued browsing the menu. He gazed out of the window watching the people of Tannersville go about their everyday business and wondering how wide he would need to search until he would find 'Spiral Architect'.

When the waitress returned Jamie ordered the works. Mike opted for bran cereal and brown toast.

'There's a clothes store across the street,' said Mike. 'And I guess there must be a drugstore somewhere around here.'

'Why are you being set up?' she asked him. The question caught him off guard.

'I'll tell you when we've booked in, not here; it's too public.'

'How long will we be here?'

'I'm staying until I've found the person who sent the e-mail. You can leave anytime.'

'We're in the middle of nowhere, Mike, that's going to be a little difficult!'

'We'll check in first but then I go to work. You'll have to entertain yourself.'

'I knew I needed a vacation but I didn't really have this place in mind.'

'You could be back in Boston,' he concluded.

When breakfast finally arrived, Jamie attacked it as though she hadn't eaten in days.

The clothes store was in need of modernisation and had a fairly basic range of garments to offer. This came as no surprise to Jamie when she considered where they were, but she had no choice. She managed to pick up some fresh underwear and three new shirts, the type that country girls would wear, but they would see her through for the moment. The storekeeper was a plain-looking woman, probably in her late 30s and Jamie felt that her eyes had followed her all around the store. Mike was checking out the body warmers as Jamie approached the cash desk.

'Allow me,' said Mike.

'No, it's OK; luckily I put my purse in my jacket before I called at your apartment.'

'I insist.'

Before Jamie could continue the discussion Mike handed his credit card over to the storekeeper.

'It's OK Mike, really.'

'Let him pay, honey,' said the woman as she swiped the card. 'You're lucky; my husband's got an old rusty key that keeps his wallet locked!'

When the transaction had gone through she put the clothes and the receipt in a bag and handed them to Jamie.

'Why did you do that?' asked Jamie as they left the store.

'Do what?'

'Look, thanks for breakfast but I can pay for my own clothes.'

'You were going to use your credit card.'

'So?'

'If the FBI knows you're with me they'll put a trace on any credit card transactions.'

'But you used *your* credit card.'

Mike pulled a silver-coloured MasterCard out of his wallet and showed it to her. As she glanced down she noticed the name on the card wasn't his.

'Where did you get that?'

'I use it for emergencies. It comes in very handy, particularly in situations such as this. I think that's a drug store along the end of the street.'

As Jamie was escorted into one of the rooms at the Hartdagen hotel just out of Tannersville centre, she smiled in relief. This time the accommodation was more conducive with her needs than the one in Cairo.

'Yes, we'll take them,' she told the hotel owner. 'I'll just tell my colleague,' she added, and then descended the stairs to reception where Mike was reading a newspaper.

'This will be fine,' she told him and so he allowed the receptionist to take a swipe of his alias credit card which was under the name of Kelvin M Toussaint. The 'M' was a safeguard to ensure that nobody would question him if he were ever addressed as 'Mike' when handing over the card for payment. The guy in the drugstore where Jamie stocked up on essentials had recommended the hotel to them. When the receptionist handed them a key each for first floor rooms 15 and 16, Mike followed Jamie back up the stairs and along the corridor to where the adjacent suites were located. Jamie was the first to insert her key.

'Shall we have dinner later?' asked Mike as she entered her room.

'Call for me at seven o'clock.'

Mike knocked on Jamie's door at 19.00 prompt. He didn't want to risk upsetting her in any way; she had been through enough already. She took a few moments to answer and then invited him in.

'Shall we get going?' he asked.

'I'm not hungry, the breakfast was enough.'

'OK, so shall I....'

'We need to talk,' she said, interrupting.

Jamie climbed onto the bed and sat cross-legged at one end and signalled for Mike to do likewise. He approached the bed cautiously.

'Come on Mike, sit down.'

Mike rested his back against the headrest and put his hands on his knees. He let Jamie open the conversation.

'Tell me what's going on, Mike. I want to know everything.'

'Are you sure about that?'

'Yes.'

'OK,' he said and then paused to collect his thoughts. 'Has there ever been a day in your life that's been indelibly marked in your memory?'

'Well, let me see... probably the day my mother and father sat me down at the age of 13 and told me after all those years that I had a twin who died at birth. Is there one in yours?'

Mike was taken aback and sat up. 'Why didn't you tell me?' he asked. Clearly she had not shared everything with him in Ashbury Falls.

'Maybe some things are better left alone. I learnt that three years later when I brought up the subject again. They wouldn't discuss it and told me never to ask about it again. I thought about it for a long time afterwards and then realised how distressing it must have been for them, so the subject was never mentioned again. Anyway I want to hear *your* story. Tell me about the day in *your* life, Mike – what happened?'

Mike looked suddenly perturbed. Jamie could see by his expression that he had probably never told anyone what he was about to tell her now. 'Tell me, Mike,' she said softly, 'tell me what happened to you.'

Mike paused for a moment and then looked up at her.

'The date was June 10th 1973 – that was the day that I came home from school with jubilation written all over my face. Against all odds we'd made second place in the Chicago junior's baseball league by winning that last crucial game. It was all down to me. Points were level; I had to make the home run. Their pitcher was something else – a new kid. We'd never played against him before. What should have been a walk in the park was in danger of slipping from us. As the ball sped towards me I just took a swing and prayed to God. I hit that ball so hard I could feel the vibrations ripple through my bones. "Go for it, Fabien!" I heard the coach yell and off I ran. I ran so fast, like I was chasing the wind. They were screaming, but when I reached second base I tripped and fell. I looked up and could see their outfielder about to pick up the ball. I jumped to my feet and just ran. What would get to home base first, the ball or me? "You can make it!" cried the coach. As I passed it the guy caught the ball. There must have been a second or so in it. We'd won! The coach grabbed hold of me and then my team mates surrounded us. I only wished my father had been there to see it, but he had something pressing to see to – something he couldn't tell me about. He had asked me to make him proud. I promised I would and I did. For that hour after the game I was floating on air; I was a hero. All sorts of people; teachers, parents you name them; they just came up and patted me on the shoulder. It was my first major achievement. I've still got the shield.'

Jamie smiled, her face now relaxed and wanting to hear more.

'I couldn't wait to get home. I had the shield in my hand already to show my mom and dad. It was a hot day and I was still in my baseball kit. We lived on the southern city limit; in fact our house was about half a mile outside. I went back there a few years ago and saw the house – it was a great neighbourhood. The driveway was sheltered by a huge sycamore; it's still there you know. I ran up it towards the house and then when I got there I shouted out to them to come and see the shield. My father's car was on the drive but there was no sign of them at first. The house seemed empty.

'Were your parents French?' asked Jamie.

'No but my father's parents were. They fled to America from a small town outside of Bordeaux before the war. They got out just before the Nazis invaded. My father was named Patrice after his father.'

'And your mother?'

'Chicago born and bred. Marion Elizabeth Wade, later Fabien.'

'Where were your parents when you got home from the game?'

'My father was upstairs attending to my mother. He came down the stairs and asked me about the game. I showed him the shield and told him about the home run. He told me he was proud of me and hugged me tightly like he'd never done before. When I looked at his face I could see that he was holding back tears. I asked him where my mother was and if I could show her the shield, but he told me that she was resting and I should leave her for the moment. I went into the lounge and turned on the TV. 'Champion the Wonder Horse' was on – boy, I loved that show. I sat there for a while but then I remember going into the kitchen to get some soda or something. It was then that I saw my father standing at the sink looking out the window and sobbing. I stood there for a while just listening to the tears, but then he must have sensed I was there because he turned around. I asked him if he was OK and he told me yes. "Son, I need to talk to you," he said and led me back into the lounge. He told me to sit down. "Got to be brave, son, we both have," he said, or words to that effect. I asked him what was wrong. It was then that he told me that my mother was sick. I knew that she had been tired and not as active as usual for several months up to that time, but I knew then that something was wrong, very wrong.'

'What happened?' asked Jamie.

'I asked him what was wrong with her and with tears in his eyes he told me that she was dying of cancer. I'll never forget those words and the way that my feelings of jubilation turned sour in a single moment. I ran upstairs and burst into her bedroom but when I got to the bed she was sleeping. I stood there wondering what to do, wondering if my father had got it wrong. He came into the room and put his arm around me and told me that I could see her in the morning. I left the shield on her bedside table for her to see when she woke up.'

'That must have been devastating for you,' said Jamie.

'I don't think that was the devastating part. For the next four months I watched her deteriorate very quickly. She was such a beautiful woman who loved life. I loved my father but I loved her more. She was my inspiration. I remember one particular day when the doctors visited her. My father led them upstairs and then turned and asked me to play in the garden for a while. I watched them all disappear onto the landing and then waited for them to go into my mother's room before creeping up the stairs. Slowly I tiptoed over to the wall by the door to the bedroom and led against it to listen to their conversation. I remember my father asking them if there was anything they could do to put her out of the pain and let her die with dignity. They told him that they couldn't and it was then that I heard my father raise his voice. He told them how wrong it was to let someone die a slow painful death and that God would want her to leave us and find peace. Again they sympathised with him, but told him that they couldn't do it. I remember him asking them to help him, he would pay them and nobody needed to know. "It wouldn't be right, Mr Fabien," they told him, and that the law would not permit it. I remember his reply to them. He told them that someday every citizen of the United States would have the right to end their own lives. Tears were rolling down my cheeks and I couldn't contain myself any longer. I burst in and ran over to my father and began to hit him with both arms as hard as I could and cried out, "No! She's not going to die, I'll never let you do it, never, never!" With that the doctors pulled me away and tried to calm me down as my father stared at me in shock. As every day passed I had to confront at a very early age the reality of death and how it comes at its own calling. I would talk to her every day and she would tell me to dry the tears. Despite all the pain and the suffering, she clung on to life with every last ounce of will left in her. She battled with death and refused to go on its terms, she fought to prolong her life as long as she could. Even the doctors were amazed that she held on for so long. One of the last things she said to me was that whatever I wanted to do with my life, I should seize the moment and follow my heart.'

'Mike, I'm so sorry,' said Jamie, taking his hand.

'On December 14th 1973 the fight was over and she passed away peacefully. That was the day that my world collapsed around me.

The following spring, we moved to Ashbury Falls when my father took a job in Manchester, New Hampshire. I had just turned 14 when we arrived. It took me a long time to settle in. I missed her so much, so did my father, but as time went on he changed. He provided for me as any good father would but he found it hard to care for my emotional needs. We slowly drifted apart and when I went to college in Albany he returned to Chicago when he got a job back with his old company. We kept in touch by letter and every so often I would call him. He came to my graduation and he embraced me, just like the day I returned home with the baseball shield. He told me he was proud of me. He asked me what I was going to do and when I told him I had been accepted by the FBI I could sense that it was not what he really wanted for me.'

'Do you still keep in touch?'

'Occasionally, but I must admit I've let things slips for a while. I guess it's my turn to call but things have been crazy over the last year.'

'What do you mean?'

'I came through the disciplinary hearing with my career in the FBI hanging by a thread. I was grounded, to put it in simple terms. During the period of the hearing I was suspended and spent my time digging deeper into the hidden secrets of the Ascension project. I kept a secret copy of the files on a CD. If anyone had found out I'd be frying burgers for McDonalds now. I'd only touched the surface during my investigation. What I found out afterwards… The scope of the project reached further than even some of my superiors are aware. I wonder how many of them knew about the victims of phase I – what they went through and how they ended up. When my suspension period ended I couldn't think straight, I couldn't sleep. Even when I did, the nightmares…'

'You don't have to continue with this,' said Jamie sympathetically.

'They put me on medication, but it doesn't stop me visualising in my mind's eye what must have happened to them. It's like an after-image in my mind that won't fade away. Weird things have been happening to me since then, things I can't explain. Have you ever heard of Senator Robert Gouldman?'

'The senator who's been kidnapped?'

'That's the guy. Who do you think they assigned to find him?'

'It's you, isn't it.'

'Give the girl an A-plus. The guy is evil – I've been following his activities for some time now. He's a pro-euthanasia supporter. If he and other like-minded individuals get their way, can you imagine how many people will start to play God, just like my father wanted to when my mother was dying? They think I was behind it. They think I'm involved with the anti-euthanasia league and they want me out of the picture.'

'Mike, what have you done?' asked Jamie.

'You think it's true then?'

'I hope not, Mike, but I want the truth.'

'They have already tried to eliminate me. They can't prove anything because it's not true, so they had Gouldman's PA murdered and set me up for it. It's the truth, Jamie.'

'OK.'

'Sometimes I wish it had been me who had abducted Gouldman. My colleague John Carlyle asked me when we started the investigation whether Gouldman had a point. What do you think, Jamie?'

She paused for a moment, feeling uneasy about answering a question on such an emotive subject.

'Well, to be honest I haven't given the subject much thought. But I can understand where you're coming from.'

'I hope they never find him, Jamie, believe me.'

'You've never forgiven him, have you?'

'I don't think forgiveness applies in Gouldman's case.'

'I'm not talking about Gouldman, Mike.'

'It's no good...' he replied sombrely.

'Let it go, Mike, holding onto the pain won't bring her back. It's not a perfect world and you can't change it because of your father.'

He pondered over her words and then looked at her for a while. For the first time since she had walked back into his life he sensed her empathy towards him, her expression seemed to convey a desire to find out who he really was. He also noticed something else that was different about her. Since her return she had covered her arms but tonight she wore only a T-shirt vest, and something was missing from her upper left arm.

'So you got rid of the tattoo then,' he said to her, returning eye contact.

'I couldn't carry it around with me forever, could I Mike?'

'Was it painful?'

'Yes, like a lot of things we do.'

She edged forward on the bed towards him, still maintaining eye contact and then began to prostrate herself over his body. Before he could respond she started to kiss him, tenderly at first and then passionately.

18

Mike and Jamie had driven about a mile from the centre of Tannersville and parked the car at the side of the road in front of the entrance to a house situated 100 yards from the gate.

'Let's see who's in,' he said to her as they simultaneously closed the doors of the car.

Darkness was beginning to fall and there was probably another hour of daylight left before the Catskill Mountains would be shrouded in darkness.

The house was small, well kept, and as they approached the porch they could see that the front door was heavily netted, almost completely obscuring the inside from view. Mike rang the doorbell and waited for a few moments until he realised that nobody was going to answer.

'Let's take a look around the back,' he said; Jamie followed him around the perimeter of the house to the rear entrance as he led the way. The door was locked.

'It has to be this one, I'm sure of it,' he muttered.

'I wonder what's through that opening at the top of the lawn?' asked Jamie, curiosity having got the better of her.

'Go and take a look; I'll be there in a moment.'

Jamie began the short walk to the opening as Mike went around to the front of the house again. He looked up at the telegraph wires that were connected to the edge of the roof and remembered Zachary's comments regarding the communications connectivity. There was a window at the side

ALUMNI

of the house and so he peered through it again to see if there was any movement inside.

'Hello!' he called, tapping on it.

Again there was no reply and so he headed up the lawn until he reached the opening that Jamie had gone to investigate.

'I think we'd better try again in the morning,' he called out. There was no reply. 'Jamie! We'd better head off now.'

He called to her again as he walked through the opening into a dense wooded area at the rear of the house, calling her name continuously. As he walked into the silent trees the only sound he could hear was the crackling of the occasional twig as it snapped under his feet. The darkness became more pronounced as the trees shielded what daylight remained in the skies above him and so he began to jog further into the trees, calling out to her periodically, but still receiving no reply. Eventually he came to a clearing and saw a figure in the distance standing by the edge of a lake.

'There you are!' he called, but as he got closer he could see that it wasn't Jamie. The figure stood there casting stones into the lake, disturbing the still waters with little pools of turbulence.

'I've been waiting for you.' said the robed figure – it was a female's voice.

'Where's Jamie?'

'Jamie?' replied the figure.

'The girl who was with me.'

'What girl? There's no one here, only us.'

'Who are you?'

'Have you forgotten me already, Michael?'

Mike began to withdraw from the edge of the lake, looking over his shoulder at the trees behind him to find the direction of a clear exit.

'It's no use going back,' said the figure as she continued to cast stones into the lake.

'Why?' asked Mike.

'Because you'll have to face up to it all sooner or later.'

'Face up to it?' replied Mike.

At that moment the sound of a motor dinghy could be heard in the distance.

'On time as always,' said the figure as the dinghy and its crew came slowly into view. 'There's nothing to fear, Michael. Remember, seize the moment, that's what I always told you, didn't I?'

The frogmen stood in the dinghy, motionless as if awaiting instructions from their mistress.

'Step into the boat, Michael, there's no need to be afraid; Mom won't force you to come this time.'

Mike felt his stomach implode as the figure lowered her hood.

'Come to me, Michael, come to your Mom, everything's going to be alright...'

Mike yelled out a deafening cry that woke Jamie, making her sit up in bed promptly. She groped for the bedside light, eventually found the switch and turned it on to see Mike sat up staring at the entrance door to the bathroom, his complexion having turned a ghostly white and his heart pounding like a drum at a parade.

'It's OK; I'm here.'

'Mom!' said Mike, shaking.

'Mike, it's Jamie, it's OK,' she said, holding him. His breathing was fast and heavy. 'You were dreaming. Come on, lie down; I'm here.'

'Water! I need some water,' he said, still looking traumatised.

'I'll get some.'

When Jamie returned from the bathroom she handed him a

glass and he drank it quickly. She got back into bed and told him to lie down.

'Are you OK now?'

'It was her,' said Mike.

'Who?'

'My mother – she's the stone thrower!'

'Whoever it was, they've gone now,' said Jamie, trying to reassure him.

'No, it was her,' he muttered, his lips quivering as his forehead perspired.

'Mike, it's OK, come on, lie down.'

As he lay back on his pillow, a tear rolled from the corner of his eye and he continued to shake, as though he was still in transcendence from the subconscious world to reality.

When morning arrived Jamie was first to surface. Mike's eyes were still closed and she didn't want to disturb him. She quickly got out of bed and took a shower. About 20 minutes later she returned and boiled the kettle to make some coffee. As she drew the curtains the light from outside caused Mike to stir.

'What time is it?' he asked, sprightly. He had been awake for about five minutes.

'About 10.15,' she replied.

'I guess we've missed breakfast.'

'Are you OK now?' she asked, still concerned.

'What happened last night?' he asked.

'No complications, hey?' replied Jamie, considering her words carefully.

'Guess not. So you'll help me find this guy then?'

'What guy?'

'The e-mail.'

'Of course, where do we look?'

'Towards the edge of town – we need to get a map first.'

'How will we know where to call?'

'We ask.'

'Won't people get suspicious?'

'Not if we pose as journalists from National Geographic.'

They finally found a map in an old shoe repair store. The owner, a tall thin man in his early 60s, gave them one that he had out the back in his storeroom. Mike asked him about the layout of the town and where the isolated houses could be found. The man commented on how the area had been featured in the magazine some 15 years previous and how he looked forward to reading Mike's article. The search would cover around a two-mile stretch to the north, but they would have to be selective. Anything that looked like a regular residence would be best omitted. Mike was looking for potential hideouts, places that were not so up together.

'Where do we start?' asked Jamie.

'Zachary said to try the northern outskirts.'

'Who's Zachary?'

'Just a guy who owed me favours.'

They got into the car and headed out of town. As they drove into the sticks the houses became fewer until all they could see was trees. Going a short distance, Mike noticed a place to his left and pulled in.

'Got to start somewhere,' he said as he cut the engine.

As they got out, Mike noticed there were no telephone lines running to the house and so he told Jamie to get back in the car. A mile up the road they saw a mailbox and again pulled over. This time they were led up a long pathway to a grey house with many ornate features that had obviously been carefully crafted by those who had built it some 60 years previous. The paintwork was wearing badly and the house looked like it had been neglected somewhat.

'What do you think?' asked Jamie.

'Possible.'

Mike knocked on the door. They only had to wait about 30 seconds before a man in his 40s came to the door. This was not the house. Mike apologised for the disturbance and asked for directions to Albany – the best cover story he could come up with. The man told him to head back into town and then follow the signs for Cairo; something Mike already knew.

At the next stop they found no door at the front and so they had to go around the back to find the occupant. An elderly woman with long grey hair tied behind her in a ponytail, wearing a distorted face and sporting a large double-barrelled shotgun greeted them.

'Don't get strangers round here, you can't be too careful,' she said as she finally lowered the gun to the ground after Mike had persuaded her that all they wanted was directions. She wasn't forthcoming. Jamie was unnerved by the gun; she had seen too many already.

'Occupational hazard,' Mike told her as they closed the gate behind them.

The last house on the road going north was derelict and so they had to turn the car around and head back into town.

'There's a turning off here, perhaps we should try it,' suggested Jamie, pointing to the map.

'Not far enough out,' replied Mike.

'Maybe there are turn offs not detailed on the map; no harm in trying.'

The homes along this road faced an area of woodland and were fairly close to each other, hardly the place for hiding out. Jamie noticed a dirt track at the end of the road and so they followed it up until they reached what looked like a small chicken farm.

'This isn't it,' said Mike.

A few moments later, there was a tap on the window.

'After chickens?'

'No, sorry, just took a wrong turn.'

'OK,' said the man. 'If you're ever in Barbara's Restaurant in town, try the chicken. It's fresh from here.'

'Maybe we'll do that, thanks.' replied Mike, and then he turned the car around.

'Shall we get something to eat?' he asked Jamie.

An hour later, Mike and Jamie walked out of Barbara's Restaurant and got back into the car.

'We should try this road here, to the west,' said Jamie.

As they reached near to the top of the road they could see the last few houses in the distance on the hill before them. 'No good?' she asked, knowing what the answer would be.

'We'll make a few calls and see if there's anywhere else around here.'

At the last but one house a redheaded woman came to the door with her two children. The girl must have been nine, the boy about six.

'I'm Agent Fabien, FBI. Nothing to worry about, ma'am, I just need some information.'

Jamie smiled at the daughter. She was like a young version of her mother, her hair an identical colour.

'Hi,' said the little girl quietly to Jamie.

'Are there any more homes around this area?' asked Mike.

'This is the end of the road as you can see. Not that pretty is it?'

Mike looked across the street and then back at the woman. 'It's home,' he replied.

'Why don't you come in, would you like some iced tea?'

'OK thanks.'

'Have you lived here long?' asked Mike as they sat at the kitchen table.

'Three years; Welfare moved us here after my husband died.'

'I'm sorry,' said Jamie.

'Accident at work. We didn't get much from the company but we get by. We're the same as the other families around here. I don't like it much, but that's the way it is.'

'What's your name?' Jamie asked the daughter.

'Martha.'

'I'm Jamie.'

Martha smiled.

'My name's Paula Sherwood, and my son here is Billy. What can I do to help?'

'You said there are no other homes around here.'

'Well there is one, a short drive up the hill behind the last house. It's more of a dirt track.'

'Can you tell me about it?'

'I've seen it once. Billy went exploring up there with one of the other kids in the neighbourhood. It's a creepy looking place. I don't care too much for the colour either.'

'There's a man up there in a wheelchair,' said Billy.

'Shouldn't be trespassing in places you don't belong,' said Martha to her brother.

'What did he look like?' asked Mike.

'We saw him working on his computer through the window and so we went in. When he heard us he came out to chase us away. His face was all burnt up on one side. He looked like the Gate Keeper from Doom II!'

'Are you looking for this guy?' asked Paula.

'I am now. Thanks for the iced tea.'

'You're welcome.'

'Take it easy, Billy,' said Mike as they left.

Martha waved to Jamie when she got to the end of the path.

By the time they reached the top of the dirt track, which must have been a good half a mile, Mike wondered whether his car still had a suspension left and Jamie was rubbing the side of her neck from the jolting. In the distance, through the trees, they could see the house. It was dark red, almost crimson in colour. Jamie followed Mike as he paced up the broken driveway towards the front door. As they arrived they saw an old Chrysler parked outside. Mike looked up at the roof and noticed that the telegraph wires were intact, hoping that they provided the correct bandwidth. It was when he saw an old brass sign on the lintel to the left of the front door that he knew this was the house.

'Well done, Billy,' he said quietly as he saw the name on the tarnished sign: 'Spiral Architectures Inc'.

'I'll take a look around the back,' said Jamie as she started to walk away.

'No! Stay with me – this is the house.'

Mike tried to open the door. It was locked. He reached into his jacket pocket and pulled out a small, wired implement. Jamie looked on as she saw Mike put it into the door lock and wriggle it around several times. A few moments later she heard the lock click and the door open slightly.

'You're not serious are you?' she asked him.

'Let's go.'

Mike cautiously entered the hallway with Jamie following close behind. There was very little in the way of objects or décor inside. The kitchen door was open enough for Mike to see that it was basically equipped, and when he peered inside he couldn't see much more than a large wooden table in the middle. There was a saucepan of stew on the cooker and so he quickly went over and felt the side. It was warm. He pulled out his gun and returned to the hall where Jamie was waiting.

Along the passageway were a number of doors, one of which was open. As they approached they could hear the sound of classical music playing quietly in the background.

'Sounds like Prokovief,' said Jamie.

'I wouldn't know,' replied Mike.

As they inched towards the door, Mike could see a figure sat in a wheelchair looking out of the window. He moved slowly into the doorway and then into the room, holding his gun out.

'What took you so long?' said the distorted voice from the wheelchair.

'Who are you?' asked Mike as Jamie moved closer.

'I think you know.'

'Are you a friend in need?' he asked.

'I would say that applied more to you, what do you think, Fabien?'

'That's what I'm here to find out.'

'Then let me cease this impoliteness.'

With that the wheelchair slowly rotated towards Mike and Jamie. As the charred remains of the occupant's face came into view, Jamie covered her mouth in horror at what she beheld. Only the left side of his face bore any resemblance to normal human skin tissue and what was left of his hair on the right side was matted and fused into the red crumpled skin on the side of his head. Both his hands were also badly burnt and disfigured.

'And you must be Jamie Farrington.'

'Yes.'

'Todman gave me the lowdown after the Ascension incident, or should I say *investigation*.'

'Who are you?' Mike asked again.

'You need information on the Haedenberg Foundation, don't you.'

'Yes, the corporate rescuers of the terminally ill.'

'Hardly. Just a façade for an organisation that is pumping millions into the campaign to make euthanasia legal in every state in our fair country.'

'Bad as that is, why the façade?' asked Mike.

'To keep the FBI away from finding out where the money comes from. We're talking drug trafficking, illegal arms sales to the middle-east, I could go on…'

'I guess you're going to tell me who manages the funds, aren't you?'

'I don't think I need to, do I?' replied the man. With each breath he winced in pain and held the side of his stomach. 'The accident has left me in much pain. Pass me those pills on the table, Jamie.'

When Jamie handed him the bottle he quickly swallowed a small number straight from it.

'Mason-Wainwright was in on this?'

'Were? Still are, Fabien. I also found out during my investigation that there is more than just a business link between them. William Calvert and Milton Porter belonged to the same college fraternity in Princeton. Guess who else belonged to it?'

'Who?'

'A prominent senator.'

'Gouldman?'

'And someone else close to your heart, Fabien.'

'What do you mean?'

The man began to laugh.

'The accident has left me in this,' he replied, pointing to the wheels of his chair. 'You could say that I am half the man I used to be!'

His laughter demented, Jamie could only look on in shock as the charred figure's body shook in the wheelchair and then suddenly bent over in pain and started gasping for air. It was when he grabbed Mike by the hand that Mike felt the rough, mangled skin and the gravity of what had happened to his colleague. The man looked up at him, breathless and pitiful.

'Calvert was on his way to meet me with his lawyer the night the plane was sabotaged. I already knew about the connection between Mason-Wainwright and Haedenberg, so it was something else he wanted to spill.'

'Riley?'

'Be careful, Fabien!'

'What was it?'

'I don't know. He never got there, did he, and even if he had he would have missed me anyway. I was killed in the line of duty. That's what they told you, didn't they? What a coincidental sequence of events. Nail them, Fabien, nail them all!'

Before Mike could respond, a large bottle exploded on the floor besides them. He pulled Jamie to the ground with him and then dragged her away from the large pool of lighted gasoline that was spreading out rapidly towards them. When they got to the wall they looked back to see a screaming Dan Riley enveloped in flames, and as they struggled to stand up the wall behind them caught fire. The flames rose quickly and almost immediately spread out over the ceiling as they ran to the door. Suddenly they heard Dan Riley cry out to them.

'Three-twenty-nine!' he screamed.

Mike watched in horror as Riley's skin began to melt before his eyes.

Without warning a second bottle landed on the floor in front of them and their exit became blocked by another instant inferno. By now the room was engulfed in flames and smoke.

'The window!' cried Mike as Jamie coughed violently.

He led her quickly through the flames and kicked a table over by the window that was blocking their escape. He quickly picked up the chair that was underneath it and smashed it against the window. The impact made only a single neat crack on the pane of glass that was the only obstacle between them and survival. Jamie coughed again as the flames were about to touch the back of her jacket. He quickly pushed her into the corner, out of the way of the approaching heat, but she slumped to the floor. Again he hit the window with the chair and a few more cracks appeared. It was only when he hit it a third time that the window shattered.

'Come on!' he shouted to her, and pulled her up.

With the legs of the chair he cleared the sharp glass that protruded from the frame, which had by now started to burn, and climbed out of the window, pulling Jamie through with him. She staggered and coughed before falling down on the grass before them and so he quickly put his hands under her armpits and pulled her a safe distance from the blazing house. He settled her on the ground and she sat up momentarily.

'Are you OK?' he asked her.

'I'll be fine,' she replied, disoriented and coughing violently again.

'Can you get up?'

'No, I'm too dizzy.'

'Just wait here and get your breath back. I'll get the car.'

She saw Mike disappear around the edge of the house and then felt a sense of nausea overcome her. She coughed several times again before her breathing normalised, but each breath became a struggle. She did not have the strength to get to her feet and felt terrifyingly exposed as she watched the flames bellowing from the house behind her.

Mike sprinted towards the front entrance to the house. He scanned the surroundings expecting to see another vehicle – the one belonging to Dan Riley's assailant. Only his own could be seen. Coughing, he approached his car and started to feel for his keys. The painful blow to his head that followed was both sudden and traumatic. In the two seconds that lapsed before his world turned black he was unable to see the face of his attacker. As he coiled to the ground the figure of John Carlyle stood over him. As he pushed Mike over onto his back with his foot he rotated the gun in his hand so as to take hold of the handle, the part he had used to inflict the almost lethal blow, and pointed the barrel at the temple of his unconscious colleague.

19

As the light began to penetrate his eyelids, Mike's head started to throb. He opened his eyes to see the shadowy forms before him take shape. He could not move; he was sat upright and realised that he had been restrained. As his vision became clear he looked down and saw that his arms and legs had been crudely tied to an old wooden chair. Standing before him was his colleague, John Carlyle.

'Found you at last,' said Carlyle.

Mike scanned the room trying to figure out where he was. It appeared that he was in some kind of wooden shack with a stove, a fireplace and a few chairs, nothing more. He was sat facing a solitary window and there was no sign of Jamie.

'Where's Henderson?' he asked, expecting him to appear at any moment.

'Who knows?' replied Carlyle.

'You're taking me in then?' he asked, still coming to terms with his situation.

'I don't think so,' replied Carlyle. 'There's someone I'd like you to meet.'

He could hear footsteps from behind him – someone had been standing in the far corner out of view. When the figure emerged and faced him he was looking at his double – the facial features were practically identical.

'This is John Markham,' said Carlyle.

'We've met,' said Markham, 'remember?'

Mike froze as he recalled the incident in his apartment – the incident that no one believed.

'Don't be shocked. It's amazing what we can do these days, isn't it? We can turn convicted murderers into FBI agents on demand,' added Carlyle. 'They get a second chance as it were, to prove they can be useful to society after all.'

'So that's why Celina thought she recognised me,' said Mike.

'Not exactly – I looked much older when I first met her, but when I killed her she died thinking I was you,' said Markham grinning.

'How much did Gouldman pay you?' asked Mike.

'Nothing,' replied another voice from behind.

Mike turned his head as best he could and caught a glimpse of another man moving towards him. As his face came into the light he recognised the voice also. Robert Gouldman had joined them – the third party in a panel of conspirators.

'So he did it for the sheer pleasure of it?' asked Mike indignantly.

'Ask him,' replied Gouldman.

Markham grinned, saying nothing.

'Why Celina? Was it just to set me up?' asked Mike.

'She was untrustworthy,' replied Gouldman. 'It was regrettable but necessary. She was given strict instructions to involve only you. Talking to Henderson was a big mistake. When she told him that she suspected your involvement I realised she would be a liability.'

'You had her bugged?'

'I gave her a very expensive emerald broach on the day of my abduction. I'm glad she was wearing it the night we contacted her. Pity for her though.'

'How did you find me?' asked Mike.

'Zachary,' replied Carlyle. 'I followed you during your little visits. When you took off in a hurry I paid him a visit; he told me everything.'

'Was he in on this too?'

'You have no confidence in your allies, Fabien. Of course not – he was just unfortunate to have been involved, like Celina. After I had extracted the information from him, he was no longer of any use.'

'So this was all a scam to get Mark Bradovich out of jail and into Gouldman's hands, wasn't it?' said Mike. 'I should have seen it.'

'But you didn't. I don't expect the medication helped the situation did it?'

'Can we bring this to a conclusion now, Agent Carlyle?' asked Gouldman. 'It's time you delivered me safely back to Washington.'

'Yes of course.'

'I'll wait in the car. Finish up here, will you,' he added and left promptly.

'You knew Riley had survived, didn't you?' said Mike.

'Two birds with one stone – it must be my lucky day. Now it's time to finish the job. Agent Michael Fabien – killed in the line of duty whilst apprehending Gouldman's captors. I'll return to DC with Gouldman and take all the glory. He's all yours,' said Carlyle, glancing at Markham. 'You know where the money is and make sure that you lose yourself. Oh, and don't forget to get a new face.'

As Mike heard the door close, Markham picked up his gun from the window ledge. He rubbed his fingers along the barrel for a while, tormenting his victim, allowing him to savour his final moments. The sound of Carlyle's vehicle skidding away down the leafy track outside would be his penultimate memory.

'It's nothing personal,' said Markham. 'Now it's time to put you out of your misery.'

Markham lifted the gun and pointed it at Mike. As he stared at the nozzle of the silencer that had prematurely ended the life of Celina McCallen days before, he thought of his mother.

'Cast your last stone,' he said quietly, and closed his eyes.

The door burst open. Before Markham could react, Jamie lunged forward and struck him at full force in the head with a large wooden gatepost. As he fell to the floor, she struck him with a second blow and he became sprawled over the wooden boards. She quickly went outside and picked up a small hand axe that she had left by the door. Re-entering the shack, she started to jab at the rope that was binding Mike to the chair.

'Be careful!' he said loudly.

Soon the rope flayed and he managed to free his left foot. She quickly did the same on the right side and soon his legs were free.

'Couldn't you find a knife!' he exclaimed, looking very worried as she did the same near to his hands. 'How did you find me?'

'You left the keys in the car, stupid!'

Markham began to stir, groaning and holding his head.

'Quickly!' said Mike.

Jamie hurriedly attacked the rope that was tightly wound around his wrist. It was proving difficult this time and so Mike got up, hurried to the door with the chair still attached to his arms.

'Can you lift that stone?' he asked as they made it out into the fresh air.

'I'll try,' she replied.

'Put it in front of the door. It will hold it for a while.'

Jamie lifted the stone that was located about two metres from the door and dropped it at the edge, just enough to prevent the door from opening.

'Good, now let's get this chair off me!'

She began to jab at the rope again and then managed to free Mike's left wrist. As she did so they heard a loud thumping from inside the shack and saw the door shake violently.

'That won't hold for long,' he said.

As Mike's other wrist became free, the door was kicked open, splitting in two from the corner where the stone had held it right to the top centre. When Markham emerged she looked at Mike in horror. She had failed to see his face at first as he had tumbled to the floor in the cabin, but seeing the evil twin just a few yards away nearly caused her knees to buckle. Mike grabbed her quickly.

There was no time to get to the car so they headed for the trees. Mike picked up the chair and hurled it with all his strength at Markham. It hit him directly in the face, stunning him and causing him to fall face down in the dirt. They sprinted away from their fallen pursuer and into the trees. Jamie was coughing again and Mike was becoming increasingly concerned about the amount of smoke she had inhaled from the fire. As they reached a good distance Markham got to his feet and began the chase. Mike pulled Jamie as hard as he could, nearly causing her to stumble as they disappeared into the dense woods with the sound of Markham close on their heels. As they ran towards a large pine they saw the trunk splinter from what must have been a gunshot. With that, Mike changed direction, pulling Jamie with him, but she was becoming breathless and was dragging him back. It was the smoke.

'Stay with me!' he called to her as she stumbled on a small log. Catching her before she fell, he lifted her and held her with his arm. Markham took another shot, this time only narrowly missing them both.

'Come on!' cried Mike as they sprinted off again.

Markham was gaining on them as they negotiated their way over a felled tree trunk that blocked their escape. On the other side was a shallow pool of dirty stagnant water and as their feet landed in it a third bullet hit the top of the trunk. A fraction higher it would have caught Mike's calf, ending the pursuit. As they splashed their way to the edge of the pool they could see an incline before them that was both long and slippery. They were now easy targets – a fourth shot would have certainly hit Mike had it not been for Markham tripping on a large stone in the pool through which he was following his prey. As he fell he dropped his gun in the water. This gave them a vital window of opportunity to clamber to the top of the incline; but the climb proved too exhausting for Jamie and before they reached the top she slipped and slid down a fair distance. Markham reached out to grab the heel of her boot as Mike started his descent. He was about to seize her when Mike kicked him, causing him to fall backwards. Jamie got to her feet but was instantly thrown down again by Markham as he quickly recovered and stood up. Ignoring her, he went for Mike. With Markham a whisker away from him he clambered up the slope again. When he reached the top he found himself trapped on the edge of a deep ravine. Moments later Markham arrived at the peak of the ridge and lunged forward to pin Mike to the ground. He ducked instinctively, causing Markham to somersault over him and land at the edge before plunging over. As he fell he caught hold of a branch jutting from the rock face a few feet from the top. Mike stood up, but before he could get his footing, the earth at the edge of the ridge upon which he was standing gave way. The cluster of mud, rock and roots disintegrated, showering Markham as he clung to the branch for his life. Mike grabbed at the large tuff of the remaining grass in front of him to pull himself up but suddenly felt Markham's hand grab his foot and pull him down. He cried out to Jamie as he likewise disappeared over the edge.

Mike slid down the branch that Markham was grasping and caught hold of it in time. His descent trapped Markham's hand under his foot and as he let go of the branch he grabbed hold of Mike's leg. Looking down he could see his assailant dangling in mid air with only Mike's foot now holding him from the sheer drop and the rocks below. Mike felt his whole body being stretched and jabs of pain striking him like needles in his joints and organs. Markham's grip slowly loosened, giving him one last opportunity to save himself. He stamped down firmly on Markham's hand and then his head. Finally Markham's grip failed and letting go, he plunged to the base of the ravine, eventually landing on a set of large jagged boulders.

When Jamie reached the top of the ridge there was no sign of either man. Fearing the worst she crawled to the edge and leant over. When she saw Mike holding onto the branch her heart stopped. She grabbed Mike's hand, allowing him to pull himself up, securing his foot on the branch as he did so. They rested for a few moments before getting to their feet. Mike peered over the ravine and stared down at Markham's lifeless body that lay far below.

'It's getting dark – we'd better go,' said Jamie, breathless as she clenched his hand. Mike remained still, his eyes fixed on Markham.

'He's gone, Mike, whoever he was,' she added, and led him away from the edge.

20

Rachel Kirby was working late, something that was now becoming the norm. She had been concentrating her efforts for the past few hours on trying to identify the central figure in the recent escalation in drug movement in and around the capital. The sudden influx had been brought to the FBI's attention by sources that had been trying for some time to infiltrate the cartels involved. Due to the insidious nature of the rise in narcotics usage, Henderson's team had been assigned to trace neither the source of supply nor the end dealers, but the middle man; the controller. With an estimated street value of some $20 million per shipment, someone else was muscling in on an already complex and highly successful network of what the FBI were now calling 'onshore suppliers'. Kirby's failure to crack the case had now brought about a premature end to the official investigation. Two days previous Henderson had been ordered to waste no further time or resources on the matter. Kirby had other ideas. For the first time in her career she was going against orders. Durrell had long gone home, giving her the opportunity she so keenly desired. Trustworthy as Durrell was in her opinion, she had no intention of revealing her exploits to him or anyone regarding this investigation that she was now secretly continuing. Sat at her computer with a breakthrough eluding her, her efforts were becoming both frustrated and tiresome.

She took off her glasses and rubbed her tired eyes before glancing at the clock. It was fast approaching 22.30 and she had lost all track of time. She shut her computer down and prepared to leave. An hour later she would be home but she had already made plans for an early start in the morning. As she got up to go the phone rang. She allowed it to continue to do so – the caller would have to leave a message. He did.

'Pick up the phone, Kirby; I know you're still there.'

She recognised the voice; it sounded nervous but without hesitation she left the receiver down. A few moments later it cut off, but only seconds passed until it rang again. She allowed her voicemail to cut in once more as she picked up her bag to leave. Glancing back at the phone she listened to the message. There was now urgency in the caller's voice, but she was no longer going to allow herself to get involved. She picked up the receiver after the caller had rang off and dialled her voicemail. When given the option to delete any messages she did so immediately. As she turned off her desk lamp her cell phone rang. This time she had no option than to take the call.

'Rachel Kirby,' she replied nonchalantly.

'You took your time.'

'There's nothing I can do for you, Fabien. Don't involve me in whatever mess you've got yourself into.'

'You're the only one I can trust right now.'

'I have to distance myself, Fabien. We've all heard what happened.'

'Whatever you've been told…'

'I can't help you, Fabien, goodbye.'

She hung up. Tempted as she was to switch it off she knew the consequences would be far worse if she was non-contactable.

She made her way promptly to the elevator that led to the parking lot. Her cell phone continued to ring without letup until she reached her car.

'OK!! Where are you?' she replied finally, raising her voice, hoping it wasn't her boss trying to get hold of her.

'You have to come to Tannersville, New York. It's out in the Catskills.'

'If anyone knew that I was even speaking to you…'

'Please, I need your help.'

'What are you doing up there?'

'I found Dan Riley.'

'But he's dead.'

'No, he never was, we were meant to believe that to throw us off the trail.'

'What trail?'

'Listen, I'm sorry, Kirby, but Riley is dead now, thanks to Carlyle.'

'Carlyle? What are you talking about?'

'He's on his way back to Washington with our missing senator; it was all a scam to get Bradovich and to eliminate me.'

'But why?'

'There could be any number of reasons; Bradovich is dead, Gouldman's about to resurface and Carlyle's a danger to us all. I didn't kill Celina McCallen and I can prove it, but I need you up here.'

'What do you want me to do?'

'I'll tell you when you arrive.'

'I don't know, Fabien, things have been happening back here. Henderson's shutting me out, he's reassigned us again and Jackson's acting strangely. I can't explain any of this.'

'Then take a rain check and get out of there.'

'Fabien, I'm up for review soon, I'm sorry…'

'Kirby, listen to me. Everything's wrong about this. I haven't pieced it all together yet but I'm getting close. We're all at risk; you, me, Durrell… They'll be no reviews, Rachel. Do this for all of us. Whatever happens nobody must know I'm alive, do you understand?'

'OK!' she cut in, again raising her voice. It's echo in the empty underground parking lot made her shudder. She looked around her, feeling suddenly vulnerable and wondering if she had been followed. Promptly, she got into her car and started the engine. 'How do I find you?' she asked.

21

Fabien's car was parked in a lay-by at the entrance to a narrow road that led into the woods where Markham had plunged into the ravine. It was a short walk from the end of the road according to an ordinance map that Jamie had borrowed from the man in the shoe repairers that morning.

It was mid-afternoon; the sky was overcast and the temperature cooler than usual. Kirby would arrive soon but as Mike randomly tapped his fingers on the steering wheel in anticipation of her arrival his thoughts were on his future. Even if he managed to clear his name regarding Celina's murder, what then? Gouldman would be after his blood and Carlyle was potentially a lethal instrument in his hands. All he had was evidence to prove his innocence and nothing else. Who would believe him regarding Gouldman anyway? He would be constantly looking over his shoulder for Carlyle once Gouldman realised that he was alive. And there was Jamie; she was involved now and the thought of disappearing with her crossed his mind for the first time. Suddenly that scenario seemed real.

As he looked down the lonely road that would eventually lead back to Tannersville he saw a car approaching in the distance. It wasn't Kirby; it was going too fast to stop and drove past him before disappearing around the bend in the road. He waited, checking his watch at close intervals and wondering whether Kirby would really come. A second car passed, going in the opposite direction, and before long there were no vehicles at all. The silence of the road intensified, so too did his doubts as to whether he could trust his colleague. He had worked with her for three years and seen her as a quietly ambitious girl who went by the book in everything. He had never seen her so unnerved and wondered if she would cave in, do the safe thing and hope it would bring her some sort of reward in the future.

Eventually a car approached and began to slow down, indicating that it was turning into the lay-by. There were two people inside, one of whom was Kirby; the other, too, was unmistakeable. He pulled his gun out of his jacket and got out, kicking the door closed as Kirby brought her vehicle to a controlled stop and cut the engine. The passenger door opened, Henderson got out and without hesitation Fabien pointed his gun at him.

'What are you playing at Kirby?' he yelled.

'It's OK Fabien, put the gun down,' she replied.

'You're in on this too, I should have known.'

'She's in on nothing, Fabien. Do as she says and put the gun down,' said Henderson calmly.

Fabien looked over their shoulders expecting police and back-up vehicles to arrive en masse at any moment, but none arrived.

'She's told me everything, Fabien. Now, where's the evidence.'

Fabien continued to point his gun at Henderson.

'Fabien, we're here to help!'

'It's true,' said Kirby.

'And why should I believe him?'

'Because I believe what you told Kirby is true. I've not been able to reconcile any of this from the start. Now show me the evidence.'

'Your weapons – throw them on the ground.'

'As you wish, Fabien.'

'Do you know something I don't?' asked Fabien as the two guns were thrown at his feet.

'I'm just trying to complete the puzzle too. I'm taking a big risk on this myself.'

'Get in the car, both of you in the front,' said Fabien as he picked up the guns with his left hand.

'I'd be more comfortable if you'd stop pointing that thing at us,' said Henderson.

'Until we reach the ravine,' replied Fabien.

'OK.'

Fabien walked to the rear door of Kirby's vehicle and then signalled for his colleagues to get in first. Keeping his eye fixed intensely on Henderson, he got in after them and then rested the nozzle of the gun on the side of the headrest and against the hair just below the bald patch at the back of his boss' head.

'Drive to the end of this road, it's a short walk from there.'

When the three arrived at the destination they could see a narrow pathway into a large wooded area ahead of them. Henderson looked along the track as he got out of the car and asked Fabien where it led.

'There's a ravine about a quarter of a mile along the track,' he replied, his gun still pointing at his boss.

'Lead the way,' said Henderson.

'No. Kirby will stay in front, you behind her. This can all become civilised again when we reach the body.'

'Very well... Kirby.'

The track eventually led them past a large pond covered in moss and leaves with a stream running into it. Fabien knew that the ravine was not far away.

'I camped in the Catskills once,' said Henderson. 'Did your father ever take you camping, Kirby?'

'No Sir,'

'That figures.'

'It's not far now,' said Fabien, his heart beating faster with every step that took them closer to the location.

Minutes later, they arrived at the top of the ravine on the opposite side to which he had almost met his death along with John Markham. To his relief their side of the ravine was not a sheer drop and they could get down the large incline with relative ease. Fabien lowered his weapon as he pointed to the base of the ravine.

'There's your evidence,' he said.

Henderson and Kirby looked down and saw the body of John Markham sprawled across a cluster of boulders, exactly where it had landed the day before. They carefully descended into the ravine and reached the bottom in about three minutes. Getting down was relatively easy; navigating their way across the boulders proved more difficult. When they arrived at the spot where Markham's body lay, Henderson approached the corpse to take a closer look.

'Markham, am I right?'

Fabien nodded and then looked away. Seeing his lifeless double right before his eyes was like seeing a precognitive vision; it could so easily have been him, he remembered.

'OK, you're off the hook, Fabien. I'm sorry I doubted you.'

'So this guy killed Celina McCallen,' said Kirby. 'Who put him up to it?'

'Gouldman,' replied Fabien.

'We'd better call the sheriff's office and get them to remove the body,' said Henderson.

'What did Riley tell you before he died?' asked Kirby.

'He found out about Haedenberg.'

'What did he uncover?' asked Henderson.

'It's a façade for an organisation that's supporting the pro-euthanasia movement. Mason-Wainwright is managing the funds and the revenue sources alone are enough to put them all away if we can prove their origin. He also told me that Calvert, Porter and Gouldman belonged to the same college fraternity in Princeton.'

'Interesting,' replied Henderson.

'Calvert was on his way to meet him the night the plane crashed, unaware that Riley was out of the picture. He told me that Calvert had intended to tell him something else but of course he never got to find out what.'

'How do we prove that Gouldman sabotaged the plane?' asked Henderson.

'Gouldman was blackmailing Calvert. I remember finding a deleted e-mail that Gouldman had sent to him when I was first checking things out with Celina.'

'Whatever he was using to blackmail him obviously didn't work,' commented Kirby.

'So his only option to stop Calvert spilling the dirt was to sabotage the plane,' added Henderson.

'We still need proof,' said Fabien.

'Then I think we'd better pay Milton Porter a visit in New York,' said Henderson. 'If we put enough pressure on him, perhaps he'll crack.'

'Gouldman and Carlyle think I'm dead,' said Fabien. 'I want it to stay that way.'

'I agree. I'll tell Jackson that you're missing. Lay low for now, meanwhile Kirby and I will go to New York.'

22

May 17th 1974

'And that, as you will see when you research this further over the coming week, will give you pointers as to why these factors cause the economic cycles we have been discussing. Do not view this as bedtime reading, ladies and gentlemen; this is research that you must ponder over, assimilate and most importantly be able to explain in your sleep. By the way a very interesting theory, Mr Porter, but I suggest you revisit your research and see if your views are really founded. Enough for today, you are dismissed.'

So ended another economics theory lecture from Professor James Stephen Eckhart, a man who had only two years previous gained his professorship at the age of 29, and, who also being an avid student of politics, had recently received a prestigious offer to lecture in the subject at Harvard in the coming academic year.

As his class of third year students filed out of the lecture theatre, Eckhart was packing his material into his worn brown briefcase before he noticed Milton Porter standing a short distance away.

'Can I help you, Mr Porter?'

'I believe my theories were right, Professor Eckhart.'

'Well we'll see, won't we?'

'Hey Milton, let's go!' called a voice from the top of the auditorium.

'You'd better run along now, Mr Porter, but a word of advice first. You have good potential, so listen to your friend Mr Calvert. He will go far, feed on his expertise. Graduation is only a year away and remember, this is Princeton.'

Dejected, Milton ascended the stairs to the back entrance.

'Come on,' said his friend as they left the theatre together. 'I think you brought out some interesting points in there,' he added and put his hand on Milton's shoulder.

'Interesting theses won't give me first-class honours,' replied Milton.

'Then spend more time in the library.'

'It's no use, William. Anyway I heard them snigger at me.'

'Some, yes, but others were listening, Milton. I'll help you.'

'Tonight?' asked Milton.

'Sorry, no can do, the inner circle is meeting tonight, I have to be there.'

At that moment Robert Gouldman arrived and patted Calvert on the shoulder.

'How are you doing, Will? Another totally boring economics lecture? Politics Will, that's the place to be; nothing's set in stone. Money is money; ideology is the opium of the gods. Come on, I'm meeting Louisa in the refectory. Janet Elmer will be there, you know?'

'Thanks, but I'll see you tonight at the fraternity house. I need to get to the library right now.'

'OK, your loss. Hey Milton; still wishing on a one?'

'I'll get there, Gouldman, you'll see.'

'Sure you will – with a little help from Daddy!'

Porter grew hot with rage. He hated those words and had still not forgiven William for telling Gouldman that his father had managed to get him into Princeton and into the Alpha Epsilon Theta fraternity on account that he had himself attended

ALUMNI

the university and had been a former fraternity president.

'I'll see you later,' said Gouldman to his friend quietly, 'and ditch that loser.'

'He's my friend,' replied Calvert emphatically.

'Who does that guy think he is?' said Milton, still angered as Gouldman turned and walked away.

'Don't concern yourself with him, Milton. Are you coming to the library?'

'No, I'm out of here.'

'I'll see you tomorrow then,' replied Calvert as the two of them parted company.

As the evening sky darkened above the Alpha Epsilon Theta fraternity house, a car pulled up into the driveway, taking the last available parking space behind a white open-top Mercedes. The driver got out, closed the door and looked up at the elegant yet enchanting house into which he was about to enter. It had served the fraternity for 13 years since the completion of its building back in 1961. It had replaced the original building after a fire had destroyed it two years prior. As he walked up to it and reached for his key he felt a slight uneasiness within himself and waited a moment before putting the key in the lock and turning it.

'Sorry I'm late,' said Calvert as he closed the entrance door.

'Late?' replied Gouldman, 'You're on the bell, Will, it's good to see you.'

Calvert hung up his jacket and then approached the others in the lounge area.

They were all finally assembled; the members of the Alpha Epsilon Theta fraternity inner circle; Calvert, Stuart Manley, Dwight Schlenzenger, Frank Sherman, Joshua Allenby, F Gregory Tillman and their leader, Robert Gouldman.

'It is time, my friends,' said Gouldman, signalling to them to follow him down to the sanctuary.

He led them along a short corridor towards the back of the house to a locked, heavy oak door. The key glistened in the light as he took it from his trouser pocket and proceeded to unlock it. As Gouldman swung the door open a wooden stairway appeared that led into a darkened basement below. He reached for the light switch and turned it on, suddenly revealing the long staircase before them. They each descended into the gloomy basement, the last of them closing the door behind them, and when they reached the foot of the stairs they entered a stone-walled lobby with beautifully carved oak benches that sat against the two facing walls. At the end was a dark wooden chest containing a number of priest-like robes with hoods and dark blue braiding along the edges. Gouldman handed one to each member of the circle in turn as they lined up in a ritualistic fashion to receive them, after which they proceeded to put them on and enter a larger circular room with opaque slatted windows near to the ceiling. The centre of the stone floor was made up of tiles that formed what looked like a circular maze and surrounding it were 12 evenly placed iron candle holders each with a solitary candle protruding from its top. As the seven members of the fraternity inner circle gathered in the centre of the room, Gouldman and Manley took firelighters and began to light each of the candles, both of them starting from a central point opposite the entrance where they had collected their gowns and moving in opposite clockwise directions from each other until all 12 candles were lit.

'Come, my brothers,' invited Gouldman. 'It is time to embrace the thread that bonds us.'

With that, each of them crossed their arms and held the hand of his colleague on either side. Closing their eyes they began to speak in one voice:

'May our brotherhood prosper and may the flame of the

cause burn brighter. Let the circle be strong and never let the chord of trust that protects us be weakened.'

There was a short pause before Gouldman addressed the circle.

'My brothers, do you vow to pursue the cause upon which this fraternity inner circle was founded?'

'We vow to pursue the cause and its ideals from now until the end of days,' the others chanted.

Releasing hands, they stood solemnly waiting for their president to continue.

'I have good news, my brothers. The Haedenberg Foundation is well pleased with our continued support, just as they have been with the inner circle of this fraternity in years past. Remember we have many brothers in fraternities across this great nation of ours who are united with us in the desire to see the day that the cause is realised and when every man and woman has the right to determine their own destiny. The foundation has expressed its generosity to a greater degree this time. Our pouch is overflowing, brothers, and in return they require more names from us.'

'We must widen our contacts network, brothers, if we are truly dedicated to the cause,' added Stuart Manley, endorsing the request of his close friend.

'Joshua, it's time to hear from you. What have you to report?'

Joshua Allenby remained silent. He had been dreading this meeting and had actually contemplated taking a leave of absence, something he knew he would regret for the rest of his college days if not into his working life. He had heard that AET's inner circle had always been from its founding a haven of safety for those who thrived within it. Not so for those who were no longer dedicated.

'Well, Joshua? The brothers would like to hear what you have to say. Did you accomplish the tasks we assigned you?'

He began to shake.

'Cat got your tongue, Allenby?' asked Tillman.

'I haven't been able to follow through.'

'You disappoint us,' replied Manley.

'It's been difficult. Please understand, it's...'

'We were counting on you. Haedenberg was counting on you,' added Gouldman. 'Those names were very important... No, *vital*, in fact. What happened?'

'I couldn't do it.'

'What are you telling us, Joshua?'

'I... I can't do this anymore.'

'Are you telling us that you are no longer dedicated to the cause?'

'Well, I believe in it... I do, I really do, but...'

'But not enough, is that right, my brother?'

'Please, I want to leave now.'

'Leave?'

'Yes.'

'Leave us?' said Gouldman, now standing only inches away from Allenby's face.

Allenby continued to shiver as he saw deep beyond Gouldman's cold expression. For the first time he really wondered what Gouldman would be capable of doing and felt a small stream of sweat trickle from his hairline to the edge of his eyebrow.

'Of course, Joshua, you may leave us.'

'Thank you, thank you. I won't say a word, really I promise.'

'We know you won't,' replied Gouldman. 'You're a brother of the fraternity. We wouldn't expect anything else.'

Allenby walked briskly out of the inner room and promptly put his gown back in the chest in the entrance room. The others then heard him run up the stairs to the ground floor where they had first assembled and close the door behind him.

'Seems we must seek a new brother, my friends.'

'What are you going to say to Haedenberg?' asked Tillman.

'Nothing yet,' replied Gouldman. 'Just that we're working on it. You and Manley must arrange to see Joshua alone; a kind of a de-initiation ceremony, you could call it. In the meantime I'll make the contacts and I'll get the names. May the flame of the cause burn brighter,' he added, 'and may your own future dreams be secured.'

'May the flame of the cause burn brighter,' they chanted as each member again crossed their arms and held the hand of their immediate brother.

'Our gathering will now disband, my brothers. Go in peace,' said Gouldman, bringing the meeting to a conclusion.

One by one they took off their robes, folded them neatly and placed them back in the chest from which they had been taken before heading up the stairs that led back to the ground floor of the fraternity house. Calvert remained as Manley and Gouldman each started to place their small metal flame extinguishers over each of the 12 candles that surrounded them, doing so in opposite clockwise movements from the ones they had made when lighting them.

'One day when I enter the senate we shall see our dream become reality, William,' said Gouldman as he gazed into one of the flames.

'You have high hopes, Robert.'

'Speaking of elections,' continued Gouldman, 'we'd better call in on Linden and get the latest on my re-election campaign.

Gouldman, in an expectant mood, parked his car outside the house where Joseph Linden and some of the other members of the fraternity were boarding. They had driven about half a mile. The others followed him up the path as he knocked the door three times and waited for it to be answered. Linden looked surprised upon seeing them but then asked them to come in.

'Guys,' said Gouldman, acknowledging the others who were spread out in the lounge reading.

'Is there something I can do for you, Robert?' asked Linden, a little concerned.

'I just came over to see how my re-election campaign is going. What's the mood in the camp?'

Linden appeared lost for words, making Gouldman feel somewhat uneasy.

'Well?'

'It's not good news, Robert,' he replied. 'I'm afraid it's going to be a close one; Thomas Jackson is in with a real chance this time.'

'Are you sure about this?' asked Calvert, joining in.

'Yes William, I am. Jackson's camp has really gone for it and many are looking for a change. Some are still wavering so we need to do some persuading otherwise the vote will go against us.'

'Then make sure Jackson doesn't get those votes! I intend to be re-elected as fraternity president of Alpha Epsilon Theta for the graduation year, do you hear me?'

'I'm doing what I can.'

'I'm sure you'll swing it, Linden.'

'Be sure to,' added Manley.

'Let's hit town, guys,' said Gouldman, signalling for them to leave. Unlike the others, Calvert knew that Gouldman had been shaken by Linden's reply. His buoyant mood to hit town was mere bravado.

As Manley and Calvert headed back to Gouldman's car their fraternity leader remained at the door for a few moments.

'I'm putting my trust in you, Joseph. Don't let me down will you? I remember my friends,' he said, concluding their meeting.

23

June 3rd 1974

Robert Gouldman entered the fraternity house with lingering doubts in his mind that had vexed him all that day and had played on his thoughts like little mind daggers stabbing at him. For the first time since entering the gates of Princeton college and taking his place in AET he could see the clouds becoming greyer against the backdrop of blue that had coloured his days to date. His morale had been boosted to a degree by a number of his fraternity brothers who, on different occasions throughout the day, had informed him of their intention to vote for him, but he knew that it was going to be close, very close. Joe Linden had been relentlessly canvassing every member of the fraternity, from freshman to senior, over the previous two weeks. Even he, after all his efforts, persuasion and threats, was unable to make the call. It was that close and he wasn't confident that everyone had been forthcoming with their true intentions.

As the some 200 members began to file into the fraternity house at the end of a busy day of exam preparations, they lined up to place their voting slips in the ballot box that was being guarded well by representatives from both the Gouldman and Jackson camps. Gouldman was becoming nervous, something that was almost alien to him because everything had been a walk in the park since entering Princeton. He was set to graduate with first class honours and his election as fraternity president the year before had seen a resounding victory over his then opponent who had held the position for three years. He became more agitated when he caught sight of this year's opponent, Thomas Jackson, looking relaxed and cheerful as he conversed with his campaign team.

'Are we going to win?' he asked Linden, letting his guard down for the first time.

'Too close to call, Robert, we'll just have to wait and see now.'

Slowly the voting line diminished until the campaign team members cast their votes. Finally, in fraternity tradition, the candidates cast their own votes before the entire assembly, the challenger first. When Gouldman dropped his paper into the ballot box the guest adjudicator, Philip T Rossitor, one of the college vice principals, stood up to conclude the vote.

'My best wishes to the candidates. Stick around, gentlemen, the results will be announced shortly.'

There was a loud cheer as the box was taken into the study by the adjudicator followed by two representatives from each campaign team.

Forty minutes had elapsed. Gouldman now knew that Linden had been right. It was neck and neck. They had to be checking the result because the previous year's count had taken just over 20 minutes. Either way, to Gouldman it would be a hollow victory or a humiliating defeat.

'Guess Joey was right, hey Will?'

'Let's just wait for the result, shall we,' replied Calvert, trying to be objective. He had never seen his friend like this. It was as though the jury was out and his life was resting in the balance.

'This will change everything.'

'It doesn't have to, Robert. Look at you; you've got a great future ahead. You've already accomplished what so many aspire to and yet fail to realise. Being AET president, even for one year, it'll go well with you.'

'Where did Jackson come from anyway? He was a nobody a few months ago and now he dares to challenge me.'

'Robert, everyone has the right to run. You should respect that, especially where you're intending to go.'

Moments later the study door opened and the noise of chatter rescinded as the five men returned from their counting. Rossitor stood on a chair and signalled for everyone present to pay attention.

'I have the results of the ballot for the AET fraternity president for the academic year of 1974. The votes were as follows: Robert Willard Gouldman, 102 votes.'

At that moment Gouldman's heart sank like a battleship that had just been broadsided.

'Thomas Emmett Jackson, 106. Spoiled papers, 11. I thereby declare by simple majority of vote, Thomas Emmett Jackson, AET fraternity president of 1974.'

The room became awash with cheers of adulation for the victor as Gouldman looked up in desperation, firstly at a despondent Joe Linden standing next to Rossitor in the centre of the room, and then at his trusted friend William Calvert, who was by his side.

'Tell me what has just happened?' he said to Calvert, barely able to get the words out.

'I'm really sorry, Robert, I know how much this meant to you.'

'OK everyone, settle down,' said Rossitor. 'Let's first hear from the defeated candidate who I am sure would like to say a few words.'

'It's not over yet,' said Gouldman to Calvert before wading through the crowd towards Rossitor.

'Let's give him a big hand; Robert Gouldman, gentlemen.'

At that, Gouldman stood up on the table to address the crowd.

'I'd like to thank my campaign team: Joe Linden, Ralph Brogan, Jim Smethers and Bobby Matheson. Good work guys, you tried your best. There's nothing else to say at this time except that under the electoral rules of this fraternity, I demand a recount.'

The assembly responded with a mixture of boos and applause before Rossitor stood up and calmed things down.

'In a vote as close as this, and under the rules of the fraternity electoral process, the defeated candidate has the right to request one recount. We shall therefore retire to do just that.'

Gouldman left the temporary podium to the sound of both applause and jeers. He did not respond, nor did he, for that matter, care.

It took a further 40 minutes before Rossitor and the others re-emerged from the study with the result of the recount and immediately a silence of greater intensity fell upon the fraternity house and all those gathered. He again stood up in the midst of the crowd and began to speak:

'I have the results of the recount of the ballot for the AET fraternity president for the academic year of 1974. I confirm the votes as final and not subject to challenge. The votes were as follows: Robert Willard Gouldman, 104 votes. Thomas Emmett Jackson, 106 votes. Spoiled papers, nine. I thereby declare again that Thomas Emmett Jackson has been elected as AET fraternity president for 1974.'

Again the cheering erupted and Jackson immediately rose to address the assembly. He had to wait a few moments for the noise to abate before he could continue.

'It's been a great campaign. My team has been magnificent and I never for a moment dreamed of ever getting close to winning, albeit by this narrow margin. I'd like to thank all of

ALUMNI

you who supported me and extend my hand to all my friends in both camps this day. It's been a close one: two votes. Robert, you ran a great campaign too and it seems like it was too close to call. From looking through the records I believe that the last time any two candidates came this close was back in 1957, so this is an extraordinary day. However, under the fraternity rules, I as victor in this election hereby call for a second ballot.'

His supporters were aghast, as was his campaign team, and there occurred a frenzy of words of disagreement.

'Listen please, my friends...'

'Gentlemen,' interrupted Rossitor. 'Please allow Mr Jackson to continue.'

'Please...' continued Jackson until the room became quieter.

'If I am to serve you as president I require a mandate from a majority of you, which today I have not received. You as a fraternity have spoken for change and I will carry it through, but only with greater backing. I urge those of you who supported my worthy opponent to reconsider your vote and for those who spoiled their papers to get off the fence and vote for change. There will be a second ballot tomorrow, same time same place.'

Gouldman glared at Linden as Thomas Jackson walked gleefully towards the entrance door of the fraternity house, shaking the occasional hand as he did so. When he had finished talking to Phillip Rossitor, Linden approached him, trying to put on a brave face. The campaign had failed badly; he felt responsible.

'Thanks, Joe; you did your best,' said a despondent Gouldman. 'But a day can make all the difference in politics, so get to work and persuade the masses, hey.'

'I'll do what I can.'

'Good,' said Gouldman, putting his arms around his friend. 'I'll be over later. There's something I want you to do for me.'

24

August 8th 1974

'You're kidding me, right… You got in? A football scholarship… That's great, man, that's just great news… Sure, I'll get to the games if or when they let me out. Next year's the big one you know… Well I'm hopeful; we'll just have to see… thanks for the confidence. I bet Marcie's real pleased, say hello to her will you… Sure, we'll meet up before I go back to Princeton…'

The chiming of the doorbell interrupted the telephone conversation William Calvert was having with a long-time friend.

'Someone's at the door. I'll call you soon, big guy, take it slow…'

He put the receiver down and got up from his father's treasured dark-red leather chair that sat in the corner of the lounge of the Calvert family home situated in one of Hartford, Connecticut's most desirable neighbourhoods. He opened the door and to his surprise he found Robert Gouldman standing at his doorstep.

'Robert!'

'Will, how you doing? Enjoying the summer recess?'

'I guess so.'

'So are you going to invite me in or am I going to have to stand here for the next hour?'

'Sure, sorry, come on in.'

'Are your folks at home?'

'No they've gone to visit my mom's sister down in Meridan.'

'I'm sorry I've missed them. You will mention that I called, won't you?'

'Sure.'

'Anyway, great news Will.'

'I'm sorry?'

'Big Dick's swinging! Way to be!'

'Am I missing something?'

'Haven't you seen the news?'

'No.'

'Nixon's resigned!'

'You're kidding!'

'Would I be this excited about the downfall of a republican president if it wasn't true?'

'No I guess not. It's crazy though to think that the arrest of five men breaking into the Democratic national committee offices in Washington DC two years ago with cameras and bugging devices could bring a president down.'

'Well it was all down to the creeps, wasn't it.'

'The creeps?' asked Calvert puzzled.'

'Yeah, Tricky Dickey's creeps, the committee to re-elect the president.'

'Of course, the creeps.'

'He couldn't deny the links forever. My hat goes off to Messrs Woodward and Bernstein. It takes investigative journalism to new heights. This is a great day for America!'

'Maybe,' replied his friend.

'Well, anyway, enough of that, I've been thinking that we ought to invite Joe Linden to join the circle, what do you think?'

'What are his views on the cause?'

'I think he's with us. I sounded him out before we left for the recess.'

'What did you tell him?'

'Nothing, we just had a conversation on the subject and his view seemed to reflect ours, and after all he did get me re-elected as fraternity president.'

'That's for sure. I still don't know how you swung that Robert. Twenty two votes!'

'I feel like I owe him, just like we will all owe each other when we take our places out there.'

'So just how did you manage to get yourself re-elected?'

'Knowledge is power, Will.'

'Apparently.'

'What do you know about Thomas Jackson, Will?'

'About as much as you really. He did well though, you have to admit that.'

'Yes, I do. Maybe we should take some interest in him next semester. See what he's all about. He's come from nowhere really – I'm intrigued.'

'Do you need a beer?'

'Never say no, Will.'

'Go and sit down, I've got a few cooling in the ice box.'

'This is a great place your folks have got here.'

'It's OK,' replied William from the kitchen. 'It's a bit sterile for me. I always figured I'd own a place like this someday, but I'm not so sure now. New York is more appealing.'

'The big apple hey?'

'There's more going on,' replied William as he returned with two cold beers.

'Sit down Will, we need to talk.'

'OK, I didn't have much else planned for the remainder of the day, except maybe taking in a movie later. They're re-showing Rollerball in the theatre in town for the next three nights.'

'What have you been doing?'

'Not much. I just got off the phone to an old friend from

high school. Have you seen Louisa during the recess?'

'We split. My decision, I couldn't see a future. Anyway I didn't call to talk about women.'

'OK, what's on your mind?'

'You and Manley are my closest friends. I always confide in you and I trust you both like we were brothers. I've travelled all the way from Providence because I needed to talk to you, Will.'

'What's this all about, Robert?'

'I want the fraternity inner circle to become members of the Haedenberg Foundation.'

'Are you serious?'

'No Will, I said it for fun. What's the problem?'

'Do you have any idea where that will lead?'

'Of course I do, I've met these guys.'

'You've met them! When?'

'A few months back.'

'But I thought you just communicated by letter, to get instructions and update them on our efforts.'

'It's time to reach out, Will. Graduation's next year. We'll be out there soon and we will need the appropriate level of backing, believe me.'

'Robert, we're making good money and we're giving them names. Let's just leave it at that.'

'Am I hearing you right, Will?'

'Look, I just think it's too risky.'

'Think about it, Will. You could leave Princeton like others in the past, and have just been a part of this, and then it's over. You take a job, you keep in contact with your brothers, you do the occasional favour and that's it. I'm talking about being part of the cause, making a difference, not to mention the financial security that will come along with it.'

'It's for life, Robert. Do you really want to commit yourself for life? You know the ethos of the foundation, you know what they expect. What if you ever wanted out?'

'Wanted out? What are you saying?'

'I'm saying I need to think about this. This is all of our futures we're talking about here. What does Manley think?'

'He's in.'

'I need time, Robert.'

'Frederick Haedenberg needed time. But time was the one thing that eluded him. He was only 47 when he died, did you know that? He had only just started to realise his dreams when the heart attack took him. His company had just achieved a major breakthrough in becoming leader in the field of advanced polymer development at the time. He collapsed in front of his board of directors, in front of his son Alexander, whom he had only days earlier appointed to the board. The moment those cronies took over the company it was doomed and Alexander knew it. Within 18 months it was taken over, stripped and broken up. Alexander was lucky; he managed to salvage one section of the corporation and use its finances to create the foundation we know today. He had a vision, Will. Sometimes the officers just can't cut it like their dying captains. He had the vision to see that, but he had little time to make that critical choice, but he made it. We all have to be dedicated to the cause, so what's it to be?'

'Like I said, Robert, I need time to think this through.'

'You disappoint me, Will. I thought you'd be in all the way. Haedenberg's vision goes way beyond what we're involved in. This is just groundwork for the boys. You could be part of a vision for the future, and you could help that vision become reality.'

25

November 23rd 1974

The campus refectory was beginning to fill up as many of the students filed in from a break from lectures in search of refreshment and conversation. William Calvert was talking with an acquaintance from the year below him who was discussing the merits of investing in a Harley Davidson once he had graduated. It would be more of a novelty than portrayal of image, or so Calvert thought, judging on the appearance and character of the student in question. As the prospective free rider left Calvert's company in search of others in his year, Calvert saw one of his own friends walking from the refectory counter with a cup of coffee in his hand and looking somewhat distracted and alone.

'Milton, there you are!'

Porter was shaken from his daze as he looked up to see who had called to him.

'What's new, William?' he said as he changed direction and approached Calvert who was standing near to one of the perimeter walls.

'I got some great news this morning, Milton. Mason-Wainwright have offered me a job on condition of honours graduation.'

'Isn't that something,' replied his friend unenthusiastically. 'What's the position?'

'It's for a junior investment consultant. I'll be on probation for the first two years but there'll be opportunities for promotion afterwards. How's it going with you, any news?'

'Nothing yet.'

'Anything in the pipeline?'

'No.'

'Hey, don't get despondent, something will come up, wait and see.'

'And what if nothing comes up, William, what will I do then?'

'You shouldn't think that way, Milton. Besides, if things go well in Mason-Wainwright I can always ask around and see if there are any openings.'

'Well that's just great, William, thanks. I'll just get on the ladder with a little help from my best friend and everything will be alright. You have no idea what it's like to feel second best, do you. Eckhart's got it in for me. Why does everything have to be so black and white? It either fits his theory or it doesn't.'

'Milton?'

'You're his 'A' student, William, I'm just one of a sea of faces who Eckhart looks at each lecture and thinks probably they won't cut it in the big world of investment and finance. I'll show him, William, but I'll do it on my own OK.'

'Hey Milton, I'm sorry, I didn't mean to…'

'Forget it. You'll be ascending to the top in Mason-Wainwright and you'll forget all about me.'

'You're my friend, Milton, I won't forget. Why do you say that?'

'Because you never got me into the inner circle, did you? Why won't they let me in, William? Talk to them, talk to Gouldman, tell them I'm worthy.'

'It's not my decision alone. We've got a meeting tonight. I'll remind them that your father was once fraternity president and that he still wields influence out there, OK? Maybe that will swing it this time.'

Before he could finish speaking he was pinned to the wall by his crazed friend who had a firm grip on the lapels of his jacket.

'You'll do nothing of the kind!' shouted Milton, causing a nearby crowd to turn their heads and look towards them.

Calvert was lost for words as he felt the coldness of the stone wall against which he was being pressed seep through his clothes and onto his skin. As Porter looked up, he noticed a seagull perched on the ledge of the large window above them. It jerked his head in small movements as it surveyed its surroundings. Now indignant, Calvert turned his head and looked Milton straight in the eyes.

'Where the eagles are gathered, the doves cannot enter therein,' he said in a strange tone.

'What? What are you talking about, William?' asked Porter, still pressing his friend firmly against the wall.

'Let go of me, Milton,' he replied, and as he loosened his grip and stepped back, Milton saw the seagull fly off into the sky and disappear from view.

'May our brotherhood prosper and may the flame of the cause burn brighter. Let the circle be strong and never allow the chord of trust that protects us to be weakened.'

'My brothers, do you vow to pursue the cause upon which this fraternity inner circle was founded?'

'We vow to pursue the cause and its ideals from now until the end of days.'

The seven were gathered within the circle of candles, this time each of them covered their heads with the hoods that were attached to their robes. Their leader was wearing a gold amulet around his neck with the Greek letters for alpha, epsilon and theta engraved in the middle. A circular two-fold cord surrounded it. Outside the circle stood an eighth figure shrouded by his hood like the others.

'We welcome our new brother,' said Gouldman as he removed his hood. 'Come, enter the circle.'

The figure walked into the centre of the gathering and faced Gouldman as the others looked on, their hoods still in place. Taking a large dagger from the stone table behind him, Gouldman approached his new brother and then stood a short distance away with his arms raised and the dagger pointing downwards.

'Do you vow to pursue the cause on which this fraternity inner circle has been founded?'

'I do,' he replied.

'Do you vow to spread our mission both now and into the future, and to use your influence in the position you will occupy in life?'

'I pledge my vow.'

'Do you vow to protect the sanctuary of your fellow brothers both now and until you pass over from this life?'

'I vow to protect the sanctuary of my fellow brothers.'

With that Gouldman came closer, lowered the dagger and placed the point just below the figure's earlobe. He began to move it slowly around the edge of the face, towards the chin and then held it just above the throat for a few seconds before continuing around to the other ear. Not a drop of blood appeared. Holding the dagger to his chest, Gouldman closed his eyes and remained silent for a moment.

'I have drawn no blood,' Gouldman observed as he opened his eyes again. 'I deem him worthy. Members of the inner circle, do you embrace your new brother?'

With that the others surrounded the figure, stretched out their arms and placed their hands on his shoulder before walking slowly around him in an anti-clockwise direction.

'We embrace our new brother, we welcome him to the cause,' they chanted seven times and then stopped in their tracks before returning to their original positions.

'Take your place among your brothers,' ordered Gouldman to the new member.

The seven expanded the circle allowing the eighth one to enter among them.

'Let us hear from you, Joseph. Have you accomplished the tasks that were required of you?'

'I have the names,' he replied, handing a sealed envelope to Gouldman, who hastened to open it.

'Good work, brother,' he said as he browsed the list before him. 'Their deaths will bring new life to those that will follow.'

'May the flame of the cause burn brighter,' they chanted and then removed their hoods, all except their new brother.

'This day, November 23rd 1974, marks the beginning of a new era for the inner circle of the Alpha Epsilon Theta fraternity. It is a move to greater activity and the realisation of our dream. Today, my brothers, I can inform you that we have all been accepted as members of the Haedenberg Foundation. Here are your letters of acceptance, and that includes you, our new brother. Please remove your hood and join us.'

'Gladly,' replied Thomas Jackson as he revealed his face and smiled.

They had returned to the ground floor of the fraternity house and had decided to stay there for the rest of the evening. Tillman and Manley were watching TV, Schlenzenger, Sherman and Calvert were going over some project work on the dining room table and Gouldman was sat reading *the ethos of the American political system* by R T Reinhardt in a large armchair in the corner of the study away from the others. Linden and Jackson had disappeared somewhere but the others neither noticed nor seemed concerned. Gouldman was in for an early night. He had a final mock examination the next day, the last before the real ones were to begin in just over three weeks. He had been starting to date Louisa Browning again since returning after the recess. She had agreed to renew the relationship after ending it months earlier and things had got off to a heavy start. With his involvement with Haedenberg of late, burning the wick at both ends could not be sustained indefinitely.

When he had come to the end of the 11th chapter, Gouldman needed to go to the bathroom, and so he emerged from the study and walked up the open staircase that led from the lounge to the first floor. Along the end of the landing was the bathroom, and he had to pass several bedrooms on the way, one of which was his own. He, as fraternity president, had guaranteed residency along with other seniors whose fathers had been prominent fraternity members or who contributed well financially to it. It was as he passed the door nearest to the bathroom that he stopped. It was Linden's room, the door was slightly ajar and he could hear who he thought were Jackson and Linden conversing in the room on the other side. He peered cautiously through the small gap between the door and the frame and saw that it was indeed them, both standing near the window, and Linden taking a drag of a cigarette. He could hear the conversation, just.

'It won't be easy, Thomas, getting those names took a lot of effort. Even though you won't know them personally it can sometimes be hard, you know, but you've just got to think of the cause. I've known others to fabricate them, just to get the numbers up.'

'Look, I'm in it for the money, that's all,' said Jackson. 'Who cares whether people live long and are a burden to society anyway? Gouldman and the others can have their cherished cause, I'm not worried either way.'

'Be careful, Thomas. If others in the inner circle find out about this, well…'

'I'm not scared of Gouldman. He'll be leaving next summer anyway and then I'll be fraternity president. I won that election and I can win it again. Gouldman is a fraud; he must have got to someone to get those 22 votes.'

'It's not good to have secrets,' replied Linden as he extinguished his cigarette.

'Clearly,' said Jackson. 'I'll need a good campaign manager for the final year. Join me, Joey, and I'll make it worth your while someday.'

'Thanks, I'll give it some thought.'

'Don't take too long deciding. I've others in mind as well, but you're my first choice, OK?'

As Gouldman listened intently from behind the door he felt something inside that he had never experienced before – a sense of betrayal that twisted inside him like a knife.

'I think we'd better go down and join the others now,' said Jackson, which was Gouldman's cue to head quickly to the bathroom.

As the two of them came out of Linden's room and headed back down the corridor, Gouldman watched them intensely through a narrow gap between the bathroom door and its frame.

'No, my brothers, it's not good to have secrets,' he said quietly to himself. 'They'll come back to haunt you when you least want them to.'

26

Robert Gouldman watched from the windows of his limousine as two officers opened the iron gates to his residency. The welcoming committee had arrived; they had been camped all morning after press rumours of his return had spread like locusts across the capital. The efforts by the security officers to suppress the crowd proved futile and even the best-laid plans to return Gouldman as discreetly as possible had clearly been fraught. Carlyle had delivered Gouldman to a FBI safe house the night before and had contacted Thomas Jackson when they had arrived. Jackson had joined them early that morning along with Ed Hamell and had made the necessary arrangements with the Washington police department to have the residency reopened in preparation. How the news of his return had leaked was a mystery. Unexpectedly, representatives of what must have constituted the entire spectrum of the capital's press and media were now ascending upon the moving vehicle as it turned into the driveway. Every cameraman, newspaper journalist and TV reporter fought to get a shot or a look at the returning senator. Activists from the anti-euthanasia league had made certain that their presence with placards and biodegradable missiles would not go unnoticed by the senator or the media.

The police fought hard to put a barrier between the crowd and the passengers in the vehicle but were no match for the news-hungry press that surrounded the car as it came to a halt by the steps that led up to the entrance to the building. As the doors of the limousine were opened the car was pelted with missiles from the protesters, momentarily distracting the reporters from their mission to get a statement from the man of the moment. Some members of the press reacted angrily causing Ed Hamell to fear that a protest riot might breakout. He reluctantly took it upon himself to be the first to surface from the rear of the limousine and looked shaken and overwhelmed by the onslaught of camera flashes and questions that flew at him as Gouldman himself followed him out. Hamell's eyes had not long recovered from the abduction incident and started to react to the photography. He turned his head away as Gouldman stood up and momentarily looked at the excited crowd in defiance, but was quickly escorted away by Thomas Jackson and two bodyguards who were desperate to get the senator inside the building as quickly as possible.

'Senator Gouldman, can you tell us at this time who abducted you?' shouted the first reporter to get a hearing above the noise of the crowd.

'Is it true that the anti-euthanasia league were responsible?' asked another.

'The senator has no comment to make at this time. A full statement will follow in due course,' said Hamell as he faced the crowd for the last time.

'Senator, are you affected in any way from the experience?'

'The senator is well and ready to get back to the business of representing the people of Rhode Island,' replied Hamell.

'Death monger!!' shouted one of the protesters as he tried to force his way through the sea of reporters at the steps to the building.

'Will the senator continue in his campaign for nationwide legislation on this issue?' cried a female reporter in a vain effort to get a response as she became entrapped in a mire of bodies swaying like the tide of a restless sea. 'Is it true that the senator would like to see euthanasia become law in every state?'

'Thank you, that's all for now,' called Hamell as he turned to flee from the ensuing media.

From his office in downtown Manhattan, Milton Porter watched intensely as the CNN news crew transmitted pictures of Gouldman and his entourage entering the building, unaware that the door to his office had been opened and that behind him stood Simone Kimball with Lawrence Henderson and Rachel Kirby. As the production team switched back to the studio for further comment from the presenter, Simone brought to Porter's attention the fact that he had visitors. Porter turned his head in surprise and then recognised Henderson from a time they had briefly met the previous year when the corporation had been under investigation.

'Leave us Simone – no calls or visitors,' he replied in a sombre tone.

As she left the room he turned back to his TV and continued watching the report.

'Look at him,' he continued, glaring at the picture of Gouldman behind the news presenter. 'He's gone too far. It was never meant to escalate to this. It's a pity his abductors never kept him.'

'That's assuming he had been taken in the first place,' replied Henderson.

'What are you talking about?' said Porter.

'Congratulations, you're the first to know that it was all a scam, perfectly staged to further his own interests. Timing couldn't have been better in view of Calvert's death, don't you think?'

Porter switched off the TV and stood up. They had now gained his attention.

'Is this true?'

'Yes,' replied Kirby.

'May we have a seat?' asked Henderson.

'Please…' replied Porter as he began a slow walk towards the window.

'I suggest you sit down, Mr Porter,' said Henderson. It was not a request.

Porter ignored Henderson and gazed out of the window. His eyes again became fixed on the activity on Wall Street.

'What is the purpose of your visit this time, Mr Henderson?'

'We know all about the Haedenberg Foundation, Milton, and we know about your illegal financial dealings,' he replied.

'I don't know what you're talking about.'

'Yes you do, Milton. One phone call and I can have this place crawling with agents who will dissect your every accounting record. This is for real Milton – they'll find it all and it won't be good for the corporation down on Wall Street. Alternatively you can tell me what I need to know and I'll make sure that the worse that happens is that your links with Haedenberg and the organisations that you have been doing business with are severed. An internal enquiry will see to the rest. The corporation will be fined for accounting irregularities, you'll resign as president of course and everyone gets a firm smack on the wrist. The choice is yours.'

'It'll be the end for me.'

'It's better than spending the next ten years in jail,' said Kirby.

'Gouldman was blackmailing Calvert, wasn't he,' said Henderson.

Porter didn't respond. Memories of that final year at Princeton came flooding back along with the hurt that he had battled to suppress for the past 24 years. It was too late for payback concerning William; but Gouldman, that was a different matter. Composing himself, he confirmed Henderson's statement.

'Why?' asked Henderson.

'Haedenberg needed more funds and Gouldman told William to diversify. For months now we've really had our fingers in the dirt. I'd rather not discuss the details – you want to know about William and Gouldman and that's all I'm prepared to discuss at this stage without my lawyers present.'

'Go on.'

'Only William and I knew about this, or so I thought. On the day of the crash I was in his office. He was getting ready for a trip but he wouldn't fill me in on where he was going or for what purpose. I confronted him about an incident the previous day when Peter Vincent, one of the board, started asking some searching questions about some of our overseas funds.'

'The dirty investments?'

'Yes. I think William could easily have spilled the beans that morning when the board met; I could see it in his eyes. I told him to get a grip – this had to stay between him, Gouldman and me. I reminded him about the fact that your department needed only the smallest of excuses to take us down. He told me to leave. It was later that day as I was passing his office that I really became concerned. I overheard him speaking to Gillian Taylor about a trip they were taking to Washington. He told her to drop everything and travel with him. She was to say nothing to anyone, including me. She wasn't happy at all. She told him that it was her wedding anniversary that night and asked him what the trip was for and why it was so important. He wouldn't tell her. I was waiting for her to leave so that I could confront him on it, but I was called away – something urgent came up. I went back later that morning but he had locked his office. I couldn't find Gillian anywhere so I checked with Simone to see if he had left. She told me that he was in a meeting and couldn't be disturbed. Why had he locked his door? He never did that when he was on site. When he finally surfaced from his meeting, I waited for him at the door to his office. He unlocked it and asked me what I wanted. He was cold and distant as though I was nothing to him any more. I asked him again what the trip was all about. He told me that it didn't concern me and dismissed me like I was some junior office clerk. When he walked out of the executive lounge he never looked back, he said nothing, no goodbye, nothing. I never saw him again after that and the next I heard was that he was dead when I got the call early the following morning. When I found out that David Forrester was on the plane with them I realised that Carlton Hayes hadn't been telling me everything either.'

'So the lawyers were in on the deals,' said Henderson.

'Yes. It became apparent to me that William got an attack of conscience and I guess Forrester did too.'

'So Calvert was on his way to blow the whistle to Dan Riley,' said Kirby.

'I don't know who he was going to meet, like I said he was very secretive towards the end.'

'Riley was one of our agents.'

'Was?' said Porter.

'Yes, he was killed in the line of duty,' said Henderson.

Kirby's stomach turned. She had had a close working relationship with Dan Riley and had been affected badly by his death. They had worked together on many cases and had always watched out for each other. Kirby would never allow the relationship to become personal, not out of choice but to avoid complications at work. Since hearing Fabien's words to her on the phone the evening he had called her from Tannersville she had become almost sick with grief. To date she had bottled it up, now she could feel herself losing control.

'How very co-incidental,' commented Porter.

Kirby glared at Henderson. He could see her out of the corner of his eye and refrained from making eye contact with her. Just how he knew about the circumstances surrounding

Riley's death she could not be certain. Now she appreciated Fabien's sudden mistrust of him.

'Agent Riley was a respected member of my team,' he replied, still aware of Kirby's burning glare.

'I've tried desperately to keep all of this from the board,' continued Porter. 'This was part of the reason I fired Vincent.'

'You think that he was beginning to suspect something?'

'Maybe, but there were other reasons.'

'How was Gouldman blackmailing Calvert?' asked Kirby.

'Celina McCallen. William slept with her. Gouldman put her up to it and arranged for a revealing portfolio of photographs to be taken. But it didn't work, did it. I can only assume that he was determined to bring us all down; the consequences of his little indiscretion didn't compare with the burden he was carrying.'

'So Gouldman had the plane sabotaged to ensure that none of the dirt on Haedenberg came out,' said Kirby.

Porter remained silent.

'Is that what happened, Milton?' asked Henderson.

'I am saying nothing further – I want my lawyer.'

27

Two long days had passed since Henderson had returned from New York, and as night fell over Washington he was sat in his office, his face illuminated by the light from his laptop and his eyes aglow with satisfaction as he closed the last of eight files he had been interrogating that evening. It had been 36 hours since his last communication with Fabien, at which he had informed his subordinate that he was on to something. He had given no further information other than that, and had told him he wanted him to remain in Tannersville with Jamie and to await his further instructions. Even an enquiring Rachel Kirby was none the wiser as to her boss' activities. He had found out that she had been moonlighting on the narcotics case and had called her into his office. Expecting a reprimand, she was surprised at his sudden change of heart. He had encouraged her to concentrate on identifying the man in the photographs and had told her he would call her if needed.

As Henderson checked his watch he realised that the visitors whom he was expecting were 20 minutes late. He nervously waited, wondering whether he would actually go through with the plan he had been devising. If he were wrong about the conclusions he had come to over the past 24 hours, his career would be over.

Henderson's anxious look was clearly noted as the meeting in his office drew to a conclusion. Underneath, however, he felt an inner satisfaction from the hour-long conversation that had just taken place. Bill Stratton and Maurice Hawthorne, two superiors whom Henderson respected and trusted, watched with keen interest to gauge his reaction to the comment about to be made.

'Go ahead with the plan,' said Stratton. 'But if you're wrong about this, then you take full responsibility, Lawrence. If this turns out to be a one way trip, this conversation never happened and we will deny all knowledge.'

'I understand.'

Robert Gouldman was sat smugly in his office with the morning papers that his replacement for the late Celina had brought him. The papers were full of reports on how the pro-euthanasia campaign had taken a boost since his return to Washington. The anti-league were being branded as extremists, taking responsibility for his kidnapping as part of a well orchestrated media propaganda exercise to bolster his popularity and that of the cause. Everything was falling into place or so he believed.

He had called Ed Hamell earlier to catch up with things. Hamell had agreed to meet him at the residency and when Gouldman heard a knock at the door he walked briskly to it expecting his colleague to be standing behind it. To his surprise Lawrence Henderson, Rachel Kirby and two police officers were stood behind Ed Hamell. They had arrived at reception only seconds before Hamell and had followed him up the stairs. Hamell assumed that the FBI were checking to see if Gouldman was OK or needed further assistance, but the presence of the two officers seemed out of place.

Thomas Jackson had always been wary of Maurice Hawthorne. When Hawthorne entered his office Jackson was unprepared for the visit. Meetings with him were usually scheduled.

'Hello Thomas,' he said. 'You were heading up the Gouldman abduction case, weren't you?'

'Yes.'

'Then you might wish to switch on CNN.'

'Why?'

'Take a look.'

Jackson picked up the controls of his office TV and switched on the CNN channel.

'What's this all about?'

'You tell me, Thomas. I saw this report earlier – it'll be coming up again in just a moment I would think.'

Jackson looked nervously at the screen awaiting the next report. A minute later the cameras switched back to the studio and behind the face of the newscaster was a picture of Robert Gouldman.

'Startling new developments came earlier today in the Robert Gouldman case. The Rhode Island senator who was recently released after being kidnapped only a short distance from the White House was today arrested by the FBI.'

Jackson stared in disbelief at the screen as CNN broadcast images of Gouldman being taken from his Washington residency by two police officers and being followed by Lawrence Henderson and Rachel Kirby.

'It is alleged,' the reporter continued, 'that Senator Gouldman was involved in a plot resulting in the murder of one of his aids and of an FBI agent, whose name is yet to be confirmed...'

'Did you sanction this, Thomas?' asked Hawthorne.

'No, absolutely not... what's Henderson doing?' replied Jackson as the report on CNN continued.

'I suggest you get on top of this, Thomas, and quickly!'

Jackson didn't reply.

'I take it that you do know who the deceased agent is?'

'No, I don't.'

'I heard it was Michael Fabien.'

'Fabien?'

'Someone was dispatched yesterday to the Catskills to identify a body that was found in the woods near Tannersville.'

'Who was dispatched?'

'I don't know, Thomas; I would have thought that you would have taken care of it.'

'Me?'

'Of course, he was your agent. Thomas, you do know what's going on in your department I hope.'

'I do, yes…'

'This doesn't inspire confidence. Report back to me at the end of the day will you.'

'Of course.'

The moment Hawthorne had left the office, Jackson scrambled to the telephone. He picked up the receiver and made a call.

'Come on!' he said impatiently. 'Pick up the phone, you know it's me!' Seconds later, John Carlyle came on the line.

'Someone has found out about Fabien. Henderson has arrested Gouldman. How did he make the connection?'

'I've no idea,' replied a nervous Carlyle.

'Do you realise what this means?'

There was a short pause. Bill Stratton waited eagerly for Jackson to comment further as he listened in carefully to the remainder of the conversation on the bugged line.

'It's over. Gouldman will do anything now,' Jackson continued. 'He'll save his career and he'll take me down. Old scores are always settled.'

Fabien's cell phone rang. He picked it up from the table and looked at it for a few moments, hesitating to answer it.

'I'd better get this, it could be Henderson,' he told Jamie. 'Hello.'

'How are you two doing up there?' asked his boss.

'We're running out of clothes,' replied Mike.
'We arrested Gouldman today.'
'Did he confess to sabotaging the plane?'
'It wasn't him.'
'Are you certain of that?'
'Too obvious really.'
'Then who was responsible?'
'It was Jackson. It all fits. He wanted you out of way from the start – the disciplinary hearing, remember? You heard him when he said that it wasn't over.'

'Just rhetoric that's all. It doesn't prove anything.'

'Was it? How have you been since the hearing, Fabien? I'd say at a low ebb, mentally and physically. The opportunity was there, wasn't it?'

'What do you mean?'

'The drugs of course. They weren't prescribed to get you back on form; they were prescribed to weaken you, to make you vulnerable. The hallucinations, the blackouts, it was all in the plan.'

'Go on.'

'Why were you suddenly returned to duty when Gouldman was abducted? Why were you assigned to the case when still under medical supervision? There were others – Kirby, Durrell – why you?'

'I'm listening...' replied Fabien.

'We know the abduction was a set-up, but who was assigned as your back-up?'

'Carlyle, to track my movements no doubt.'

'Then there's the false lead, almost fatal. Just a co-incidence?'

'Of course, to have me killed in the line of duty. That fails so he has to try something else; the photographs, they were of John Markham. He gets Markham to kill Celina to frame me.'

'Kirby gets taken off the Mason-Wainwright case because

she's digging too deep, and there's something else.'

'What is it?'

'Guess where Jackson went to college, Fabien?'

'Princeton?'

'It gets better. He belonged to the same fraternity as Calvert, Porter and Gouldman.'

'Then Riley must have found out something about the fraternity.'

'I think we've just found ourselves a rotten apple, don't you?'

'Just what did he uncover?'

'That's what I want you to find out. I want you to return to Washington. I'll arrange for a safe house for Miss Farrington. I'm not taking any chances. Jackson's missing and nobody has seen Carlyle all day.'

'OK, where do we go?'

'You'll receive instructions after you leave. I'll speak with you later. Meanwhile Kirby and I have a fish to catch.'

Mike ended the call, put his phone back on the table and turned to Jamie.

'We have to return to Washington.'

28

The car carrying Jamie drove speedily across the outer suburbs of the capital and out towards open country. She was on edge; she had no idea where she was being taken as the driver turned off the freeway. They reached a main road that led through a quiet town on the outskirts, its name she could not recall; her mind was elsewhere.

She was tired after the night's drive from Albany with Mike. They had stopped for a few hours in Wilmington, Delaware to pick up supplies for her. Eventually they had completed the first leg of the journey at which point she and Mike had separated and he had told her that he would meet her at the safe house later but had given no indication as to when. Little conversation had taken place between her and the two agents in the front seats since she had left the designated rendezvous point with them just north of Baltimore earlier that afternoon.

She asked them how much further they had to go and was told they would arrive shortly. As the driver turned the car into a side road Jamie's eyes met with those of a young boy riding a bike on the sidewalk. The boy stared at the car until it was well along the road. As it passed out of view the road descended down a hill until it reached a junction with a set of traffic lights. Before them the road continued on a shallow incline and Jamie noticed the houses were becoming fewer the further they drove out. Eventually they turned off the road down a steep driveway surrounded in trees, at the end of which was a single-storey sand-coloured house with a car parked in front of the garage. The house looked as though it had been renovated, most likely for the purpose for which it was now needed. It appeared to her as having been part of a small farm or holding in the past. Waiting for them at the entrance was a man in a suit who walked towards them as they pulled up. It was Henderson. He opened the door for her and she was very glad to get out and stretch her legs. He asked her if she had had a pleasant journey and if everything had been OK. All she wanted was to lie down. He escorted her to the entrance. The house was basic yet tasteful – minimally equipped yet comfortable.

'Try to stay indoors as much as you can, but if you need some air you can take a walk outside in the fields. There's nothing for at least five miles,' said Henderson, pointing to the views out of the kitchen window. 'When the rest of the farm buildings were demolished in the early 80s, this was renovated by the government. There's still a cesspool out towards the fields somewhere that used to provide natural drainage for this and some of the other buildings, so be careful if you should go out walking. There are enough supplies to last a week but if you need anything just let these gentlemen know and they will be pleased to oblige. I suggest you stay low for a few days to give us time to bring this affair to a conclusion. We'll keep you posted on developments. Don't answer the telephone. Don't answer the door under any circumstances. Agents Thorpe and Merrill will take care of everything.'

Rachel Kirby and Sam Durrell were huddled around the computer in the corner of Durrell's home office as Mike made his entrance.

'Heard you were dead, Fabien,' said Durrell without lifting his eyes from the screen. 'Henderson said you needed use of an offsite computer; what's this all about?'

'What do you know about college fraternities, Durrell?'

'The least the better.'

'Bad memories from college?'

'Let's just say I didn't get much choice as to the fraternity I got into.'

'Me neither,' added Mike.

'Guess you were OK though, Kirby,' said Durrell, 'with your old man and all.'

'Let's get on with this,' she replied, ignoring the comment.

'Any news on Jackson or Carlyle?' asked Mike.

'I wish. Henderson's after their blood,' replied Kirby.

'What did Gouldman tell you?'

'Enough to bury Jackson alive!'

'And in return?'

'Exoneration. What are we looking for?' she asked.

'Princeton.'

Durrell began typing as his colleagues looked on.

'OK, here we are.'

'Let's see if we can look up the graduation classes of '75 and get some names,' said Fabien. 'How's the case of the mystery man in the photograph, Kirby?'

'I may be on to something.'

'OK Fabien, here they are,' said Durrell.

'May I?' asked Mike. Durrell got up, allowing Mike to continue. He sat down and started to examine the files. Gradually, one by one, he began to pull out the photographs of his famous four as though he was compiling his own rogues' gallery.

'There they are: Jackson, Gouldman, Milton Porter and William Calvert.'

'What are you looking for?' asked Durrell.

'Let's check out which fraternity they belonged to,' he replied.

Moments later, the information came to the screen.

'Here we are, Alpha Epsilon Theta. Impressive, let's check out the alumni.'

Fabien looked up the files on AET and before long a list of names appeared.

'Ethan Hawkins, let's check him out,' said Durrell, rubbing his chin.

The Hawkins file came up. Kirby and Durrell looked closely at the contents for a while.

'Anything?'

'No, not on this guy,' replied Kirby. 'Wait a second, Joseph Linden. I dealt with a case involving him.'

'Didn't he commit suicide?' asked Durrell.

'Let's pull up his file, see if it mentions anything about his college days.'

Mike switched to another screen and integrated the FBI files on Joseph Linden.

'Take a look at this.'

His colleagues looked on. Kirby began to read aloud. 'Joseph Linden, prominent businessman, found dead in his secluded woodland home... No sign of foul play... Conclusion, suicide... Member of the Haedenberg Foundation...'

'This is interesting,' she continued. 'Uncovered comprehensive details of miscellaneous terminally ill patients' medical records and those with degenerate conditions on his personal computer records... Close associate of Stuart Manley, a business director of the Sterling Medical Research Corporation... Remember what Jackson said about Haedenberg?'

'Yes,' he replied.

'Look. Manley was in AET too,' commented Durrell.

'I think Dan Riley uncovered something big here, don't you?'

'Can we access any of his case files?' asked Kirby.

ALUMNI

'I would suspect that they've all been moved by now,' replied Durrell.

'Maybe we can still retrieve them,' said Mike, confidently.

'How?'

'You were close to him, Kirby. Think – where would he have kept information as sensitive as this? Online?'

'No, you're right; it would be somewhere safer, somewhere…'

'Somewhere only his closest and trusted colleagues would know?'

'Yes,' she replied, and then thought for a moment before her face went blank.

'Come on, Kirby, you must remember. He must have told you or you would have seen him…'

'Wait… Get the car, Fabien.'

Kirby eventually found the entrance to the small lockup complex where she believed the information they needed would be found. Located in an alleyway in the downtown area and dwarfed by the surrounding buildings, it had not been the easiest of places to find, something she had expected from the moment they had left Durrell's place. The lobby was tiny, enough for four, maybe five, people to cram into at once. There were no seats, just a front desk in the corner and a door that presumably led to the storage area behind.

'How can I help,' asked the guard, who by now looked ready to clock off, eager for his replacement to arrive.

'I need to look in a box that belonged to one of my colleagues. His name was Daniel Riley.'

'Do you have the locker number, lady?'

'No, I just remember him mentioning this place to me once.'

'You got a security pin number?'

'No.'

'Then I can't help you. This is a secure lockup facility. Unless you've got a locker box number and a pin, you ain't looking at nothing.'

'But this is urgent.'

'It always is, lady.'

'Our colleague is no longer with us,' said Mike interjecting.

'Then he would have passed the information over to someone else.'

'He didn't have time.'

'Locker and pin – no numbers, no access.'

'We're FBI,' said Kirby, holding her badge up.

'Can't you search by name?' asked Mike.

'We don't keep records of names. The client comes in. They enter a code right here to verify that they are the key holder. This unlocks the door to the vault and then they are escorted to their box. To open it they put in a six-digit pin known only to them. Not even I can override that.'

'So what do you do if a client dies and doesn't pass over his numbers?'

'They have to renew their access code every two years. If they don't the system will automatically unlock the box, we empty the contents, destroy whatever comes out and then reset the box ready for a new client.'

'Look Fabien, I'm not 100 percent certain we're going to find anything in here so maybe…'

'If he had anything on Haedenberg it will be here. Where else would he keep something like that?'

'But how will we get access?'

'If we knew the box number I could use this to decipher the pin number. You can get us inside the vault, right?'

'Yes,' replied the guard, suddenly looking impressed.

'You shouldn't be using that stuff,' said Kirby, referring to the CD that Mike had taken out of his pocket.

'Where is your main computer server?' asked Mike.

'Inside the vault.'

'May we?'

'I shouldn't be doing this.'

'This is important.'

'OK, follow me.'

The guard swiped his vault access override key and slowly the large metallic door opened revealing the space inside. There were rows of vault boxes before them. Each row held 20 closely located boxes that looked like safes on stilts. Every box was located at the average eye level of an adult human and the doors contained a keypad and digital display for its owner to enter the pin number.

'How many boxes are there?' asked Kirby.

'A thousand,' replied the guard.

'Great. Now all we need to do is figure out which one belonged to Riley.'

'Are you sure he never told you the number, Kirby?' Think. He told you about this place; try to remember.'

'He never mentioned a number.'

'He must have found some way to pass it on. Did he leave you a cryptic e-mail or anything?'

'We're clutching at straws, Fabien. There's nothing I can tell you.'

'Then he must have told someone else.'

'When could he have done so?'

'Maybe before he fled. The trouble is, he wanted everyone to assume he was dead.'

'Not everyone,' replied Kirby. 'He made sure that you found him. It must have been you.'

'He didn't say anything about this before the fire…Wait!'

'What is it?'

In his mind's eye he remembered Riley engulfed in the flames that had nearly killed him and Jamie. The vivid images of his colleague's melting flesh made the hair on his neck stand on end, and then he remembered something he had neither understood nor paid any attention to moments before the second bottle of gasoline fluid had hit the floor before them.

'Three-twenty-nine,' he whispered and turned to the guard.

Mike's CD had done its job. In his hands was a file with Haedenberg written in large black rapid marker ink across its cover.

'Is there somewhere we can take a look at this?' asked Mike.

'There's a table and chair at the end of rows D and E.' replied the guard.

'Give us a few minutes, will you.'

'Sure, I'll be back in the foyer. I guess you will be wanting me to reset box 329 then.'

'No, not just yet. I'll hold onto it until it expires.'

Fabien and Kirby reached the table and spread out the contents upon it.

It contained a dossier and other notes that Riley had compiled over a series of months.

'Here it is. A list of the names of the members of Haedenberg,' said Kirby.

As Mike scanned the list each of the main players were there: Gouldman, Calvert, Jackson and Milton Porter.

'All members of AET at Princeton,' he said.

'Take a look at this,' said Kirby, handing him another file.

He read for a while as Kirby watched his reaction to the words on the paper. Then she found something that caught her own eye.

'It's just like Jackson described at one of the briefings,' said Mike. 'Riley must have found the names of the organisations that Haedenberg had taken over.'

'Except he wasn't giving us a clear picture,' replied Kirby.

'What do you mean?'

'It wasn't just corporations that Haedenberg were concerned with. Riley discovered something else. Look. The CEOs that were terminally ill were taken to various Haedenberg medical facilities that supposedly nursed them until their deaths. These are documents authorising lethal injections to patients. The names match up with the CEOs listed. Riley discovered that they were being terminated within hours of their arrival.'

'So they went to Carousel.'

'Where?' asked Kirby, perplexed.

'Logan's run. When anyone reached 30 years of age they went to Carousel to be terminated.'

'I never read the book. Now, look at these.'

'They're just a list of names.'

'Look closer. Look at their ages.'

'They all seemed to be around 70 years of age.'

'Look at the dates that these names were passed to Haedenberg.'

'Looks like a period covering the last 40 years.'

'Now take a look at this letter.'

As Fabien read the contents his blood ran cold. It was a letter from a young Robert Gouldman dated March 1975. In it Gouldman explained how he had managed to obtain the medical records of a number of elderly patients from hospitals in New Jersey, and that after careful consideration he believed that the attached names were in his view suitable for termination. He had attached a projection as to the future medical costs that would be incurred and had given details of a revised account into which payment for the information given should be wired.

'Riley uncovered more than just corporate euthanasia,' added Kirby, 'I believe he uncovered a systematic elimination of thousands, maybe tens of thousands of innocent people who were robbed of their final years of life, as Gouldman put it, to reduce the burden on the system. Look! Numerous members of the medical profession have been involved in this too.'

'And,' added Mike, 'AET alumni, old and new, have been providing the names to Haedenberg; loyal to the last to their alma mater and taking a cut of the savings that the medical institutions and insurance corporations would make.'

'So why has Gouldman taken this above ground with his crusade for euthanasia?' asked Kirby. 'Surely this would put an end to the whole of Haedenberg's operations.'

'I guess to him it's taking the whole ethos to its logical conclusion. He, his fraternity brothers and Haedenberg have made their money, now its time to make the dream a reality, a cause, an ideology. It's simply evolved, Kirby, and he's the man to take it all the way to the top of the political agenda.'

'So how did Dan Riley get hold of all this?'

'I suspect it was leaked to him over a period of months from the victim of a recent plane crash.'

29

With the radio playing AOR songs from the 80s quietly in the background, Jamie reached for the novel she had picked up at a bookstore in Wilmington. She had already read the first four chapters and deciding that there was very little else she could do, she started chapter five in an attempt to pass as much time as she could before Mike returned. It was early evening, she was still feeling tired but she knew that if she went to bed she would find it difficult to settle. The sterile environment and the uncertainty regarding when the ordeal would end began to play on her mind and she knew that when the lights went out later, fear of the dark would come back to torment her as it had when she had been a child.

She was trying to absorb herself in the book when her concentration was sidetracked by a knock at the front door. She remembered Henderson telling her not to open it and that Thorpe and Merrill were outside. Maybe they were being polite and didn't want to just walk in on her; after all, she thought, it was her home albeit on a very temporary basis. There was a second knock and so she walked cautiously into the entrance hall and saw the door before her with shadows in the glass.

'Is that you, Agent Thorpe, Agent Merrill?' she called out.

'Miss Farrington?' said a voice.

'Who is it?'

'Agent Merrill,' replied the voice. 'I left my keys inside, I'm sorry to alarm you.'

'OK, just a moment,' she replied and then she stopped – something didn't seem right.

'Agent Merrill?'

'Yes.'

'What was I wearing when I arrived?'

'Why do you ask?'

'Just tell me what I was wearing, you must remember.'

'Your clothes?'

'Yes, … my clothes,' she replied as she felt her voice begin to tighten.

'I don't recall.'

She needed something to grab hold of, to use as a weapon but there was nothing in sight. As she backed away from the door towards the lounge the man outside knocked the door again. It rippled through her.

'Aren't you trained to observe things like that?' she added, stalling for time.

'You've got me this time, Miss Farrington. I appreciate your caution but please let me in,' said the voice again.

There was no way she would let the big bad wolf in but seconds later the decision was out of her hands; three loud gunshots suddenly rang out and the door was kicked open. From the other end of the hallway she saw two men she did not recognise standing in the doorway, one of them pointing a gun straight at her. She ran into the kitchen and headed straight for the rear exit. One of them pursued her into the kitchen and reached the entrance in time to find her struggling in vain to open the locked door at the rear. Immediately and without thinking she darted for the only other means of escape. John Carlyle chased after her as she swung open the door that led into the garage to the side of the house. By the time he had made it out, Thomas Jackson was holding her at gunpoint. He flung Jamie at his subordinate and Carlyle grabbed her with gratitude, pulling her arms behind her in an agonising grip. She writhed in pain and started to tremble again as Jackson stepped forward and began massaging the underside of her chin with the nozzle of his gun.

'Fabien will be here soon. Then you can say goodbye to each other,' he said.

'How do you know he's alive?' she asked.

'Markham never collected his money,' replied Carlyle.

'Take care of her,' ordered Jackson coldly before re-entering the house.

Dusk was turning to darkness as Mike swung into the driveway that led down to the secluded dwelling where Jamie was being sheltered, the beams of his headlights providing a needed source of light along the darkening trail. As he approached the house all the lights were switched off, which seemed a little strange to him, and what was more he had expected to be met by his two armed colleagues. There were two other cars, one belonging to Thorpe and Merrill and another he couldn't properly identify. Something's wrong, he thought.

He reached for his gun and slowly got out of the car, closing the door yet avoiding shutting it to attract attention. Cautiously he walked towards the entrance door, his pupils fully dilated and his ears open to the roaring silence that surrounded him. As he got closer to the house he could just see that the front door was ajar, but as he headed towards it he stumbled over a large mass and fell to the ground. As he picked himself up he felt an arm brush against his foot and turning his head to look behind he noticed a body lying still on the lawn. There was another one about two metres away and it was then that he realised why Thorpe and Merrill had not met him when he had pulled up. Now he needed to stay focused, to forget the things that Henderson had revealed to him about his condition; to forget the stone thrower and the frogmen that were waiting for him inside. Jamie was in there and retrieving her dead was not an option. With every second that passed, however, he began to feel himself being detached from the situation; to walk away would mean to stay alive, but Jamie was firmly in the equation.

As he reached the entrance door he stretched out his arm and moved his hand across the wall trying to find the light switch. His hand brushed against a plastic plate and so he knew that the switch was a fingertip away, but when he eventually found it and pressed it down there was no response; the electricity had been cut. He knew that he had to move into the house slowly without making a sound and at first his frozen body refused to move. Then, slowly, he began to enter in the knowledge that each step he took could be his last.

Carlyle and Jackson were watching him from different locations within, waiting for him to step into the perfect position for one or both of them to make the fatal shot. Jackson was standing in the corner of the lounge facing the doorway that led into the hall, completely sheltered from what little light remained, and watching the space in the doorframe into which Fabien was about to enter. Carlyle was behind the kitchen door and could just see the figure of their target approaching.

Fabien called out suddenly. 'We have everything we need to put you away. We know Calvert was going to expose the fraternity so it's over now. Jamie is of no use to you – release her.'

There was no reply. Fabien, now inches from death, called out again as Jackson, knowing that he had been sifted out and that his façade had been torn away, waited for the precise moment.

'Riley discovered what was really going on. Joseph Linden, Stuart Manley, all of you members of Alpha Epsilon Theta or should I say Haedenberg. We know all about the names, Jackson. You were trading information on dying CEOs, taking over their companies, using their assets and then relieving them of the burden of their painful existence. Not to mention the thousands of others. They were just ordinary people hoping to live out their days before you snuffed out the flame. Riley found it all – the links with Sterling, the euthanasia products, how and when they were administered right from the days you were in college at Princeton. Seems your brother William finally had an attack of conscience, just like Joseph Linden. He was going to let the world know, wasn't he, and you just couldn't allow that to happen.'

Jackson could now see the dim outline of Fabien's body in the doorframe and that was all he needed.

'Take him!' he called out, and with that Carlyle fired three fatal shots at Fabien's chest causing him to fall to the floor like a felled tree. Jackson emerged from his corner and approached Fabien's body.

'And here's another to make sure,' he said, firing a fourth shot. 'Hit the lights.'

Carlyle ran to the garage to switch the electricity on, leaving his boss standing guard over Fabien's motionless body. As he entered the kitchen, his adrenaline pumping, he collided with the corner of one of the units and winced in pain before moving on again to find the rear door to the garage. The master switch was just to his left in the corner as he entered and as he reached for it he suddenly heard a further three gunshots fired from within the house. He quickly flicked the switch and instantly the lights in the garage and in the house came on. Running back into the kitchen he headed towards the hall. There a body lay sprawled on the carpet; the eyes terrorised having experienced a sudden and fatal shock moments earlier. Carlyle looked down in horror to see his boss, Thomas Jackson, dead and motionless with no sign of Fabien. Before he had time to contemplate his next move he felt a gun at his head.

'Where's Jamie?' asked Fabien with the look of a crazed man.

Carlyle paused as his eyeballs rolled sideways to look at his colleague.

'OK, Fabien, take it easy.'

'Take me to her, now! And if anything has happened to her...'

'You'll shoot me, right?' replied a fear-stricken Carlyle.

'You got it.'

'OK... She's outside.'

'First take that gun you're hiding and place it on the floor... Slowly now.'

Carlyle bent down and as his hand reached the floor he gently loosened his grip allowing his weapon to slip out of his hand and onto the carpet.

'Let's go,' ordered Fabien.

Carlyle led Fabien towards the rear entrance and then around the edge of the garage towards the grounds at the rear of the house. From the outside floodlights that were attached to the rear of the garage, Fabien could see the fields behind and a small garden house in the distance as darkness enveloped the sky. As Carlyle began to walk over to it Fabien realised that Jamie would be inside.

'Finish me off, Fabien, that's what you'd like, isn't it?' said Carlyle, now goading him.

As they approached the garden house Fabien held back as Carlyle opened the wooden door and switched on the lights. He kept Carlyle within the sights of his gun as he retrieved Jamie from a chair in the corner. She was bound and gagged with silver duck tape.

'Get that tape off her.'

'With what?' replied Carlyle, thinking he had stalled things for a moment.

In the heat of the moment Fabien reached into one of the pockets of his jacket and pulled out a jack-knife set he would carry in case of emergencies.

'Use this,' he said, throwing the set to Carlyle.

First he ripped the gag from Jamie's mouth causing her to cry out, then he reached down and quickly cut through the tape holding her feet together. He stopped for a moment and glared back at Mike.

'I have contacts, Fabien. I was just following orders, misguided or deceived they might say.'

'Hands... Now,' replied Mike.

He started to tear through the tape around Jamie's hands when without warning, he swung at Mike with the jack-knife, striking the corner of his forehead above his left eye.

'Big mistake, my friend,' he said, as Mike fell to the ground.

Blood started to trickle from the wound. Jamie screamed as Carlyle kicked Mike hard in the stomach, winding him. He flung Jamie against the wall of the garden house and then proceeded to deliver yet another painful and winding blow to Mike causing him to reel with pain on the floor. Jamie desperately tried to get the tape off her hands as she saw Mike let go of his gun. It was as Carlyle bent down to grab it that she felt her hands loosen in the tape. Mike crawled along the floor until he reached the door and as Carlyle picked up the gun Mike dived out of the garden house. As Carlyle aimed his gun Mike managed to kick the door closed as he opened fire, causing the glass to shatter and the bullet to miss him, but only just. Carlyle flung open the door in rage and aimed the gun again at Mike who lay helpless on the ground. As he was about to fire again Jamie lunged at him from behind causing him to fall to the ground and drop the gun. Mike grabbed it just before Carlyle could get to his feet.

'Hold it, Carlyle,' he said and then looked at Jamie as she got to her feet. 'Jamie, get out of here, now!'

She hesitated.

'Now!'

Looking around her and feeling suddenly disoriented, she paced slowly away from the two men.

'Go, go now!' cried Mike, his gun still firmly pointed at Carlyle.

Jamie hesitated again. She knew the safest route was to head for the fields; there she would be obscured by the darkness. But as she started to run she remembered Henderson's warning regarding the cesspool and quickly changed direction, sprinting instead towards the house.

'I ought to finish you too,' said Fabien, returning to Carlyle and clutching the trigger.

'Then do it.'

Mike paused – something from within restrained him. Facing off, the two men stared into each other's eyes. Fabien felt a cold shiver as though Carlyle could see into his very soul knowing he would fail to pull the trigger.

'I thought so,' said Carlyle. 'You're too noble to shoot a defenceless man; and that, my friend, is your downfall.'

Before Mike could answer, blood trickling from his head wound ran into his eye and blinded him momentarily. The distraction was enough for Carlyle to kick the gun out of Mike's hand. It fell to the ground somewhere behind him, concealed in the dark. The pain in Mike's hand flared up as though it had just been put in a heap of fiery coals. Carlyle wasted no time in inflicting another painful blow to Mike's stomach, and when his colleague fell to his knees, the second to the face was enough to incapacitate him. He had no time to find the gun; this was his one opportunity to escape and he accepted it with gratitude.

In her panic, Jamie had made the mistake of assuming that one or more of the cars parked on the drive would contain ignition keys. She desperately groped for a set in the car parked second nearest to the entrance door of the house. She knew she had a little time left – Mike had everything under control now. If she could just get away in one of the vehicles she would be safe. She could find Mike later. Her second mistake was failing to realise she was sitting in the driver's seat of the pool car that Jackson and Carlyle had obtained in their hasty retreat from the capital.

'Looking for something?' asked Carlyle as he dangled the keys in his hand and stared at her gleefully. She turned to stone.

With the small pointed blade of Mike's jack-knife set resting against her neck, she was ordered to move slowly across to the passenger seat and not to say a word.

As Mike staggered to the edge of the driveway he heard Carlyle start the car and saw it pull away with Jamie remaining still in the adjacent seat. His vision blurred, he was unable to see with any clarity the license plate. As he felt the warm fluid trickling into his eye again he took off his jacket and used it to stem the flow of blood from his forehead. Covering his shirt was a large bullet-proof vest with four gaping indentations in it.

Jamie remained calm. Carlyle's perturbed expression grew more intense as he drove the car at pace out into open country. Within him the realisation that he was alone now with no protection from his superiors began to tighten its grip as though unseen hands were suffocating him. Deducing that something had clearly happened to his colleague gave Jamie reason to assume that the net would soon close on her captor and that she was of no real use to him in the present scenario. Nevertheless, entwined within her thoughts was the stark reality that she was still in great danger and that she had to play it cool and try to reason with him.

'Where will you go?' she asked, bucking up courage to address him.

He remained silent and kept his eyes fixed on the illuminated road.

'Surely the best thing you can do is just get as far away as possible. Mike won't know where you're heading and neither will Henderson.'

He glanced at her for a couple of seconds.

'True,' he replied.

'Then you don't need me, do you. All you need to do is pull over, let me out and then you can disappear.'

'You're my insurance.'

'What insurance? I'll only be a liability to you. You'll drag me from place to place, threatening me with what, a jack-knife? You have no gun.'

Her simple yet clear words of truth cut through his veil of wishful thinking like the knife through the shower curtain in his favourite movie. But his reply caused her to shudder, making her wish she had kept her mouth shut.

'Then you, Jamie, are the spoils of the battle.'

Now he had silenced her. Memories of her final encounter with Reuben Stein at the hotel the previous fall returned like a ghost from the past. The difference now, she realised, was that Mike would not be there to save her. He glanced at her again, this time with a warped smile.

'Did you know that during my time at the academy I learned how to temporarily paralyse a person in one simple grip of my hand in just the right place,' he said to her. 'Extra curricular research can come in very handy. I used it once to disarm a suspect. I will never forget the fear in his eyes as I caressed his face with the nozzle of my gun. You see, he really didn't know what I was going to do to him. I sometimes wonder whether that was more effective than the touch of my hands. Who needs a gun, Jamie? I could stop this car any time. We're on a deserted road; it's dark, no other traffic in sight. Before you could open the door your body will freeze, you won't be able to scream or call out. You're mine to do with as I please. I'm sure it would destroy Mike Fabien, just as he's destroyed me. You aren't just some innocent bystander caught up in all this. You mean much more to him than that. I saw the rage in his eyes in the garden house. Touching you is like touching his eyeball, and well… wasn't I sloppy with that jack-knife. I wonder how you are going to feel when I caress its cold, sharp blade over that soft delicate face of yours as you lie there unable to move and wondering where the next cut will be.'

In that moment of terror all scenarios flashed before her. How they would find her, what she would look like. And then it came to her – she was not going to allow this to happen. Moments after he had concluded his words she realised that there was a way out of this. The opportunity would come soon; it was only a matter of time. She calmly turned her head to face the windshield and spoke no longer, allowing him to keep on driving – far away from the safe house. Whatever he was going to do with her, it wouldn't be in the car in the dark. She sensed in him a man who would choose his moment carefully; in a special place, dignified almost in its own perverse way. So she sat and watched as the trees flashed by in the headlights and focused her eyes on the dark before her.

Five miles later came her moment of release. It came in the form of two bright lights on the road ahead. It came when the lights grew larger, big lights that started to blind her. All it took was for her to grab hold of his tie and pull. Pull as hard as she possibly could. It all happened so quickly yet to her it was as though in slow motion. His head hit the steering wheel with such force. His hands let go of the wheel and now it was hers. Just a little turn to the left and it would all be over. As John Carlyle raised his head and caught hold of the wheel again, the deafening sound of the horn of the truck, now less than six feet away from the windshield, awoke his senses in time for his face to be showered in flying particles of glass and his body to be pulverised as the front of the car was crushed in an instant. As the driver continued with every ounce of strength in him to bring the truck to a halt, Carlyle's vehicle exploded in an inferno and was catapulted into a ditch by the side of the road. When the truck eventually came to a stop, the traumatised driver stared at the carnage before him, unable to move a muscle.

By the time Mike had managed to stop the bleeding, 40 minutes had passed since Carlyle had fled with Jamie. It had taken several large band-aids with applied pressure to attempt to seal the wound above his eyebrow. All he could hope was that they would prevent further blood flow. He would need medical attention before the night was through – an inch lower and he would have been blinded. Every fibre in his body was going through 'cold turkey' now and at that moment he knew it was the medication. If Carlyle returned he would be no match for him. He had to act quickly.

The safe house looked like a place of carnage. With the electricity restored, he now surveyed the grounds trying to find his cell phone. He saw properly for the first time his two dead colleagues on the lawn outside – a sober reminder of his own vulnerability. Faced with the possibility that his cell phone had dropped from his pocket during the struggle with Carlyle, he entered the hallway through the forced door. Jackson was lying on the carpet and he knelt down besides the lifeless body. With emotions bereft he searched the inside pockets of the suit jacket and found what he needed. He called for reinforcements and paramedics, and lastly for Henderson. Had fortune gone his way he would have been well on his way to pursuing Carlyle. The keys to Merrill's vehicle were missing, most likely, he believed, taken when he had been shot. Now overspent on adrenaline, he looked in a mirror that hung on the wall in the corner of the hallway. The band-aids were now soaked through with blood. There was nothing he could do now except wait for help.

Twelve miles from the safe house, one of two of the police officers who had arrived at the scene was taking a statement from the driver of the truck as he watched the fire crew put out the remains of the blaze from Carlyle's vehicle. In the back of the patrol vehicle, wrapped in a blanket and giving a statement to the other officer sat a cut and bruised Jamie. The flickering lights of the vehicle cast coloured shadows across her drawn face as she recounted how the driver had suddenly lost control of the car in which she had been travelling, and how she had, by seconds, managed to cheat death by opening the door and throwing herself onto the road – missing the oncoming truck by only a metre or two. When she had concluded her statement she asked the officer if she could use a phone. There was someone she needed to contact.

30

Jamie had collapsed onto the bed in the spare room of Mike's apartment upon their arrival home. With his head still sore from the stitches that the nurse in the emergency room of Washington General had skilfully implanted, Mike had been sat up in his lounge for most of the remainder of the night, unable to sleep. Jamie had also been brought to the ER to be checked and when both she and Mike had been given the OK to leave, they had been accompanied by Henderson to headquarters to give statements regarding the deaths of Jackson and Carlyle. During the car journey back to the apartment she had been incapable of talking due to what Mike had perceived as delayed shock. Mike had been ordered to report in the next morning and, as he reflected on events, the realisation that the frogmen and his disgraced colleagues were finally gone had yet to sink in. Sleep, be it sporadic, had come to him eventually.

When he surfaced later that morning he went into the spare room to check on Jamie. She was still there in the position in which he had left her. He checked his voicemail as he switched on the coffee machine but there were no messages, and that meant nothing new to report from Henderson. As the aroma of fresh coffee began to fill the apartment, he went over to the window and opened the blinds to let in the morning light and allow the cool air to circulate before heading into the bathroom to take a shower. When he had dried he opened the cabinet and picked out the bottles of medication that he had been taking and proceeded to throw them all into the small plastic trash bin beneath the basin. He stared down at them long and hard wondering how much damage they had done to him. For a moment he felt as though he had been violated and deceived by the organisation that was supposed to have protected him, yet despite all that had happened since his return from Ashbury Falls, he suddenly felt calm within himself. It's a brand new day, he thought as he started to close the door of the cabinet. As the mirror came into view, he saw a face looking at him from behind; it belonged to neither Carlyle, John Markham nor his mother; it was Jamie.

'Can I take a shower?' she asked.

'Sure, I'll fix us some breakfast.'

Jamie looked at him with a strangely calm, friendly demeanour.

'I need to check in at headquarters. Can I borrow your car for a couple of hours?' he asked her. 'In case you've forgotten, the police have probably impounded mine.'

'Go ahead,' she replied, smiling through her wet hair. 'Go and do what you have to do.'

FBI headquarters was abuzz with activity as Fabien walked through the main entrance doors and across the long hall towards the elevators located on the opposite side. He had managed to stay clear of the film crews and reporters that were starting to descend upon the gates outside looking for confirmation that a senior official had been killed in an incident the previous night. He wondered how the story had been leaked so soon as he continued past a small group of officials who had clustered themselves together a few minutes prior to his arrival and who stared at him as he approached the elevators. As he hit the call button he could feel their prejudiced eyes upon him. The facts would take time to be disseminated through the organisation but it wouldn't make much difference in some quarters even if a sworn statement had been made and verified. He turned around and looked back at them in defiance and after a few moments they looked away and continued the discussion that they had formerly been engaged in. When the elevator arrived at the destined floor, Fabien stepped outside and looked around nervously. A few of his colleagues began to pass him and one of them stopped him to enquire regarding Jackson. Mike told him he had an urgent meeting and couldn't stop. When he arrived at Henderson's office he knocked the door. When ordered to enter, Stratton and Hawthorne, with whom he and Jamie had met the previous night, greeted him.

'Have a seat, Fabien,' said Stratton.

'We'll keep this brief,' said Hawthorne. 'Have you spoken to any of your colleagues about last night's incident?'

'No.'

'Good,' said Hawthorne, rubbing his chin. 'Mr Henderson has already filled us in on the details leading up to and including the events of last night. This has come as a shock to us and whilst we now accept that Jackson was a bad apple we must adopt a damage limitation position on this and make sure that his involvement with Gouldman and the Haedenberg Foundation is never disclosed. Is that understood.'

'Agreed,' replied Fabien.

'Certain information will, however, have to come to light,' added Stratton, 'mainly in connection with Miss Farrington's abduction. We will also report that since the Ascension incident, Jackson has had an apparent vendetta towards you and that his judgement had been clouded as a result.'

'What about Agents Kirby and Durrell? They were assisting me in the Gouldman abduction and know about Jackson's involvement with Haedenberg.'

'We've already spoken to them and debriefed them.'

'For a while things may not be easy for you, Agent Fabien,'

added Hawthorne, 'but hopefully the dust will settle in time.'

'Maybe,' replied Fabien.

'Between the three of us, you're to be commended,' said Hawthorne smugly. 'Exposing Haedenberg is a major gain for us. Whether it will stem the tide of Gouldman's vision, that's not for us to concern ourselves with. You must not get involved in any political backlash. We know your views on the subject and if we find any links between yourself and the anti-euthanasia league, there will be serious consequences. We are not on personal crusades, Agent Fabien, is that clear?'

'Perfectly.'

'If that's all, I have to be somewhere else. Mr Henderson asked me to give you this,' said Stratton, handing Mike a note.

'I think we're done here,' said Hawthorne. 'Good luck, Fabien.'

With that the two men left promptly, leaving Mike alone in Henderson's office.

The grounds of the White House were starting to fill with tourists as Lawrence Henderson sat waiting on a bench on the edge of a grass verge that held an impressive view of the dome in the distance. As Mike approached along the pathway that led towards it, he stood up to greet his subordinate.

'Thank you for coming, you must be exhausted. How's Miss Farrington?' he asked.

'Difficult to tell at this stage.'

'I suppose I should say good work,' said Henderson, 'but what a mess.'

'Shame about Carlyle,' said Mike. 'I never liked the guy.'

'Me neither,' replied Henderson. 'How's the eye?'

'It'll mend.'

'They've given me Jackson's job.'

'Congratulations; it's what you've always wanted.'

'Well it's too early to start celebrating yet. I'll be on probation for a year so they can always transfer me back if they don't like my methods. With Jackson gone the department can start to move on and that includes you. You'll be back on full operational duties once you have been cleared by the medics.'

'Did you know about the drugs?' asked Fabien. Henderson hesitated. 'You knew, didn't you?'

'Yes.'

'What else were you aware of?'

'Only the drugs, the rest I had no knowledge of, that's the truth. Jackson was threatening to reveal a misdemeanour of mine from the past. It could have had serious consequences for my career. That's the reason he got the job over me, but I guess that's not the issue anymore.'

'You, stepping out of line? I'm shocked.'

'I was like you once, Fabien, but I learned to toe the line. You should do likewise. I apologise for using you to protect my interests.'

'I want one month's leave,' said Mike assertively.

'This wouldn't have anything to do with that Farrington girl would it?'

'And I want a transfer. I think that's best, everything considered – you owe me.'

'We'll discuss this when you return.'

Mike turned to leave.

'I'll be sorry to lose you, Michael. But remember this; there'll always be the likes of Thomas Jackson somewhere in this organisation – the trick is not to awaken them.'

Mike stopped and looked at his boss momentarily.

'By the way, I have some news regarding Kirby's narcotics case,' added Henderson. 'The man in the photograph – it was Ed Hamell. He was in league with a local drugs syndicate and the funds received went straight to the Haedenberg account at Mason-Wainwright. Hamell would rendezvous with the traffickers occasionally when the shipments came.'

'How did she make the connection?'

'When she and I visited Gouldman after his return, Hamell turned up. She caught his profile as we walked up the stairs and remembered the photograph. I sent a team up to Manhattan to investigate. They found the deposits and traced their origin. She never lets go, that girl – just like her old man.'

'Will Gouldman be implicated?' asked Fabien.

'Yes, I'm confident of that. In fact, I'm already on the case.'

'Eager to impress.'

'I have to go; Washington police need to speak to me about a homicide of a Joshua Allenby. They said it was a high priority.'

When Mike reached the top of the flight of stairs that led to his apartment he stopped for a moment before walking towards the door. He had no idea as to how he would find Jamie since their brief encounter that morning. He hesitated to open it at first but then turned the key and went inside. Jamie's bags were on the floor, evidently packed and waiting for their owner to come and collect them. The place was quiet and felt strangely empty until Jamie came out of the spare room with her jacket on a few moments later.

'How did it go?' she asked.

'All sewn up. Time to move on. I thought maybe you'd like to go out for dinner or something later but I can see that you need to be somewhere else.'

'I have to get back to Ashbury Falls; Stella's expecting me and it's going to be a long drive.'

'Of course.'

'I've decided to go back to the hotel. It just seems that's where I belong. It's safer there.'

'From me or from Boston?'

'Both. Besides, things were never going to work out at the bank. I've known that for a while.'

'You're probably making the right decision.'

'Have the demons gone?'

'I wait by the water's edge but she hasn't returned. Neither have the frogmen. I don't think they'll be coming back.'

'Maybe it's time you stopped trying to change the world, Mike. Just get the bad guys and move on, right?'

'I don't think you can separate the two. People like Gouldman and those in Haedenberg have to be stopped. If we all just did our jobs it would be like healing the wound without curing the disease.'

'But what if Gouldman was right? His methods may be extreme but what if his ideology has some merit?'

'Do you believe that, Jamie?'

'No I don't, but who are we to decide whether it should or should not be on the agenda?'

'Stay a while,' said Mike, touching her face.

'I don't know, Mike. Every time I'm around you I nearly end up getting myself killed.'

'Things change.'

'Maybe they do, Mike. What will happen to you now?' she asked.

'They want me back in the front line.'

'That's what you do best, isn't it?'

'I have other plans.'

'What do you mean?'

'I've requested a transfer and I'm also thinking to move out of Washington. Like you said, it's safer.'

'What will you do?'

'I don't know yet. I'm taking a month's vacation to rest my battered body and my cluttered mind. I was thinking to head up your way. Can you recommend a good hotel?'

Jamie lowered her head and then peeped back at him through the shaggy hair that had partially covered her face. Then she smiled at him.

'Well I know a nice hotel, quiet, good service, excellent food, all your comforts taken care of.'

'Does the owner make good pasta?'

'Yes.'

'And where would this hotel be?'

'The Beverley in Montpelier, Vermont.'

'Oh I see.'

'You'd like it there, why not try it out?'

'Maybe I will.'

Jamie picked up her bags and walked to the door.

'Take care, Jamie,' he said.

'You too,' she replied, turning to him.

'Leave the door. This place could use some air.'

When she had left he wandered into the bedroom to change. He was in the mind to pay a visit to Rockfields later but needed to take a rest for a few hours. With the after effects of the medication still causing an unquenchable thirst, he went back into the lounge a minute later to grab some water. Jamie was stood by the sofa.

'That hotel I was telling you about,' she said, smiling. 'It's a great place… But it's not as good as the Farrington in Ashbury Falls.'

'So what happens now?' he asked.

She looked at him, fingers on her lips.

'Didn't you mention something about a vacation?'

'I did.'

'Well then, I guess you could use a ride.'

Epilogue

'…We are here for but a moment,' said the priest quietly as he stood over Nile Hawke's grave and cast a handful of dirt down onto the coffin. 'Then blown away like grass in the wind.'

His words, although true, were no comfort for his grieving widow, watching through her black veil as the tiny dark particles of earth were scattered across the brass plate bearing her late husband's name. As one of his colleagues tossed flowers into the shallow pit she closed her eyes for a moment of solitude and felt a single tear flow from her eyelid to the corner of her face. There was silence at the graveside as the priest concluded the ceremony with a prayer that asked Hawke's creator to receive his servant to the afterlife, watch over those he had left behind and help his colleagues bring his killers to justice.

'Amen,' they all said in one accord before beginning a dignified walk towards the cars.

'Nile came very close to flushing out those dealers, so we're going to finish the job for him,' said Giles.

'Like a moth that went too close to the fire,' added Mitchell.

'That's what we all do when we carry the badge. We will nail them, mark my words,' replied Giles. 'But right now Amanda needs us.'

They turned to their colleague's widow as she conversed with the immediate family under the protective and comforting arm of her father. Her sister joined the party and started to lead her towards the awaiting hearse that was parked on the tarmac a short distance away. Nile's colleagues followed the party towards the cars but as they reached the edge of the grass Mitchell looked back at the priest as he was about to leave the graveside. The two men's eyes met for a few moments and it was as if the police officer of 17 years, who had seen many deaths, including those of colleagues, could find no answers to why this had happened, and the priest could offer none either.

'Mitchell!' called Giles from behind him. 'Let's go.'

He turned to his boss and then looked back at the priest for one last time before walking back to the cars. Giles patted him gently on the shoulder as he passed him and watched his subordinate walk slowly towards the parked vehicles, remembering the one and only time he too had lost his close friend and partner in a shooting incident ten years previous.

'I know what you're going through,' he said, and left him to deal with it in his own way.

As Giles approached the cars Amanda was getting into the family hearse. When she had settled in her seat she pushed the switch to open the window as he came near.

'I'll call you soon, Amanda, and meanwhile I'll get things rolling with the benefits,' he said.

'Will you join us at the house?' she asked.

'Thank you, but no. I have to be somewhere else and I'm not good at these occasions.'

'Of course, I understand. Goodbye for now, Lieutenant.'

'Goodbye Amanda.'

Giles stood alone as the cars pulled away and headed back down the silent road that led to the entrance gates of the cemetery, knowing in his heart that he was partly responsible for Nile's death. What remained now was how he would deal with the questions and whether the oversight in security that had led to one of his most respected officers losing his life would come to the attention of the investigators...

The sound of the phone on Mike's desk caused him to jump. He had been engrossed in the final chapter of his latest novel and the sound of the phone had derailed his train of thought. It was time to finish anyway and he felt unable to put any more words to paper. Closing and saving the Microsoft word document on his laptop, he reached for the phone. Only another two to three pages and *Circle of Fortune* the sequel to *Scenes of Yesterday* would be finished. How Lieutenant Giles would fare in the impending investigation was something best left for the final part of the trilogy. His immediate priority was finishing this one and preparing for some final editing before his agent would submit it to the publishers. Expecting it to be her, he picked up the phone, almost knocking over an empty glass on the table to his right as he did so. She was probably calling him again to remind him that his publishers were more than eager to see the finished manuscript. He had asked her for another week and she had reluctantly agreed.

'Mike Fabien,' he said into the receiver.

'How are you, Michael?' asked a voice at the other end. It took a few moments before he recognised the caller.

'James Stephen Eckhart, this is an unexpected pleasure. I thought you were my agent.'

'How's the book going?'

'Almost done. I hear you're having success with yours too.'

'Indeed I am. This call has to be brief as I'm sure you'll understand.'

'Of course,' replied Mike. 'It would be damaging to me too if anyone in authority was aware of my involvement.'

'So, cutting to the chase, Michael, can we rely on another donation to the cause soon?'

'Don't worry, you'll get some of the royalties from the new book.'

'Thanks. A brief update for you; we're making inroads in Congress since Gouldman resigned. The newly elected senator for Rhode Island has very opposing views to his predecessor and is going to champion our cause in a big way. Euthanasia is becoming one of the most controversial debates in the country, Michael. There are some that still carry Gouldman's vision but I feel very much that we in the anti-league will put sufficient brakes on this to take it off the agenda. We do need more funds though, so please keep those contributions coming in, won't you?'

'You can count on my continued support,' replied Mike. 'Before you go there is something I would like to ask you.'

'Go ahead,' replied Eckhart.

'You know I can still be influential despite my transfer to Washington PD.'

'So it's *Detective* Fabien now.'

'Do you trust me Stephen?'

'Of course – you've been a loyal supporter of the cause for many years.'

'I have fond memories of our meetings at rallies. When they suspected my involvement with the anti-league they managed to dig up a photograph of us together. Back in '94 wasn't it?'

'I remember.'

'Don't worry – I persuaded them that it was an impostor.'

'I'm glad to hear it, Michael. So, what do you want to know, my friend?'

'I need you to tell me who's next on our hit list.'

* * *

Anathema .*n., pl* -mas. **1.** a detested person or thing. **2.** a formal ecclesiastical excommunication, or denunciation of a doctrine. **3.** the person or thing so cursed. **4.** a strong curse ...

*

The Mike Fabien trilogy will conclude with:

ANATHEMA

**For further information visit:
www.davidlloydauthor.com**